KU-201-908

THE YEARS TO COME

Following her Irish-born father's brutal murder in New South Wales, the beautiful Erin Kelly finds she must fend for herself and her siblings in 19th century Australia's dark and dangerous land. To survive she is forced to compromise her virtue, but she vows that her spirit will never belong to Brett Wilde, the passionate and notorious adventurer – or any man. But she will make many sacrifices for her dearest family.

Recent Titles by Janet Tanner from
Severn House Large Print

THE DARK SIDE OF YESTERDAY
MORWENNAN HOUSE
NO HIDING PLACE
PORTHMINISTER HALL
THE REUNION
THE TRUTH GAME

THE YEARS TO COME

Janet Tanner

WOLVERHAMPTON PUBLIC LIBRARIES	
XB000000148102	
Bertrams	03/05/2012
	£20.99
SNU	01497502

Severn House Large Print
London & New York

This first large print edition published 2012
in Great Britain and the USA by
SEVERN HOUSE PUBLISHERS LTD of
9-15 High Street, Sutton, Surrey, SM1 1DF.
First world regular print edition published 2009 by
Severn House Publishers Ltd., London and New York.
Originally published 1983 in Great Britain only,
in paperback format only under the title
A Scent of Mimosa and pseudonym of Jade Shannon.

Copyright © 1983, 2009 by Janet Tanner.

All rights reserved.
The moral right of the author has been asserted.

British Library Cataloguing in Publication Data

Tanner, Janet.
  The years to come.
  1. Irish--Australia--Fiction. 2. Australia--Social
  conditions--19th century--Fiction. 3. Love stories.
  4. Large type books.
  I. Title
  823.9'14-dc23

  ISBN-13: 978-0-7278-9875-3

Except where actual historical events and characters are being
described for the storyline of this novel, all situations in this
publication are fictitious and any resemblance to living persons is
purely coincidental.

Severn House Publishers support The Forest Stewardship Council
[FSC], the leading international forest certification organisation. All
our titles that are printed on Greenpeace-approved FSC-certified paper
carry the FSC logo.

MIX
Paper from
responsible sources
FSC
www.fsc.org   FSC® C018575

Printed and bound in Great Britain by the
MPG Books Group, Bodmin, Cornwall.

CHAPTER ONE

New South Wales – January 1802

The storm would come before nightfall.

All day the heat had intensified and now it was evening the air hung hot and heavy over the parched land. Along the banks of the mighty river that could wash away crops and livestock when it was in flood, cattle stood disconsolately on the cracked mudflats, swishing their tails at bush flies, and even the sheep, foolish creatures that they usually were, sought what little shade there was.

At the narrow window of one of the farm-houses that had been built along the rich banks of the river, Erin Kelly stood watching the chain lightning that flickered in ceaseless waves along the ridges of the distant mountains.

It was ten years since she had come with her parents to this wild country to settle the land, ten years that had seen her grow from child to woman and turned her life upside down. But still its moods fascinated and over-awed her – the scorching summers with the dust and the flies, the torrential rains of autumn that turned the eucalypts a dull, faded green, the cold breezes that blew down from the mountains to drive icy fingers through the pale springs, and the thunderstorms, almost tropical in their intensity, such as the one that was threatening now.

As the lightning flickered more brightly Erin leaned forward on her elbows, craning to get a view down the broad drive that was flanked on either side by eucalypts and acacia in the hope of seeing a horse approaching. Both Paddy, her father, and Patrick, her young brother, were still out, and if they did not soon return they were certain to get a soaking. Patrick, she supposed, would not mind much. At fourteen he was a dreamer over whom life's discomforts rolled like heat haze over the mountains, and he was not likely to be far from home. As the first raindrops splashed onto the leaves of the eucalypts he would come galloping in, demanding to know what the fuss was about if she chided him.

But her father was a different proposition. A soaking would send him into one of his thunderous rages and by the time he had dried off both himself and his horse he would be claiming his need for a drink – that first drink of the evening that would lead him, as likely as not, to the rum-soaked stupor Erin so feared.

She sighed, catching her lip between her teeth and biting it hard. Why, oh why, did it have to be this way? Once it had been so different. Her warm-hearted, quick-witted father, with a laugh as loud as his temper was fiery, had gone now – gone these three years. Since the death of the wife he had worshipped, Paddy Kelly had drunk more and more and nothing, it seemed, could stop him. The farm that had once been prosperous had fallen into disrepair, the bush was

6

beginning to reclaim the small grant of land, and ruin was facing them all. But still the stack of empty rum kegs at the rear of the property grew, and still Paddy seemed to care for nothing but the oblivion that came from a bottle.

Erin drew a weary hand across her face and tucked a strand of glossy dark hair behind her ear. How much longer they could go on this way she did not know. So far they had survived – just. With a small band of convict labourers to work the land and her sister Grianne to help her in the house Erin had somehow managed to keep the family above the bread line. But now there were only two convict labourers left – all they could afford to keep – and one disaster would mean the end for them and all they had tried to do. If the river flooded and the crops were washed away, or if the livestock sickened, there would be no second chance. And with Paddy's drinking bouts becoming longer and more frequent and the debts mounting it might not even take that. Even now he was out begging for more time to settle accounts, Erin knew, though as always he had tried to hide from her and the others just how serious their situation had become.

Erin sighed. She was only eighteen years old but sometimes she felt as if she carried the cares of the world on her slender shoulders. It was not easy being the eldest in the family. The others depended on her so: Grianne, two years younger than she but with no thought for anything but her sweetheart, David Percy, and when she could get downriver to see him again; Patrick the dreamer;

eight-year-old Brenna; and yes, even her father when the drink was in him. It seemed a lifetime since she had been as carefree as they were and yet it was only three years – three years since she had seen her mother die, three years since that night she had sat by her bedside wiping the beads of fever from her brow and praying that Paddy would find a doctor and ride back with him in time to save her. He had not, and Erin had been alone with her when the fever had broken for a few moments and her mother's eyes had opened wide and her fingers fastened round Erin's wrist.

'Look after them, Erin,' she had whispered.

Even now, too clearly for comfort, Erin could remember the chill that had run through her then.

'Don't talk that way, Mama.' she had begged. 'Father will be back soon. Everything will be all right, you'll see.'

But her mother's fingers had only gripped her wrist the tighter.

'Promise, Erin.' Her voice had been weak but urgent. 'The little ones – and your father. He needs you, too. Promise.'

The tears that had blurred Erin's eyes brimmed over, running down her cheeks and splashing onto her mother's hands. She had always thought of Paddy as the strong one of her parents, Paddy with his loud laugh and his roaring temper. But that night as she looked down at the gentle face, deathly white but for the high spots of fever, she knew she had been wrong.

'I promise, Mama,' she whispered.

Now, across the years, she heard the echo of her own voice as she had heard it a hundred times.

'I promise, Mama.'

Well, she had tried. The Holy Mother alone knew how she had tried. But it had not been easy. And it seemed to be getting harder all the time...

'Erin, Erin, Patrick's home. Can we have dinner now, or must we wait for Father?' Brenna's voice broke into Erin's thoughts and she turned away from the window to see her youngest sister dancing across the room towards her, dark curls tumbling about the pale oval face that would one day be very like Erin's own, eyes sparkling like blue pools when the sun glints on them after rain.

Erin smiled. There was something about Brenna that could always make her smile, even when she was very tired and very worried. Perhaps it was because Brenna reminded her so much of herself at that age, carefree and happy back home in Ireland and excited by her parents' talk of going to Australia, the new land on the other side of the world. Or perhaps it was just that Brenna was sunshine and showers, laughter and tears, with pains that could be kissed better and troubles that disappeared overnight.

'You're hungry, are you?' she asked.

The little girl nodded, her eyes going longingly to the cold pork and pickles already laid out on the table.

'I'm always hungry.'

Erin laughed. 'Even in this heat?'

9

'Of course.'

Of course. Brenna was the native-born Australian. That was where she and Erin differed.

Erin lifted the knife and began to carve slices
of cold pork. 'It will be just the three of us then.
You, me and Patrick. Grianne is staying another
night at Painswick with David's family.'

'She's always with David.' Brenna sneaked a
small piece of pork from the tip of Erin's knife
and stuffed it hastily into her mouth. 'Why
haven't you got a sweetheart, Erin? You're older
than Grianne.'

'Don't be inquisitive.' Erin reached out to tap
Brenna's nose. 'And don't eat the meat before
we're ready, either.'

Brenna giggled but Erin's blue eyes were
thoughtful as she continued serving dinner. Perhaps it did seem strange to the child that while
Grianne had a sweetheart she did not. But then
Grianne had time for such things. There had
been someone once, when her mother was still
alive – Alistair Percy, David's older brother,
whose parents farmed at Painswick, some miles
down the river. For several wonderful, magical
months he had courted her, and sometimes, even
now, when she lay sleepless with anxiety she
coaxed her mind to rest remembering the way it
had been – the shy pleasure in seeing him, the
tiny trickles of awareness that had whispered
over her skin when their fingers accidentally
touched, the trembling pressure of his lips on
hers in the hidden places behind the mimosa
bushes. It had seemed to her then that she was
standing on the brink of a whole new world and

she had caught her breath at the wonder of it. But after her mother had died things had changed. At first he had been kind and understanding, but as the weeks became months and her new duties caused her to neglect him time and time again he had become impatient. One day when she was delayed and late in reaching their meeting place by the river she found him gone, and a few days later she heard he had found a new sweetheart – the daughter of a Parramatta trader.

Since Alistair there had been no one, though Erin had certainly never lacked the chances. With the years she had fulfilled all her early promise with looks that would turn any man's head. Her black hair was thick and glossy around a creamy-skinned face, and her blue eyes were smudged like mountain mist – 'put in with a smutty finger', Paddy would say when the rum made him poetic. Her body, too, slender yet rounded, drew admiring glances wherever she went, for here in the new country there was no shortage of men to admire her. But Erin ignored them all. She had no time for courtship – it could end only as her affair with Alistair had ended, in disillusion and hurt. Perhaps when the younger ones were able to take their share of responsibility she would be free to live her own life again. For now all her energies were needed to keep the promise she had made to her dying mother.

As Erin carved the last of the pork the door opened and Patrick came into the kitchen, stripping off his shirt. Like the others he was slender and dark, but there was a dreaming quality in his

11

blue eyes that made Erin wonder sometimes how he would fare here in the hard, practical world of the settler. But for all his slightness of build, there was the promise of wiry strength in his rippling shoulders and he could ride all day and never tire.

'Food.' He flung himself down into a chair, wiping away the sweat that trickled down his neck with the flat of his hand and wiping it on the knee of his breeches. 'Are we not to wait for Father? Well, perhaps that's just as well, since he's gone to visit Brett Wilde at Mia-Mia.'

His voice was lazy, teasing almost, but at his words Erin stiffened.

'How do you know where he's gone?' she asked sharply.

'Sure, didn't I see him with my own eyes turning into the drive – and him in his best breeches too.' Curiosity was mingled with mischief in his blue eyes. 'Now why should that be? Can you tell me?'

Frowning, Erin piled cold pork onto her brother's plate. Did he miss nothing?

'He's gone on business.'

'What business?'

'Oh, how should I know?' Erin snapped, turning away to avoid Patrick's shrewd gaze. They were too alike, the two of them, able almost to read one another's thoughts, and she had no wish for Patrick to read hers at that moment.

'Did he not tell you?' Patrick persisted.

'No, he did not! Now eat your tea. I've no appetite in this heat. I'm going outside where it's cooler.'

'So that you won't have to tell me why Father's gone to see Brett Wilde!' Patrick threw after her, but she ignored him, untying the strings of her apron and tossing it down on the pile of unwashed dishes.

As she emerged onto the veranda that ran along three sides of the farmhouse the heat came at her in a haze, drying her eyes and throat almost before she had time to draw breath. She had been wrong to say it would be cooler here – until the storm broke there would be nowhere to escape the heat. But at least she was away from Patrick's persistent questioning. He suspected the truth, of course, but suspecting was better than knowing, as she did. Patrick was too young yet to be worried by the prospect of the ruin that faced them if Paddy was unable to persuade Brett Wilde to extend his credit. And though he might put two and two together and conclude that the bills for provisions from Brett Wilde's Sydney stores had not recently been paid, she would move heaven and earth before she allowed him to realize that the rum kegs came from the same source – and it was them that had stretched their credit to its limits.

Erin's hands tightened over the wooden veranda rail, her fingers biting easily into the rotting wood.

Damn Brett Wilde and his kind! Damn all the arrogant, ambitious officers of the New South Wales Corps who had granted themselves the best land, set themselves up as local gentry, and grown rich on the backs of small farmers like her father. Between them they controlled every-

13

thing from the price of grain to the sale of cargoes that were landed in Sydney harbour. Worst of all, they controlled the rum. And too many men in this wild new land would sell their souls for a daily tot – her father included.

Unexpected sharp tears stung Erin's eyes and angrily she brushed them away. Crying would do no good. It was not a luxury she could afford. But sometimes, for all that, she was overwhelmed by the unfairness of it all. They had come with such hope to the new land, so full of determination to build a better life. Although she had been only a child, Erin had sensed her parents' excitement and shared in it. As if it were a dream she remembered the long sea voyage when she had been sick, day after day, the boards heaving beneath her feet and the cold salt wind whistling about her ears when her mother took her on deck for fresh air and exercise. Most of all she remembered the convicts who were being transported for crimes that varied from sheep-stealing to murder. She had rarely seen them – for most of the voyage they were securely battened down in the hold like cattle – but on the few occasions they had been allowed on deck she had been shocked yet fascinated by their matted hair, their filthy appearance and the rags that passed for their clothing. Always her mother had drawn her away as if she could be contaminated just by looking, and one of the greatest shocks on landing in the new country had been to discover that not only would convicts be assigned to them to help build their house and work their land, but some were even pardoned or remitted and allowed to take land and build houses themselves.

How young and innocent I was, thought Erin. And how excited when I first saw the house Father had built for us.

'We'll call it Kinvarra, to remind us of home,' he had told them.

The house had not reminded Erin of home, but she had loved it none the less. With his Irishman's sense of romance Paddy had built it so beautiful that it caught at the heartstrings, with its thatched roof and veranda, high, narrow windows and wooden pillars, and the vine that spread across its walls growing in just a few short years from a tiny sapling to an expanse of soft green. And the mimosa! Best of all, she loved the mimosa with its sweet scent and the bright yellow blooms that brought the sunlight down to earth on warm spring days. All this had been part of Paddy's vision in the days when he had cared for the future, and if he had lavished time and money on it that should have gone into the land, Erin could not find it in her to blame him for it. She loved Kinvarra, every stick and stone of it. Now, watching it fall into disrepair was a weight of sorrow around her heart.

A soft rumble like distant thunder penetrated Erin's reverie and she looked up sharply. Was the storm beginning? But as the rumble grew louder and more insistent she recognized it as the sound of a horse being ridden hard down the track that followed the river.

'Father!' she thought, and her heart sank a little. When he rode that way it usually meant

15

the drink was in him. And on a day as hot as this one there could be no other reason for driving his poor horse as if the devil himself was after him.

She shaded her eyes, looking down the avenue of eucalypts and mimosa, and saw him turn into view. From this distance he cut a handsome figure and she thought that no one could sit a horse as he could. But as he came closer there was no hiding his disarray – shirt flapping, hat gone – nor the high colour in his now paunchy face, and she bit her lip in distress. It was as she had feared. Paddy might have gone to Brett Wilde to plead for leniency; he had come away, at the very least, with enough rum to warm him through the night.

She picked up her skirts and ran down the steps of the veranda, half-expecting him to gallop past her to the stables, and she was surprised when he reined in so abruptly that Bess, his black mare, reared up on her hind legs.

'Father!' she admonished him, then broke off as he raised his whip hand to her, his eyes wild in his flushed face.

'Lock up the house!' he cried hoarsely. 'Drop the shutters and be quick about it!'

Erin's heart sank still further. Drunk as she'd seen him, he hadn't been this bad before. How much rum had that devil Brett Wilde given him?

'Come on, Father, down you get,' she said, speaking as if to a child, and she reached out to take the reins from him. But Paddy Kelly wrenched them away again impatiently.

'Don't you understand what I'm saying, child?

Get into the house and lock the door. Are your sisters and brother there?'

She squinted up at him. The shimmering heat seemed to have put a halo around him.

'Patrick's there, and Brenna,' she soothed.

'And Grianne?'

'Grianne's at David's. You knew that.'

'Ah, sure I'd forgotten. Please God she'll be safe there.'

'Safe?' she repeated. 'What are you talking about, Father?'

He leaned forward on Bess's lathered neck.

'Erin, will you listen to your father for a minute? Don't go thinking I'm drunk, because I'm not. There's been a break-out on the other side of the river. McClusky's convicts are on the loose, with all the guns they could steal. His overseer has ridden for the soldiers, but heaven alone knows how long it will be before they arrive. So get into the house this instant and lock the doors, do you hear?'

The blood seemed to drain from Erin's body, leaving her cold and trembling. A break-out – the thing most feared among the settlers! Convicts might be the cheapest form of labour, but they were ruthless men with nothing to lose; you could no more turn your back on one than you could on a wild animal. One slip, one moment's weakness, and they would spring. The two convicts they had been able to keep were docile enough, but she had sometimes seen the resentment burning in their eyes when they looked at her, and shuddered.

As if reading her thoughts Paddy pulled his

17

pistol from its holster and cocked it.

'Where are Higgins and Turvey?' he asked, naming their two assigned convicts.

Erin swallowed at the knot of fear in her throat, willing herself to be calm. 'They were at work in the vegetable patch. Why – you don't think...?'

'If they get wind of what's going on they'll be gone to join the others in no time,' Paddy stated. 'I'll lock them in their hut for safety. Now do as I say, girl, and get inside the house!'

Digging his heels into Bess's flanks, he cantered off along the side of the farmhouse and Erin hurried inside, her mind churning in crazed circles.

There were two guns in the house, she knew – Patrick could take one and she could fire the other if she had to. And her father had his pistol. But would they be enough? Paddy had not said how many convicts were on the loose, but Mc-Clusky's was a big farm with almost as many workers as Brett Wilde had at Mia-Mia. And they could be freeing other convicts as they went, swelling the band to a small army.

Erin shivered. If that were the case, three guns would be worse than useless. But it was no good to think that way. Better to simply do as her father had said – lock the doors and pray that the soldiers came quickly. They were the only ones with any hope of rounding up the rebels.

As she went into the kitchen Brenna looked up from her tea curiously.

'Was that Father? Why was he riding so fast?'

Erin drew a deep breath to steady herself.

There was no point in frightening the child unnecessarily.

'We're going to play a game, Brenna,' she said gently. 'We're going to lock the doors and the windows and pretend the soldiers are coming.'

Brenna's eyes widened. 'Lock the *windows*? But it's so hot!'

'That'll just make it more fun,' Erin told her.

'Erin...' Patrick had put down his fork and was staring at her intently. She tightened her lips and sent urgent messages to him with her eyes. She couldn't hope to fool him, of course, and in any case, she was counting on him to take a gun.

'Brenna, will you run upstairs for me and fetch my wrap?' she commanded. With a look of utter surprise the child did as she was bid, and Erin was able to repeat to Patrick what Paddy had told her.

For a moment Patrick stared at her in horror, then his slight frame relaxed.

'They won't come this way, Erin. Not if they're on the other side of the river. They'll make for the mountains.'

'You can't be sure of that,' Erin protested.

'It's what I'd do,' Patrick said reasonably. 'And if they do cross the river, why should they come here? We've get nothing. They'd do better to go for richer pickings at Mia-Mia.'

Erin's lips tightened a shade. That would be no more than Brett Wilde deserved – his grand house ransacked and his ill-gotten gains looted. But the convicts would know he was an officer of the New South Wales Corps and if they had a grain of sense they would steer very clear of

19

Mia-Mia.

The door slammed and Erin almost jumped out of her skin. But it was only Paddy.

'I've locked Higgins and Turvey in their hut out of harm's way,' he told them. 'Now there's nothing to be done but wait and pray.'

Erin nodded, taking down the guns and handing one to Patrick.

'Eat your tea, Father,' she suggested. 'It'll help no one if you go hungry. I'll go up and keep watch from the window.'

Without waiting for a reply she turned and climbed the rickety staircase that led to the upper storey of the farmhouse. Brenna was just coming down with her wrap; she took it from her and motioned the child to go down and join her father and brother.

It was an effort to remain calm, but somehow she managed it. Living in this wild new country had taught Erin a great deal about self-control. And as she positioned herself at the window that commanded an uninterrupted view of the drive and the rich river flats she felt sharply, breathlessly alive, with all her senses honed to a fine edge of waiting.

Strangely, it reminded her of the way she had once felt about Alistair – fear blended with excitement and the knowledge that something momentous was only a heart's beat away. Yet there was no similarity in the situations. Alistair had been her sweetheart – and a pretty poor specimen at that. While the waiting now was for something that could mean the difference between life and death, normality and terror.

But at least while her heart beat this crazy, irregular pattern she knew she was alive. And sometimes in the last months while she had scrubbed and cooked and worried about making ends meet, that was something she had begun to wonder about.

Over the mountains the lightening still flickered ceaselessly in the lowering sky. Without a doubt the storm would come before nightfall. But what would it bring with it?

CHAPTER TWO

'Erin – Father says you're to go down and have something to eat. I'll take over the watch for you.'

At the sound of Patrick's voice, Erin moved stiffly from the position she had set herself at the window and spared him a glance before once again scanning the vista her vantage point afforded her.

'It's not easy to see now it's getting dusk, Patrick. You've to watch like a hawk.'

'Are you saying your eyes are better than mine?' he teased, pretending to take offence. 'Go on down for a bit, Erin, or you'll give yourself such a squint no self-respecting man will look twice at you.'

'Oh, get on with you!' she scoffed, but she stretched her cramped limbs gratefully all the same. In the hour she had sat at the window she had scarcely moved a muscle for fear of missing a creeping danger in the shadows of the acacia trees. It would be good to relax for a while and let Patrick do the peering into the hazy dusk.

'Just as long as you don't wander into a dream and not notice what's going on out there,' she warned, moving away to let him take her place.

Patrick grinned, his thin face lighting up with

mischief. 'As if I would! Not that there's a thing to worry about if you ask me. They've gone the other way, like I told you. They're more than likely in the mountains by now.'

'You may be right,' Erin conceded. 'But *watch* all the same. Do you hear me?'

His laughter followed her as she went down the stairs and it cut her oddly. He was only four years younger than she, yet he could make her feel old and staid with his carefree view of life. She thought it was how they regarded her, too – well, he and Grianne, anyway. But there was no other way she could be. Their mother had gone and someone had to take her place.

Brenna had gone to bed now and in the kitchen Paddy sat alone sprawled in the low chair. His shirt was still open and a lock of greying hair fell limply across his flushed face. Sadness touched Erin as she looked at him. Once he had been so strong and handsome. Now he sat staring into space through rum-sodden eyes. He had not even taken off his riding boots.

'How did your visit to Mia-Mia go?' she asked softly, dropping onto her haunches beside him.

He turned bleary eyes to look at her. 'Oh, sure, 'twas fine.'

'The debts, Father!' she pressed him. 'Will Brett Wilde give us more time to pay?'

He waved his hand airily. 'Of course. Of course.'

'Father!' she said sharply. 'It's useless to pretend with me. I know Brett Wilde strikes the hardest bargain of any of that blamed trading ring. I've seen him ride by on his fine horse like

23

the lord of the manor though he never so much as spares a glance for the likes of me and I've heard of his hard heart when it comes to closing a deal. Please tell me the truth – how much longer will he allow us supplies before he takes back all we owe him?'

For a moment Paddy remained bleary yet defiant, then his body seemed to sag.

'Not much longer, I fear. Mr Wilde tells me today that he intends resigning his commission in the Corps to concentrate on his business interests.'

'Well, that's honest of him at least,' Erin said spitefully, and Paddy's hand fumbled for hers.

'You do see what it means, don't you? With no salary from the Corps to back his enterprises, he'll be more anxious than ever to make a quick profit. Not that he and his friends have ever dragged their feet on that score...'

'Oh Father!' With a small sob Erin buried her face in his hands, then raised it with a quick, determined movement. 'We must raise the money, Father – get out of his debt. If we can't there's no telling where this will end. We'll talk about it in the morning, for it can be left no longer.'

Paddy nodded, obedient as a child now. 'You're a good girl, Erin,' he murmured. 'But it shouldn't be this way for you. You're too young and lovely to be worrying your head about such things. Now if your mother was only living...'

His words were almost drowned as the first sharp crack of thunder rent the simmering sky and the farmhouse seemed almost to shake with

24

the reverberations of it. Then the rain began, hammering a rhythmic tattoo on shutters and roofs, and ricocheting in sharp arrows off the baked ground to rattle once against the walls of the farm, and a small sigh escaped Erin. It was a relief that the storm had come – more than that it likely meant that Patrick had been right when he had said the convicts would not bother them this night. Wherever they were now they would be wise to stay and take shelter.

She dropped to her knees in front of Paddy, taking hold of one of his boots.

'Let me help you with these, Father,' she said gently. 'You won't need to go out again tonight.'

But Paddy hardly seemed to be listening to her.

'I'm sorry, Erin,' he muttered humbly.

'Sorry? Whatever are you talking about?' she asked briskly, pulling off one boot and setting it beside him.

'For the way things have turned out,' he went on. 'Maybe we should have stayed in Ireland. Maybe if we'd never left your mother would be with us now. I miss her, Erin...'

'I know,' she soothed. 'Now give me your other foot, Father.'

'Wait!' He stiffened suddenly, cocking his head to one side as if to listen. 'What was that?'

'It's nothing, Father, just the storm...' she murmured.

But he was sitting bolt upright reaching for his boots once more.

''Twas Bess! Sure, wouldn'a I know her whinny anywhere! The best horse a man ever had...'

25

'The storm'll be making her nervous, that's all,' Erin said, trying to urge him back into his chair. But he was adamant.

'I must go to her. The stable needs repairing and if harm came to Bess, I'd never forgive myself.'

Sighing, Erin let him go. She had heard nothing but he would not rest until he had satisfied himself all was well with his horse. She was all he really cared for now, taking the place of the wife he had lost and, yes, his children too, in his affections.

'Take care then, Father,' she said gently.

The gusting wind snatched the door from him, slamming it shut, and with a grimace Erin began clearing away the remains of the meal. What was Grianne doing at this moment, she wondered? Sitting with David's arms about her, no doubt, pretending to be afraid of the storm and enjoying the attention the Percys always showered on her. Five sons there were and Mrs Percy always treated Grianne like the daughter she had been unable to bear.

It could have been that way for me, thought Erin, but there was no bitterness in her, only relief that Grianne would not have to endure what she had endured, mingled with an inescapable ache of longing. Oh, to be feted and waited on! Oh, to have someone to feel about her as David felt about Grianne...

A sudden sharp crack brought Erin upright, her senses tinglingly alert. What was that? For all the world it had sounded like someone firing a pistol! Oh, it couldn't be, surely! A thunderbolt, maybe, but someone firing...

The sharp crack came again and again, and she stood, her eyes wide with alarm. Then a clatter on the stairs made her turn. Patrick stood there, his face ashen.

'Did you hear that, Erin? It was a shot, wasn't it?'

Hearing him voice her fears made them real. 'Three shots.' Her hand went to her throat. 'Patrick, Father's out there. You don't think...'

Brother and sister stared at each other for a moment, then Patrick reached for the gun lying among the dirty dishes on the table.

'I'll go and see.'

'No!' Erin said swiftly. 'I'll go. You stay here, Patrick. Brenna's upstairs and asleep. I don't suppose it's anything, but just in case...'

She broke off, taking the pistol from him. Then, before the boy could argue – or before her nerve could fail her – she crossed the kitchen and opened the door.

The wind was not so high now and already the storm was almost spent. The occasional fork of lightning still split the dark sky and the thunder rumbled in the distance, but it was calm enough now to hear the sounds of the river – the normal, reassuring sounds that were woven into the pattern of everyday life.

Tonight, however, they did nothing to reassure Erin. She closed the door after her, shutting off the friendly lamplight, and stood for a moment, her lip caught tight between her teeth as she cocked the pistol. How many times had she fired it? Half a dozen at most. Even out here in the

27

wilderness Paddy had not been keen to teach her, clinging with typical blind stubbornness to his dream that one day the farm would prosper and determined she should learn from the start to act the lady she would become.

''Tis not right that my daughters should shoot like a man,' he would say. 'As long as I've life and strength, sure *I'm* the one to take care of them all.'

Now, as Erin looked down at the pistol, she was frighteningly aware of her inexperience. But undeterred she took a step into the darkness. What did one need to know about firing a pistol so long as it pointed in the right direction at the moment the trigger was pulled?

Around the farmhouse she went, one hand steadying herself against the rough wall, the other holding the cocked pistol. Her eyes soon grew accustomed to the dark and she moved quickly towards the dark bulk of the stables.

All was quiet. It was hard now to believe the shots had existed except in the imagination, but her breath still rasped in her throat and her skin tingled with sharp awareness. The barn door stood ajar; as she drew level with it she thought she heard a rustle within and froze, the pistol butt pressed tight against her breasts.

'Father?' she called softly. 'Father – is that you?'

There was no reply and a bolt of lightning showed nothing but blackness within. But for some reason Erin was not satisfied. She crept forward into the barn, straining her eyes into the silent dark.

'Father!' she whispered again, her voice low and hoarse.

Suddenly, in the stillness, the rustle came again, and with it a low moan. Sharply Erin twisted towards the sound, then, as her eyes made out the huddled form, a gasp escaped her.

'Father!'

He was half-lying against a bale of hay, and she felt a swift uprush of relief. The drink had been too much for him. She'd have to fetch Patrick to help her get him back to the house and together they would put him to bed.

'Come along, Father,' she said gently.

She crouched down beside him, putting her gun down in the hay and slipping her arms around him. Then her heart seemed almost to stop beating and she drew back sharply staring in horror at her hands, sticky and dark in the half-light. Blood! Her father's blood!

'Oh God!' It was half-scream, half-sob and it seemed to stir Paddy. With a supreme effort he raised himself against the hay, his face working, his fingers clawing at her urgently.

'Get back in the house, Erin. They've got me!'

'Who, Father?' She was almost too shocked to think straight.

'The convicts – who else? Get inside. Lock the door...'

'Father, I can't leave you here like this! Can you walk? Here, I'll help you...'

Desperately she tried to raise him but he pushed at her with weak impatience.

'Warn your brother and sister. Leave me – I'm done for anyway.'

29

'No!' she sobbed. 'No!'

'Yes.' His voice was weak, barely more than a whisper. He was failing fast. 'Never mind me, Erin. Look after them...'

Into Erin's crazed brain came a nightmare sense of history repeating itself. First her mother, now her father! Dear God, it was more than she could bear! But she wouldn't let him die. She couldn't!

'Father, please try!' she urged desperately. 'We've medications in the house. Now, lean on me.'

Again she passed her hand around his waist, not flinching this time when the warm blood oozed over her fingers. But as she tried to lift him there came the sound of fists pounding on wood and boots squelching in the muddy yard and a rough voice called: 'It's their convicts – let 'em out to join us!'

'Hush – stay still now!' Paddy whispered, his hand finding Erin's mouth and pressing hard against it. She crouched against him until the footsteps died away once more. Then he gave her a weak but urgent push. 'Go now! Go quickly! 'Tis your only chance!'

For a moment longer she hesitated, feeling as if she was being torn in two. But she knew he was right. Patrick and Brenna must be warned.

'I'll not be long, Father,' she promised. Then she ran to the barn door, peering out. The men had gone, long shadows disappearing in the direction of the convicts' hut a hundred yards from the house and hidden from view by the stables. Moving like a cat, she ran crouching under the barn wall as far as she was able, then, when she could remain under cover no longer, she lifted her skirts and darted across the yard.

But as she neared the kitchen door her blood seemed to turn to ice. She had closed it after her – she knew she had! Now it stood ajar, with light spilling through it to make a golden pathway on the wet yard.

'Oh dear God, no!' she sobbed.

Her flying feet took her the last few yards and up the steps of the veranda. Then, as she pushed the door wide, a scream of horror rose in her throat.

The kitchen was in turmoil – chairs and table overturned, drawers pulled out, crockery smashed on the floor. Against the dresser Patrick slouched, half-stunned, blood trickling in a thin river down his chin. And in the centre of the chaos two strange men were filling their pockets with everything they could carry.

At her scream they stopped their vile work, looking up at her so that for a moment they were frozen like alabaster statues. The one was small and wiry with a sharp, resentful face; the other was swarthy and thickset with eyes like pieces of jet above a rough growth of beard. And although Erin had never seen either before she knew their faces would be with her in nightmares for as long as she lived. If she had a gun in her hands now she would have used it, she knew. But the pistol she had taken to defend herself still lay in the barn beside her father and the other was out of reach amid the smashed crocks on the floor.

The big man straightened up, his mouth twisting to an evil red gash within the thick growth of hair.

'What have we here? The mistress of the house? Just the one to tell us where the treasures are hidden!'

Erin stood frozen with horror, clutching at the wooden doorpost, and he reached out with an impatient movement, twisting his fingers into her hair and yanking her towards him.

'Come on, come on! Where are your riches hidden?'

'We have none!' she spat at him. 'We're settlers, not gentry.'

He laughed, lips curling back from sharp white teeth, but the smell of his breath was fetid, mingling with the sweaty odour of his unwashed body.

'We'll see about that! Look upstairs, Wrigley, and look well! I'll stay here and see what milady settler has to offer!'

'No!' Erin cried, her thoughts flying to Brenna asleep in her bed and defenceless. As the man named Wrigley made for the stairs the big man laughed again, his fingers tightening in Erin's hair until she almost cried out with the pain.

'So there *is* something of value! Search, Wrigley, while I try to find out its whereabouts in another way!'

Erin shrank from him in terror but he held her fast, casually raising his free hand to her throat. The thick fingers spanned it easily, and as he pressed upon it Erin felt as if she were choking already. With the last ounce of her courage she kicked out at his shin, but her slippered toe was too soft to have any effect and he only laughed at her, holding her the tighter.

'You beast!' she sobbed, struggling helplessly. 'Let me go! D'you think I would tell you even if I had anything of value? I'd die first!'

The black eyes glittered. 'You have spirit, I see! A hell-cat indeed! If I had more time, my pretty...'

Still holding her hair fast, he jerked her head back so that her throat was taut beneath his fingers. Then he let his hand move slowly downwards to the curve of her thrusting breasts. Her cry of shock and outrage seemed to rouse Patrick and somehow he found his feet, struggling, still half-dazed, across the kitchen.

'Leave her! Don't touch my sister!'

With a sneer the man caught at the thin fabric of Erin's gown, ripping it viciously so that her breasts were exposed, full and white, with their rosy tips risen from his touch. A low, throaty growl escaped him and his hands clawed greedily at the soft flesh. Vainly Patrick tried to drag him off but he brushed the boy aside with a blow that sent him reeling once more.

'Pig! Leave me!' Erin screamed.

The man's face was close to hers now, the fetid breath making her heave. 'Do you know how long it is since I had a woman? Do you know...?'

'Erin!' The sob came from close at hand, making them both start. It was Brenna, emerging from behind the sofa where she had been hiding, and the distraction gave Erin a moment's grace. With all her strength she slapped at the man's

33

bearded face but she might have been swatting at flies for all the good it did her.

'You little hell-cat!' he snarled, and nausea rose in her as he lunged for her once more.

'What do you think you're doing?' From the stairs the voice of Wrigley arrested the big man. 'Leave her, you fool. There'll be time and to spare for women when we're away from this place. The storm's spent now. It's time we were gone.'

The big man jerked around, though his fingers in her hair still held her prisoner.

'Did you find aught of value?' he asked.

The man Wrigley opened his hand and Erin gasped as she saw the few precious guineas she had managed to save as insurance against her father's debts lying in his filthy palm.

'These only and a worthless trinket or two. There are no rich pickings here.' His voice was scornful.

'You see?' Erin cried. 'How can you take what little we have? Have you no conscience?'

Wrigley turned his small, mean face to her.

'Lady, my conscience went for naught on a convict transport, battened in a hold while the likes of you slept in comfort. No, I have no conscience. That's a luxury I cannot afford.'

'Oh!' she squealed. 'You criminals! Get out of our house and leave us in peace!'

The man Wrigley crossed to the door.

'Do as the lady says, now. Leave her and let us be on our way.'

For a moment the bearded face came close to Erin's and she choked at the foul breath. Then

34

with a laugh the man released her hair, catching instead at the locket that hung about her neck.

'Very well. But I'll take this with me. Count yourself lucky to escape so light!'

With a jerk he snapped the slender chain and Erin's hands flew, too late, to her throat.

'Oh, not my locket!' she whispered. It was one of the only things remaining of her mother's. 'Not my locket, please!'

But her plea fell on deaf ears. With a last greedy look around, the two men were gone, leaving the door standing open behind them.

For a moment the brother and sister remained motionless with only the sound of Brenna's soft sobbing to break the stillness. Then Erin pulled her torn gown about her and turned wildly to Patrick.

'Father's been shot!' she gasped. 'He's in the barn. I think he's badly hurt.'

Patrick's already pallid face turned even whiter.

'You don't mean ... he's not *dead*, Erin?'

She bit at her lip till the blood ran but she did not notice.

'I'm going back to see if he can be moved. Stay here, Patrick, with Brenna, and lock the door behind me.'

'But they've taken everything of value,' he protested.

'Lock it all the same!' She did not tell him of the fear that still nagged at her – that they might return and fire the house for spite at finding nothing of value.

On shaking legs she slipped outside and heard

35

Patrick lock the door after her. Thank God he was still child enough to obey her instructions without question!

With a quick look around she lifted her skirts and ran back across the yard. The barn was as she had left it, her father still propped against the hay. But his head had fallen forward, lolling onto his chest like a rag doll's, and Erin's heart seemed to stop beating.

'Father!' she whispered, dropping down beside him.

There was no reply, no sign of life in the still form.

Paddy Kelly was dead.

For a moment Erin remained beside him, cradling his lifeless body in her arms while tears blurred her eyes. It was a nightmare, all of it, surely! Soon she would wake to find herself in the narrow bed she shared with Grianne, and know that her father and brother were sleeping safe and sound in the next room. Life had been hard, yes, and fraught with dangers. It had been that way since they had come to Australia and she had grown to accept it. But not this, not this...

The sudden clatter of horses' hooves outside brought Erin sharply from her reverie. Could it be the soldiers? McClusky's overseer had ridden for them, Paddy had said. Or could it be...

Our horses! thought Erin, a shaft of anger penetrating her grief. Not satisfied with murdering her father and stealing every penny she possessed, they were going to take the horses as well!

All fear for herself forgotten, she jumped up and ran to the barn door. Yes! It was Bess, her father's precious mare, with her own pony, Starlight, strung on behind. And astride Bess was the bearded man who had robbed and defiled her, and torn her mother's locket from about her neck.

At the sight Erin's last vestige of caution flew away. It was too much! First her mother's locket, now her father's horse – and him not yet cold. The thought of this beast ill-using her father's treasure was more than she could bear. She would stop him taking Bess if it was the last thing she did!

As the horses approached the barn door she darted forward, grabbing at the reins and dragging Bess to a halt. With an angry shout, the rider lashed out at Erin and as his booted foot caught her shoulder she released the reins, sobbing with pain as she staggered backwards into the barn. Then, as her heel caught against a bale of hay, she lost her balance, landing close to where her father lay.

From the doorway she heard the man's triumphant laugh and she saw his dark form silhouetted against the night sky.

'Pig!' she sobbed, trying to rise, and as she did so her fingers encountered something cold and hard in the hay. It was the pistol! Automatically her hand closed around it, her finger searching for the trigger. The man was still there in the doorway, still laughing, and Erin did not hesitate. With a swift movement she brought the pistol up and fired.

For a moment she thought she had killed him, for all was confusion. Bess reared and whinnied and with a cry of surprise and pain the bulky body slipped from the saddle, clutching wildly at his own arm. Then, before she knew what was happening, a dark form hurled itself towards her, the pistol was wrenched from her grasp and a fist struck her full in the face.

For a moment the world spun around her. Then, as it righted itself, she felt rough hands tearing at her clothing.

'You bitch! You'll pay for that – and pay my price!' The man was astride her, thrusting her back against the hay, and as she felt his greedy nails rake the soft skin of her breasts she realized they were bare. A sob escaped her throbbing mouth and she beat at him with her hands, but scornfully he thrust her back once more, catching at the torn fabric of her dress and ripping it from bodice to hem.

The fetid breath was in her nostrils once more, making her want to heave and, terror-stricken, she shrank away. But there was no escape. The feral face came close to hers, his teeth finding her mouth and sinking deeply into her soft red lips. She tried to cry out but she could not. It was as if her voice was frozen within her and she would never make a sound again. Then the hair-masked mouth slid down her throat, sought and found the tip of one full breast and fastened onto it, biting and sucking with an intensity that sent arrows of pain shooting downwards to the deepest parts of her belly. Helplessly she writhed, trying in vain to drag his head away by tugging at his matted hair. But when he raised his head at last the moonlight illuminated the naked lust on his face and without a word he raised himself to his knees, one hand at her throat, pinioning her in the hay while he bared his body. Then, with a swift, rough movement he had what was left of her skirts about her waist, forcing her legs apart with one muscled knee and lowering himself between them.

The scream she had thought would never come escaped her then, forced from her lips as his hard body sought her most virgin places and drove searingly home. Pain cut through her, pain so sharp she thought her body would split in two beneath his merciless pumping, and though she plucked and pushed at him still her movement seemed only to excite him more. One hand he slipped beneath her, raising her buttocks to aid his frenzied working, and as his mouth closed over hers once more, his tongue forcing its way deep into her throat, the bile rose in her.

He's going to kill me! she thought, one conscious fear emerging from the welter of terror that possessed her.

Then, with a loud cry, he thrust himself even deeper into her and a sob broke in her throat. He had done, she knew – finished what he had been tempted to begin in the house – and relieved himself of the vile seed that had burned in his loins for God only knew how long. Now, it was in her, in the deepest, most secret parts of her body, and the knowledge was almost more than she could bear.

If he killed her now it would be nothing but a

blessed release. She wanted him to – anything rather than face the world with the knowledge of what he had done to her.

She closed her eyes, lying back against the hay and waiting for the hands around her throat; the hands that would squeeze the life from her. But instead she was aware of the lessening of the weight upon her and she opened her eyes again to see him standing up, fastening the clothing over his vile body and grinning down at her.

'Would that I could stay to drink twice at the same well,' he sneered. 'Now give me something to bind my wound.'

She stared dumbly, not comprehending, and he grasped at her torn petticoats, ripping a strip from them and winding it around his forearm. So she had hit him when she had fired at him and perhaps the pain had heightened his desire for her.

There was a stickiness on her belly. She had thought it was more of his vile seed. Now she touched it tentatively with her fingers and knew it was blood – his blood.

'Get out!' she cried in anguish.

In the doorway he paused, looking back at her. 'The damned horses have gone!' he snarled. 'Ah well, 'twas an exchange worth the making.'

Then he was gone and Erin was left sobbing softly as she tried to wipe away his blood and seed from her body.

She had saved the horses, she thought dully. They would come back. But what a price she had been forced to pay for them.

40

CHAPTER THREE

A night and a day and a night passed and still Erin felt that the nightmare would never end.

There was so much to think of, so many things to worry about, and no one to share the burden any more. Drunken though Paddy had been most of the time, at least he had been there. Now Erin felt quite alone.

Grianne was no help. Since she had arrived back from David Percy's and found the devastation at Kinvarra she had hardly stopped crying and her wailing sawed at Erin's already frayed nerves. As for Patrick, he had been a dreamer always and now, guilt-ridden as he was over allowing the convicts to enter the premises without him noticing, he was less use than ever. So it was left to Erin to make the arrangements for Paddy's funeral, round up Bess and Starlight, and try to bring some order back to their lives.

But mercifully she had been able to keep from them the truth of the fate that had befallen her that night in the stable and for that, at least, she was grateful. It had been her first thought after the convict had left her, for she thought she would have died of shame if Patrick should guess how she had been used. Bad enough to have to live herself with the memory of his grasping hands and sweating, pumping body and the knowledge that his ugly thrusting lust had taken her virginity. Bad enough to lie sleepless with the throbbing of her jaw echoed by the burning between her legs and the sickness that came from feeling that she would never be clean again. But if the others had known, their horror – and their pity – would have made it a thousand times worse.

Before crawling back to the house Erin had managed to tie her gown about her so as to conceal the true extent of its damage and she had wetted a handkerchief in the bucket of water that always stood in the stable and cleaned the worst of the blood and dirt from her hands and face. The cuts and bruises she could not hide, but she had explained them away by saying she had got them trying to save the horses and Patrick had accepted that.

Perhaps, she thought, he had *wanted* to accept it. The burden of guilt he carried was heavy enough already, without adding to it.

'I'll never forgive myself, Erin,' he sobbed over and over again. 'I thought they wouldn't come and I suppose I didn't watch as closely as I should. Now Father is dead and we've lost everything and I'm the one to blame.'

'How could you, Patrick? How could you be so stupid!' Grianne wept and Erin had to bite her tongue to keep back the sharp retort she longed to make to her sister. Accusations and recriminations would do no good now. Somehow they had to go on living.

'Don't blame yourself, Patrick,' she comforted

42

him, smoothing the tumbled hair back from his brow. ''Tis too late for that. It was getting dusk – anyone could have missed seeing them come. And they knew every trick of concealment, rogues that they are.'

He nodded wordlessly, snatching at the crumb of comfort, but Erin knew it would not be long before his thoughts had turned full circle and he was once again torturing himself with the charge that it was his inadequacy that had brought about the disaster.

'What are we to do?' wailed Grianne. 'We'll starve, all of us!'

Erin straightened her back, looking her sister straight in the eye. 'We shall do nothing of the sort!' she said with more spirit than she was feeling. 'The convicts may have taken all they could carry, but we still have our grant of land. No one can take that away from us.'

'Brett Wilde could,' Patrick muttered, and Erin looked at him sharply.

'What do you know about Brett Wilde?'

'Do you take me for a fool, Erin?' Patrick snorted. 'I know Father went to see him the day he died and it can have been for one reason only. We owe him money, and if he's not paid he'll take our land in its place.'

Grianne began to wail again, the tears filling her china-blue eyes and spilling down her cheeks.

'You'll have to go and see him, Erin,' she sobbed. 'Tell him we can't pay – beg for his help. Though what good 'twill do I don't know. Everyone knows Brett Wilde has a heart of stone.'

43

'*I* know that – and I'll do no begging,' Erin said impatiently. 'For goodness' sake, stop snivelling, Grianne. I'll think of something.'

The younger girl rubbed her face with the back of her hand, but above it her eyes were resentful. 'Why do you have to be so proud, Erin? Father went to Brett Wilde, didn't he? Why can't you?'

'It was different for Father,' Erin said shortly.

'Why? Why different?' Grianne pressed her tearfully.

Erin did not reply. With her father newly buried she had no wish to desecrate his memory by explaining that his craving for rum would have driven Paddy to sink to any depths to obtain it. But however great their need she would not do that. To have folk grovelling would be exactly what Brett Wilde would enjoy. He and his kind liked nothing better than to hold the strings of power and make poor settlers dance like puppets to his tune. Well, she would not do it. The very thought made everything in her cry out against it. There must be some other way – there must!

'I told you I'd think of something, and I will!' Erin assured her sister. 'Now, look in on Brenna for me while I clear these dishes and see if she's sleeping peacefully. She's had such nightmares these past days, poor lamb.'

'I still say you fancy yourself too much,' Grianne shot at her unpleasantly as she went up the stairs and Erin sighed as she began to stack the dishes from their meagre evening meal.

Perhaps it was true – she did have too much pride. But it was the only thing left she could

44

call her own and she could not let it go too easily even if they starved as Grianne had suggested.

Not that that fate was likely to befall Grianne. She could always go to the Percys, for Erin was sure it was only a matter of time before David proposed marriage to her. But there was still Patrick and Brenna to consider. They had to be taken care of and no one on the river was rich enough to take the family under their wing however much they might sympathize with their plight. And while it was easy enough to say that she would think of something, in reality Erin was at her wits' end to know which way to turn.

Damn Brett Wilde! she thought for the hundredth time. As if it was not bad enough to be destitute, knowing that he was living in luxury at Mia-Mia on the profits he had gained from his power-grabbing was almost insupportable.

As she cleared the dishes from the roughly made table, Erin's mind ran back over what her father had told her of Brett Wilde and his kind.

They had come to New South Wales as officers of the militia, and in a new country with a weak Governor they had made their own laws. The best land they had granted to themselves, and with their influence in Sydney they had been able to monopolize trade. Between them they had set up a buying ring, taking their pick of the commodities that arrived in the harbour from all over the world and selling them to the poor settlers at prices they themselves set. There was hardly a pie that the buying ring did not have a finger in, and successive Governors had not been able to weaken their grip on the throat of

45

New South Wales trade. Even the price of grain was under their control. But their greatest power lay in the lucrative rum trade.

They made their fortunes trading on the weakness of people like my poor father, Erin thought, dashing away the tears that pricked at her eyes as she remembered him. He would have kept himself in rum though the property tumbled about him. That would be the last to go. Yet he had been the dearest, sweetest father in the world...

She stopped suddenly, setting down the dishes with such a clatter that Patrick almost jumped out of his skin.

The rum! Her father would never have been without it, but he kept it judiciously hidden so that it was not too apparent to the rest of the family. Once she had found a keg concealed beneath the hay in the barn; sometimes, she suspected, he mingled full kegs among the empty ones at the rear of the property. If that were the case, the rampaging convicts might have missed it! And it would give her something to barter with – something of undoubted value to gain a breathing space...

Swiftly she untied the strings of her apron, tossing it down onto the table.

'I won't be long, Patrick.'

'Where are you going?' he queried.

'Just outside for a moment. I need a breath of air.'

He nodded. He was used to Erin and her 'breaths of air'. Besides, he was too preoccupied with his guilt to worry too much about any-

46

thing else.

She slipped outside. The heat had returned and with it the mosquitoes. She flapped at them absently as she went around to the rear of the property. She would try the stack of kegs first. Hopefully his store would be concealed here, for she did not want to have to go into the barn ever again.

With a furtive look over her shoulder she began tapping the kegs, listening for a thicker, duller sound than the rattle of an empty one. But she was disappointed. The kegs were empty every one. She straightened, biting her lip. She would have to go into the barn. There was nothing else for it.

As she crossed the yard her heart hammered painfully into her ribs. The warm smell of hay came out to meet her as she pushed open the door and bile rose bitter in her throat. She had always loved the smell of hay. No more. Now it would always evoke for her the memory of violence and death and that evil man thrusting between her legs. But she could not give way to these finer sensibilities, she knew. Steeling herself, she went right into the barn, kicking and pulling at the hay for the tell-tale hollow or the loose bale.

For endless minutes she searched, then at last she straightened up, brushing her black hair away from her face with a weary hand. There was no rum here either. Or if there was she could not find it. A sense of hopelessness welled up in her and it was all she could do to keep herself from sinking into the hay and weeping.

Had Paddy really run his rum stock so low? Had he visited Brett Wilde that day in sheer desperation? It was beginning to appear that might be the case. Yet she would have staked her life on Paddy having one keg at least stashed away somewhere. For him it had been as necessary as breath. He could not have survived a night without it.

The stables! The idea came to Erin in a flash and new hope surged through her as she remembered his eagerness to go out that last night to see Bess. He had said then he had heard the horse whinny but she had heard nothing, though with all that had happened afterwards she had assumed it had been she who had been mistaken and the horse had indeed been disturbed by the convicts.

Now, however, it occurred to her that it might have been an excuse on Paddy's part. Perhaps there was rum concealed in the stable and he had pretended to hear the horse so that he could go out and down a tot of it.

The top half of the stable door was still open; she had not yet shut up the horses for the night. When they heard her coming they fidgeted within their stalls, thrusting with their noses to greet her. Again she felt a stab of triumph that she had saved them from the fate that would no doubt have been theirs if the convicts had taken them – ridden hard until they could go no further, and then eaten when supplies ran low. And it was a mercy, too, that they had not fired the stables. The convicts' hut had gone up, but there were no convicts now to live there, and it was far

48

enough from the other outbuildings that the fire had not spread. Thinking about it, Erin's nose seemed once more to be full of the acrid smoke that had filled it that night and she wondered if there would ever be a time when the memories, with all their attendant horror, would be any less vivid.

The moonlight slanting in through the stable door made it almost as bright as day and eagerly Erin began her search. At first it revealed nothing and she had just begun to think she must have been mistaken when she saw the rum keg hidden behind the tack at the farthest corner of the stable.

Quickly she pulled it out, tapping at it, and to her delight it seemed to be almost full! This was it, then, wealth unsuspected by either the family or the marauding convicts. But what to do with it?

I'd sell it back to Brett Wilde if I thought he'd give me a fair price for it, Erin mused. But it was a certainty he would not. Why should he pay good money for what he could undoubtedly get more cheaply from the East Indian traders? No, the only way was to play him at his own game – find a buyer for the rum and sell it for just a little less than it could be obtained from the buying ring. But who? Who was there who would deal with a mere girl?

Anyone, Erin thought shrewdly, anyone in this colony would deal with me if they could get a bargain.

But there would be plenty who would seek to cheat her, and also those who could not afford to pay. If that happened she did not have the where-withal to be her own debt collector. She must sell to someone whose credit was good, someone she could trust...

For a moment she stood nibbling her lip and thinking. Then, in a flash, it came to her. There was a rum parlour in Blackley's Tower, a hamlet a few miles upriver – a neat, thatched cottage that was run as an inn. Erin had only seen it once or twice when she had been out riding with Paddy, for their excursions more often took them downriver than up. But she remembered how bright and clean it had looked, compared with her hazy recollections of taverns in England, with its thatched roof, tables set out on the veranda and the golden mimosa blooming in its neat patch of garden. She remembered, too, the woman she had seen leaning, arms akimbo, against the veranda. Paddy had hurried her past and she guessed the woman was no better than she should be. But she had looked a pleasant soul for all that, and plump and dimpled in her neat white cap and the cotton gown cut low to expose a huge expanse of creamy white breasts.

With her need to buy rum cheaply to sell again, the woman would surely make an ideal customer. Yet she would be more trustworthy than some poor soak crazy for the rot-gut liquid that could destroy bodies, minds and lives.

Erin smiled triumphantly to herself, all troubles momentarily forgotten. Oh yes, she would show Mr Brett Wilde she was not so easily beaten! She wriggled the keg back into its hiding place and pulled the tack over it. Better that the

50

others should not know what she was about. But if she did not soon go back inside the house, there would be questions asked.

With an affectionate pat for each of the horses, she left the stable, securing the door behind her. Little did anyone know what a valuable haul was guarded by those quiet beasts.

Next day Erin was up early, hurrying through what chores could not be left so that she could get out on her errand before the sun rose too high in the sky. The heat was something she would never grow used to, she thought. It seemed to drain her. But for all that she was determined not to let such a little thing thwart her.

'I have someone to go and see,' she explained to her brother and sisters and, although they pressed her curiously, she refused to be drawn.

'It's Brett Wilde, I expect,' Grianne suggested maliciously. 'She's realized it's the only way but she won't admit it.'

Erin ignored the barb. Tempting though it was to refute the suggestion, she preferred the others to think she was visiting Brett Wilde than that they should know the real purpose of her mission.

'What are we to eat today?' Patrick asked.

'There's a little of the salt pork left and some damper bread,' Erin told him, and when she saw the hungry expression on their faces her resolve deepened. If she could bring off a good deal today there would be mutton and perhaps potatoes – maybe even a duck. It was a tempting thought, although she herself had had no appe-

51

tite since the night of her ordeal and all food tasted like wood pulp in her mouth.

Leaving the others still muttering curiously she went out to the stables and saddled Starlight, conquering the temptation to pull aside the tack and peep at the keg of rum. Then, hoisting up her skirts, she mounted the little bay and trotted her out of the stable yard and down the drive towards the river road.

Already the air was singing with heat and the flies buzzed annoyingly around Starlight and Erin. But at least beneath the avenue of trees they were shaded from the direct heat of the sun. Down the river track she trotted, riding more sedately than Paddy or Patrick ever did, but her mind was a ferment at what she had to do.

Could she summon the necessary hardness to strike a bargain, or would she allow herself to be ridden over rough-shod? As yet she had no way of knowing. Only the gritty determination within her gave her confidence. No tavern woman was going to have too cheaply what was rightfully hers. That she was decided upon. But how to explain her possession of the rum and offer it for sale?

By the time the first straggling cottages of Blackley's Tower came into view Erin had decided her best approach was to ride in boldly and take the bull by the horns. On the one occasion she had seen Alice Simmons, the owner of the rum shop, she had formed the opinion she was a woman who would prefer straight talking to deviousness – a woman who, for all her dimpled roundness, was more at home in the company of men than of women.

Through the hamlet Erin rode, past the smithy where the blacksmith sweated rivers as he worked over his anvil, past the tower that had given the hamlet its name, built as a folly by a romantically inclined settler. The man, Blackley, had long since gone, bankrupted by his notions, but the tower remained to overshadow the row of cottages, thatched and white-painted beneath the film of summer dust.

Erin urged Starlight over the rutted road until Alice Simmons's cottage came in sight. There were two or three men in the garden drinking as well as a couple of soldiers, and her courage almost failed her. But she trotted purposefully to the gate, dismounted and hitched the pony to a convenient rail. Then, lifting her chin, she marched through the gaggle of men to the cottage door.

Their appreciative eyes followed her. She was unable to help overhearing their incautious remarks and the colour rose in her cheeks. Could they tell she was no virgin just by looking at her? she wondered uncomfortably. Did men have some way of knowing when a woman was no longer a pure, untouched maid? No – it was too ridiculous. The bruises were fading and she had scrubbed herself over and over again with all the water she could carry from the river. Yet still it seemed to her that she was different and it must be obvious to anyone who looked twice in her direction.

The door to Alice Simmons's cottage stood ajar; she knocked on it and a heavy jowled man with a face like the rising sun appeared from the gloomy interior.

'Yes?'

'Could I see Mrs Simmons, please?' Erin asked demurely.

The man's eyes narrowed in his over-ripe face. 'What do you want with her?'

'I'll tell Mrs Simmons that,' Erin returned tartly.

For a moment the heavy features darkened, then the man threw back his head and laughed.

'All right. You'd better come with me. Mrs Simmons is laid up, but if you've come to rail at her for selling your man rum, I warn you, a broken leg has done nothing to dull her wits – nor her tongue!'

He turned away, leading Erin along a cool, dim passage to a small but spotless parlour. A young man in the uniform of a subaltern of the New South Wales Corps lounged against a window seat, and in a chintz-covered rocker, one leg propped up onto a footstool, sat the woman Erin recognized as Alice Simmons.

'Here's someone who'll not go away till she's seen you,' Erin's guide said by way of introduction. Alice Simmons raised small bright eyes to rake Erin from head to toe.

'Is that so?' she inquired. 'Well, now you've seen me, girl. What is it you want?'

Erin lifted her chin, holding the older woman's gaze with a confidence she was far from feeling, and gestured towards the soldier.

'My business is private.'

Alice Simmons's lips twisted; for an unnerving moment Erin felt sure she was going to laugh. Then she nodded abruptly.

'You heard the young lady, Joe. You can come back when she's done, if you've a mind to. Though from the way you're looking at her, I reckon it's more likely you'll choose to follow after her.'

Erin flushed, tossing her head unconsciously so that her dark hair bounced beneath her bonnet, and the young subaltern pushed himself away from the window seat with a lazy movement.

'She's a beauty, Alice, I'll say that for her. But you know my tastes well enough. I like a wine that's matured, do I not?'

His hand reached out to tweak at the older woman's muslin cap as he passed her and though she jerked her head away in mock impatience Erin had the feeling she was well pleased.

When they were alone, Alice turned inquiringly to Erin and the girl knew the moment had come. Determined not to allow her nervousness to show, she launched into her proposition and as she finished there was a faint speculative smile on the older woman's lips.

'I'll do business with you,' she said shortly. 'Though if I were to pay what you ask you'd have me bankrupt. For that amount I would want more than a keg of rum.'

Erin stiffened. ''Tis a fair price!'

Alice smiled. 'And you, my dear, are in a buyer's market. If the trading ring knew what you were about they'd run you off the river before you could say Jack Knife, so it wouldn't be wise for you to advertise your wares too freely. Think on't...'

'I have no need to think,' Erin said spiritedly. 'I won't be bamboozled into a raw deal, so don't imagine I will.'

'Wait, now, don't be too hasty!' The smile was back, playing among Alice Simmons's plentiful dimples. 'I've a proposition to put to you. I'll pay you what you ask if you will come and serve here at the tavern for me for a week. And I'll give you half the same amount each week you're here until my leg is healed. Now, how does that sound to you?'

For a moment Erin was so taken by surprise that speech eluded her and the older woman went on. 'It's awkward here for me, laid up as I am. Jud does his best, but 'tis a woman my customers really want to see and you're bonny enough to satisfy the most finicky of 'em.'

'I couldn't!' Erin said sharply. 'I'm no bar wench. Thank you for the offer and your time, Mrs Simmons. But the answer is no.'

She turned away, but the older woman's voice arrested her.

'What is a bar wench, my proud queen? Have you not heard the saying "needs must when the devil drives"? That is how it is with you unless I am much mistaken. A wage, I'm offering you, every week until my leg is healed. Surely that must mean something to you?'

Erin hesitated, biting back the refusal that sprang to her lips. She did not want to serve rum here at Alice Simmons's tavern. The very thought of having to act pleasantly towards men such as the ones who stood outside drinking now made her insides curl with distaste. No decent girl would do such a thing. And if Erin could have crawled away and never seen a lustful man again she would have been well pleased.

But Alice Simmons was right. Even if she obtained the full price she was asking for the keg of rum it was but one amount and when it was gone it was gone. Whereas if she took the offer of work it would mean a regular wage that would buy food and the other few necessities for their meagre life.

Erin raised her blue eyes to meet the bright, birdlike hazel ones.

'I'll take it we have made a deal, Mistress,' she said. 'When do you want me to begin?'

CHAPTER FOUR

Next day Erin took up her new appointment at Alice Simmons's.

As she had expected she encountered fierce resistance from both Grianne and Patrick, who were horrified at the depths to which she had been forced to sink.

'You can't, Erin! Father would turn in his grave!' Patrick protested, white-faced, and Grianne chipped in.

'The shame of it! Everyone on the river is bound to get to hear of it and I shall never be able to hold my head up again!'

'You'll be the first to complain if there's no food on the table,' Erin said shortly. 'I promised you I'd think of something. Just be glad I have.'

'Glad!' Grianne snorted. 'I never thought it would come to this. What David and his folks will say I can't imagine.'

'They would be wise to say nothing,' Erin retorted. 'The Percys haven't much more than we have. A bad harvest and they could be in the same position. And they haven't exactly come scurrying with offers of help, have they? Like everyone else, they're likely waiting for us to become so desperate they can acquire our land cheaply.'

Grianne's eyes grew round with indignation, but she said nothing and Erin rushed on.

'The thing that worries you most, Grianne, is that you'll have to do your share of work here at Kinvara.'

'What a shrew you've become, Erin!' Grianne snapped, stung by a statement that was too close to the truth for comfort, and Patrick turned troubled blue eyes on them both.

'It's all my fault. See what I've brought you to.'

'What rubbish!' Erin retorted, thinking that however distasteful her employment, it would not be unpleasant to get away for a little while each day from their moans and complaints. Grief, anxiety and guilt had brought them to this – a once happy family squabbling and blaming each other and themselves for their misfortune. Only Brenna seemed unaffected by all that had happened. Although more than once Erin had found her sobbing in her sleep for her dead father, the worst of the disaster seemed to have flowed over her as troubles had used to flow over Patrick, and in between she was the same sunshine and showers girl she always had been.

It had been arranged that Erin should work at Alice's from midday till early evening, serving the customers who came looking for refreshment during the hot daytime hours.

'I don't want you leaving here too late at night,' Alice had told her. ''Twould not be safe for a maid to ride along the river alone after dark.'

Erin had been heartily grateful for this con-

59

sideration, but when she arrived on her first day it seemed the bar owner was not enamoured of her new assistant riding the river at all.

'You cannot serve the customers in that condition!' she told Erin briskly, taking in the crumpled skirt and the way the thick bush dust clung to the folds of her bodice. 'Could you not bring a fresh gown with you and change into it here?'

Hot colour rose in Erin's cheeks. A large wardrobe had never been a luxury she could afford and since that evil man had ripped one of her good gowns, the one she was wearing was the only other one presentable enough to use for her new employment.

Perhaps she could persuade Grianne to loan one of hers, she thought, but Alice was shrewdly summing up the situation.

'Maybe I could cut down one of my own,' she suggested. 'As they are you'd be lost in them, slip of a thing that you are, but a snip here and a stitch there and I could likely make it fit well enough.'

'But I couldn't trouble you...' Erin began stiffly.

Alice laughed, one of her loud, merry laughs that her customers warmed to.

''Twould be no trouble. Sitting here as I am till my leg's healed I'd be glad enough of a distraction. I was a seamstress, you know, back home in England before I fell from grace. A good seamstress I was, too, though poorly paid for what I did. 'Twas no wonder I took a fancy to the lady's fine brooch – and she so careless of it to

60

send the gown to me for alteration and leave it pinned to the bodice!'

Erin caught her breath. She had heard talk that Alice had come to Australia as a convict. But who would think it to look at her now?

'The gown will be altered and ready for you by tomorrow,' Alice went on smoothly. 'But I shall of course expect you to leave it here each night. If I cannot persuade you to take a room and reside here, that is.'

Erin shook her head firmly. 'I couldn't leave the others alone. Things are bad enough for them without me deserting them too.'

Alice nodded thoughtfully. ''Twould be best if you all came to live in the hamlet,' she suggested. ''Tis not right for you to be out at that place alone.'

But again Erin shook her head.

'Later, maybe. But the land is the only thing of value that we have. I don't want to let it go too hastily. And there are four of us needing a roof over our heads. The farm's the only home we know.'

'You've a shrewd head on those pretty shoulders,' Alice told her. 'And while we're discussing business matters, how am I to get my keg of rum? You'll hardly want to ride in with it strung up behind you on that pony of yours.'

'Oh!' Erin caught her lip between her teeth. She had not thought beyond making the deal.

Alice Simmons laughed merrily. 'I'll send out for it, never fear. My man Jud can collect it when he next rides down to Sydney. Now, to work. We've customers already. And don't forget they'll expect a smile along with their tot of rum or glass of wine.'

Erin did as she was bid and soon she was too busy to think. How Alice had managed since breaking her leg she could not imagine, for customers came in a steady stream – and many more of them than she had expected.

There were settlers come into the hamlet to buy provisions or have their horses shod, there were ex-convicts, their faces haggard and their eyes greedy for the rum that had been their daily ration when they worked in chains, and there were soldiers – off-duty officers and men of the New South Wales Corps – and it was they who caused Erin the most trouble, ogling her dark good looks and bonny body, making the kind of remarks that brought the blood rushing to her face, and even trying to fondle her as she passed by.

'It's a pity there were not more of you here when the convicts broke out,' she suggested tartly to one young man as she moved away from his adventuring hand.

But it was as far as she dared take her complaints. If the men thought she was to be bought along with a tot of rum they were much mistaken. But with her father had died the luxury of telling them so in the terms she would have chosen. They came to the tavern expecting a pleasantry or two and, although the indignity of it burned like a fire in her veins, Erin knew that if she wished to keep her new employment and the wage that went with it she must restrict her disapproval to the pert remark and rely on her nimble feet to whisk her away from the more amorous of the men.

That afternoon as she stood in the neat little kitchen polishing glasses Erin was startled by a sudden commotion outside. She ran to the window and the sight that met her eyes drew a gasp from her. A small detachment of soldiers was riding along the sunbaked track and behind them, in chains, were three prisoners. Their feet dragged as they stumbled along behind the horses, their clothing hung in filthy rags from their unwashed bodies, and as Erin stared in fascinated horror she realized the detachment was reining in outside the cottage.

Surely not even the New South Wales Corps had begun to drink on duty! she thought, but she hurried dutifully to the front door, knowing they would not be able to leave their prisoners to come inside.

The captain, a young man down whose dirt-streaked face the perspiration was running in rivers, dismounted as he saw her and came forward, brushing the dust of the track from his uniform.

'Could you spare us a drink of water?' he asked.

Erin went into the cottage to fill a jug and when she returned she steeled herself to look at the prisoners. Then she started with sudden shock. For in spite of the dust and grime, she was able to recognize one of them as Turvey, who had been one of their own assigned convicts before the break-out.

'These prisoners – where did you get them?'

63

she asked before she could stop herself.

The captain looked at her in some surprise. 'A strange question, my lovely.'

She caught at her lip to keep it from trembling. 'They're the convicts who broke out, aren't they?'

'Aye – some of them,' he agreed. 'But they'll not break out again. We're taking them back for hanging.'

'Hanging!' Erin's hand went to her throat. On the night of the attack she would have killed them herself if she could; now in the light of day there was a raw finality about the word that shocked her.

'That's right,' the Captain confirmed. 'And when we get the others, their fate will be the same. They're murderers and looters, every one, and we have to make an example of 'em if folks are to sleep sound in their beds.'

Erin nodded, half expecting Turvey to make some plea to her to intervene, but he did not, though his rheumy, resentful eyes never left her. And as the soldiers formed up their horses once more and moved off he looked at her over his shoulder with an expression of hate twisting his unshaven features.

Shivering in spite of the heat Erin watched them go. Perhaps one of them was the evil coward who had killed her father, and if so hanging was too good for him. But of one thing she was sure. The man who had raped her had not been among those recaptured. Unless he had been taken elsewhere and returned to Sydney by another road, he was still at large.

A week went by – a week when Erin slowly grew accustomed to her new life. Every day when she had done with as many of the chores as she could manage she rode the river road to Blackley Tower, and every evening as dusk fell she rode home again. The work was more wearying than she could ever have imagined, for she was on her feet for hours at a stretch and always there was the need to present a cheerful face or fall foul of Alice Simmons.

For all her rough kindness, Alice was a hard taskmaster and Erin knew that if she failed to fulfil her obligations to the satisfaction of her employer she would dispatch with her services in less time than it would take to tell.

But for all that she found much of it distasteful there was at least one consolation, Erin decided, and that was that she was left little time for brooding. The ache of grief for her father was still there, a leaden weight within her, and so was her shame at what the convict had done to her. But for the most part her mind and body were either too busy or too weary to do more than reflect dully as Starlight trotted with her along the river road.

Why was it, she wondered in one of her rare moments of reverie, that there were such sharp divisions in this new country? Why could some, like the hated officers of the New South Wales Corps, lounge in Alice Simmons's parlour drinking rum while others fought desperately to scrape a living from the land? But then – that was life the world over. On the one hand were those like themselves, not knowing where the

65

next meal was coming from, while on the other the profiteers lived in comfort and perhaps even extravagance.

One evening, just before it was time for her to leave, Erin was tidying the small kitchen when she heard Alice calling to her from the chair she occupied nowadays near to the window.

'Erin – don't go yet. Looks like we've got important company.'

She gestured towards the road outside and, following her gaze, Erin saw three horsemen reining in at the gate. About all three was an air of wealth – even if one disregarded their fine clothes it was there in the confident way they sat their thoroughbred horses. But as she recognized one of them, Erin's heart seemed to miss a beat.

Brett Wilde – her father's creditor!

Although she had never met him face to face she knew who he was – everyone on the river knew Brett Wilde. Although it was only five years since he had come to the colony as a young officer of the New South Wales regiment he had soon become the most notoriously successful member of the 'rum corps' and now, as her father had learned to his cost, Brett Wilde held half the river in the palm of his sunburned hand. The stories of his ruthlessness were legion – he cared for nothing but his profits and the speed with which he could buy up land from struggling settlers to add to the empire that was Mia-Mia. Why, even the house itself, which was now as grand as an English mansion, or so she had heard, had once been some poor settler's tumble-down dream, and Erin was only surprised that he had not yet come to Kinvarra with a derisory offer for the land in payment of her father's debts. The land adjoined his own, after all. It was the next natural extension for him, the only way he could now expand his borders. But he had not come, and now she stood watching, heart pumping, mouth dry, as he hitched his horse to a convenient post and turned to wait for his two friends to do the same.

'Come now, girl, stop gawping!' Alice Simmons advised her roughly. 'He's a handsome man as well as a wealthy one, but he's not for the likes of you!'

Quick colour rushed to Erin's cheeks. Brett Wilde for her? Such a thing hadn't entered her head – and never would, no, not even if he was the last man on earth. Handsome he might be. Grudgingly she accepted that he was – tall and well made with a skin that had been tanned to a rich, golden brown by the hot Australian sun, thick brown hair springing from a strong and angular face, and eyes of steely grey – but she hated his kind with all the strength of her being. He had made his money at the expense of the likes of her father and, for all his wealth and position, she detested and despised him.

'It's time for me to go home,' she said, grasping at the only excuse that could release her from Brett Wilde's hated presence, but Alice shook her head.

'I know by rights it should be. But I'd be obliged if you'd stay a little longer. It's not often I get customers as important as these. Mostly they can afford to drink in their own homes. And

I'd not like them to go away thinking Alice's hospitality is a myth.'

Erin's heart came into her mouth. She felt trapped, suddenly, like a caged bird. She longed to tell Alice she would not stay and toady to these profiteers, but she knew that if she did her poor livelihood would be in danger, with the threat of hardship and disaster for not only herself but her brother and sisters too. She stood in an agony of indecision watching them stride up the path, laughing and talking together.

'Move, you lazy chit!' Alice ordered her sharply. 'They'll choose to sit outside, no doubt, on a warm evening such as this. Go and see what they want and quick about it!'

With an effort Erin gathered herself together. The three men had stopped in the garden; they lounged now at one of the tables Alice had set beneath the mimosa trees, and as she approached them Erin was aware of the way their eyes appraised her slim figure and swelling breasts.

Tiny spots of colour rose in her cheeks and she wished, not for the first time, that she did not have to wear the gown Alice had made for her. It was pretty, certainly, in flower-sprigged muslin trimmed with blue ribbons that reflected the colour of her eyes, but its low-cut neckline left little to the imagination and Erin blamed its immodesty for the number of advances made to her by male customers.

Resisting the desperate urge to cover her breasts with her hands Erin took their order and brought the rum they required to their table. It was not the first they had drunk today unless she was much mistaken – the heightened colour in the cheeks of the two strangers bore witness to that, and even Brett Wilde, it seemed to Erin, reeked of spirit fumes. As she placed their requirements on the table she did her best to keep her distance, but one of the men shot out a hand to trap her wrist.

'Not so fast, pretty one! The company of a comely wench would be a fitting end to a good day's business.'

Erin's flush deepened. 'I'm sorry, sir, but I'm afraid I must disappoint you,' she said tartly, trying to free her wrist. But her captor had no intention of letting her go so easily. With laughing ease he pulled her towards him, forcing her down onto his knee.

'Come now, I've never known a tavern wench who was averse to a kiss!' he chortled. His companion, who still chose to wear an old-fashioned powdered wig in spite of the heat of the Australian summer, laughed as heartily as he and, made bold by his encouragement, the first man allowed his hand to slide up Erin's side until his fingers encountered the fullness of her breast, stroking and squeezing gently.

The touch was enough for Erin. With a quick movement she twisted away and at the same time she brought her palm up to meet the man's cheek with a sharp slap.

'This is one tavern wench who does not act so!' she snapped, and as he pressed his hand to his stinging cheek, his bewigged companion broke into a fresh gale of laughter.

'A lass with spirit, I declare! What say you,

69

Wilde?'

Brett Wilde did not answer, nor did he join in the laughter. For a moment his eyes lingered on the girl and they were thoughtful. He had decided the moment he set eyes on her that she was lovely; now, flushed with anger and her eyes sparkling like blue pools in sunlight, she was quite beautiful. And different, too, to the usual tavern wench. As his pompous friend Farthing had said, she had spirit, but it was more than that. There was a dignity about her too that was at odds with the place where she found herself and a sense of her own worth that instantly made a man place a higher price on her than the run-of-the-mill whores who frequented the rum parlour to make a quick shilling. And there was something else ... the promise of hidden depths that could make a man forget his sorrows better than a whole bottle of rum. And Heaven only knew, he would give a great deal for oblivion such as that this night...

With an impatient movement he drained his glass and set it down. 'Another of the same, girl, and quickly!' he ordered.

She turned the full fire of her blue eyes on him as if she resented being spoken to thus and the look of her stirred his blood.

'Make haste!' he said roughly, turning back to the others. But when they too finished their rum they pushed their glasses away.

'We'll drink no more tonight, Wilde,' the first said, scraping back his chair. ''Twould have been a thirsty night for us had we not had one jar to toast the success of our business venture, but

70

we've a long ride ahead of us back to Sydney.'

'And the girls there are more accommodating,' the bewigged Farthing laughed, still determined to make capital of his friend's rebuff. 'However, do not let us take you away if you wish to stay, Wilde.'

Brett nodded, lighting a cigar and watching the smoke curl up into the air that seemed to dance with a million mosquitoes. He had no wish tonight to return too soon to the lonely splendour of Mia-Mia. All day as he had wrestled for the best business deal he could get from these two traders whose wits were every bit as sharp as his own, he had been grateful that he had no time for the personal matters that weighed so heavily upon his heart. But now the deals had been struck and the traders were leaving and he knew that there was nothing now to come between him and his thoughts, except, perhaps, a girl with sparkling blue eyes and a voice with a lilt as haunting as a half-forgotten melody...

When the others left he sat alone waiting for her to return with his rum. His companion's approach had plainly not been to her taste and Brett thought that a good business sense did not necessarily make a man a good lover. With a girl such as her something more was needed, even if the price she set upon herself was met, and generously.

With a veiled smile he took a pouch of guineas from the pocket of his buckskin breeches, laying them on the table before him. He had yet to meet the tavern wench who could resist the sight of such wealth within her grasp. And to his gratification, as she approached him he noticed how her blue eyes fastened upon the glinting golden coins. So he had been right. Like all the others, she had her price.

As she set the drink on the table he pushed enough towards her to pay for the drink twice over.

'Take something for yourself, my sweet. If it means I can be served by a lass as comely as you, it's cheap at the price.'

Her chin came up and a wary look flickered across her face.

'There's no need to hurry away,' he went on. 'The others have gone now – we're quite alone. Stay awhile and talk.'

She leaned over, taking the price of the drink only, and her breasts strained tantalizingly against the low-cut neckline of her gown.

'I'm sorry, Sir, I have no time to spare for talking,' she replied tightly.

He sat back in his chair, his mouth curving slightly. 'What's your name?'

'Erin. If it's anything to you.'

'Erin.' His eyes narrowed behind the screen of cigar smoke. 'An unusual name. Yet somewhere I've heard it before.'

He sensed the tightening in her, though he had no way of knowing the indignation and hate that were flaring through her with the speed and ferocity of a bush fire. He only saw her chin pucker beneath her full red lips with the effort of keeping silent, and as her eyes, hard and bright, met his with scornful defiance, something deep and painful twisted within him.

'If there's nothing more I'll beg you to excuse me,' she said shortly. Then, without giving him the chance to reply, she turned, and with a swish of her skirts, flounced away.

Brett drew deeply on his cigar and watched her go. Outwardly he was calm but within him anger was mingling with unexpected desire and the anguish that spread and festered from the deep, hidden wound within his heart.

Women! How they thought they could play with a man! Take this one – a tavern wench for all her fancy ideas about her station, in a gown designed to display her charms for the titillation of all her customers, yet with an opinion of herself that would grace a queen. It was insupportable that she should be employed here to lead men on and then leave them cold and certainly not in keeping with what he had heard of Alice Simmons.

With a movement that suggested the lazy strength of a coiled spring, he pushed himself up from the chair and walked towards the cottage. Just inside the door he saw Alice, sitting on the windowseat with her leg straight out before her. How much had she seen of the exchange? he wondered.

A moment later his unspoken question was answered.

'You won't think us too inhospitable, I hope,' she said, her dimpled face unusually serious.

He shrugged. 'Your serving wench has a sharp tongue.'

Alice's eyes narrowed to shrewd bright points. 'But that only adds spice, does it not?'

73

He drew on his cigar. 'You mean...?'

Alice eyed him speculatively. Brett Wilde was an occasional customer only, but his presence added quality to her establishment. And she could not afford to fall foul of the trading ring. Tonight Erin had disappointed her. She had slapped the face of one gentleman and insulted another. Perhaps it was time she learned her business the hard way – broken in as one would break a mettlesome horse.

Again her eyes ran over Brett Wilde, taking in the breadth of his shoulders and the hard, lean strength of his buckskin-clad thighs. Were she not incapacitated by this cursed leg she would accommodate him herself, and though she might not be so young or so darkly beautiful as Erin, she warranted he would have no cause for complaint. Alice's talents had been well practised over the years, her lessons in loving learned long ago. But as things were she could do nothing except perhaps lie and moan as his jolting shook her poor shattered shin bone. No, if Brett Wilde was to leave her house satisfied there was but one woman who could please him.

Alice jerked her head in the direction of the stairs.

'You'll find her up there.'

Brett's lips curved though he said nothing. He turned and ground out the butt of his cigar. Then, two at a time, he took the stairs.

CHAPTER FIVE

In the bedroom she used for changing from Alice's gown to her own, Erin stood for a moment looking at her reflection in the mirror that topped the dressing table.

At home, at Kinvarra, she had scarcely stopped to give a thought to her looks since the day she had finally acknowledged that her body was determined to develop from child to woman whether she wanted it to or not. There had never been time for primping – her toilet consisted of washing in clear river water and combing the tangles from her thick black curls. But now, before taking off the hated muslin gown, she stopped to take stock.

Without realizing it, and certainly without meaning to, she had begun to attract the attentions of men. They seemed unable to leave her alone, raking her with their eyes so that she felt as naked as when the convict had exposed her breasts, and touching her when they could. Partly, she supposed, this gown was to blame. It was a strumpet's gown, with its immodest neckline and hip-skimming skirt – and so thin she felt sure the strong sun must shine right through it, exposing the shape of her legs for all to see. But it was not only the gown. She had not been wearing it, after all, the night the convicts had attacked. And her own poor gown had not saved her from that disgrace.

She tilted her head to one side, trying to see herself as they saw her, but she could not. Her pale oval face was just as it had always been, but for the high spots of angry colour, and there was nothing new in the tip-tilt nose or the mouth she thought too large to grace a lady. Her breasts, perhaps, were fuller, and her hips slimmer, since the days of hard work had melted away the childish roundness, but otherwise she was much as she had been when Alistair had courted her. And Alistair had left her.

Unexpected tears sprang to her eyes and she turned quickly away, pulling the gown over her head and letting it fall in a heap to the ground. She had not thought the memory of Alistair could still hurt her. Perhaps it was that the experiences of the last weeks had left her so raw that any small thing could reduce her to tears. Well, she'd have to get over that. Weeping would not help her keep her promise to look after the younger ones. Hard work would.

Brushing away the tears she reached for her own dust-stained gown, but a heavy step on the stair made her hesitate. Who could that be, taking the stairs with such vigour? Not Jud, and certainly not Alice. Then, with a crash that made her jump violently, the door burst open and spinning round she saw the tall figure of Brett Wilde framed there.

A gasp of horror escaped her and she gathered her gown in a bundle in front of her, thinking

76

only for the moment of her embarrassment at being caught in nothing but her chemise. She waited for him to back out of the room with a blush and an apology and when he did not she stared at him in confusion, not knowing what to make of the brooding look that narrowed his eyes and the faint smile that played about his lips. Then, to her utter amazement, he came into the room, closing the door behind him.

'What do you think you're doing?' she squeaked angrily.

He leaned back against the door, hands on hips, buckskin-clad legs splayed, while his eyes moved lazily over her smooth bare shoulders and the slender thighs that could be seen behind the loosely held curtain of her gown. The depth of his gaze unnerved her even more than his sudden entry into the room had done and a rosy warmth seemed to suffuse her body, as if she were blushing from head to toe.

'Get out!' she cried. 'If Alice knew you were here...'

He threw back his head and laughed, and the sound raised her Irish temper.

'Don't dare to laugh at me!' she exploded. 'Get out, do you hear?'

'Not so fast, my sweet!' His voice was low and amused and with a lazy movement he reached out and jerked the bunched-up gown from her hand. So taken by surprise was she that the fabric slipped through her fingers. Then, outraged, she flew at him.

'Give me that! Give me...'

One strong brown hand caught her flailing

77

fists, the other closed over her shoulder. She opened her mouth to scream, but he covered it with his own so that the sound was lost in her throat and she fought breathlessly to free her lips from his hard, insistent kiss. But with ease he held her pinioned against him and the more she struggled, it seemed, the closer their contact became. Just when she thought her lungs must burst he raised his head and, as she drew bless-ed air into her lungs, she felt his hands on her breasts, pushing down the brief and lacy chemise that covered them.

Panic exploded in her then. The convict had bared her breasts before taking her – surely, dear God, this monster did not intend to do the same? Frantically she twisted this way and that, hitting out at him with her hands. But almost without effort he lifted her bodily, carrying her across the room and throwing her down onto the bed. Then, while she sobbed in an effort to regain the breath that had been knocked out of her, he swiftly divested himself of shirt and breeches.

Erin had a quick glimpse of a flat, muscled stomach and a matt of crisp brown hair above it before his body descended on her, squeezing the breath from her once more.

'No!' she gasped, raking with her fingernails at his bare back. As the warm blood flowed he raised himself to look down at her with fire in those brooding eyes.

'Have I to teach you submission, my dear?' he inquired roughly. 'Enough is enough, and in your trade...'

'Oh!' she cried, pummelling at him helplessly

78

as realization dawned. 'I'm not – I'm not what you think!'

But he seemed not to hear her.

'If that's your way, mi'lady, so be it!' he grated. 'You'll soon see who is master here!'

Again his mouth covered hers, drinking deeply, while his hand travelled the length of her body till it came to rest on the outer side of her thigh. His fingers felt to her like branding irons, burning into her flesh, and involuntarily she jerked in an effort to dislodge them. Not so. He shifted the weight slightly from the lower part of her body, sliding his hand to the soft inner side of her thigh and using her own momentum to part her legs. Then his weight descended on her once more and she screamed deep in her throat as the burning tip of his manhood found its way into the petalled orifice.

For a moment Brett held back, startled. There were strumpets who fought and men who liked them to. But never before had he known one to scream. Her head jerked away from him, her eyes tight-closed, and her black hair lay fanned out across her face. Mastery provoked in him a strange tenderness and he raised his hand to brush her hair aside. But at his touch she twisted abruptly, sinking her teeth deep into the heel of his hand.

The pain – and anger at the wildness of her – set light to his desire once more. As her body writhed beneath his he thrust deep into her and the tightness of her enclosing him drove all else from his mind. For a few frenzied moments while his passion mounted he forgot her scream

79

as he forgot his own pain; there was room for nothing but the sweetness of her angel flesh, the scent of her hair and the response of his own body as she moved ceaselessly beneath him.

But too soon it was over. The exultant apex came like a burst of stars in a midsummer heaven, but as its echoes died and he rolled away from her she lay without moving.

'Erin?' he murmured.

Her hair still lay across her face and again he tried to brush it away, wanting to look at this girl who seemed too good to be a tavern wench and yet who had brought him such sweet oblivion. But at his touch she shrank away and to his surprise he saw that her shoulders had begun to shake.

He raised himself on one elbow, letting his eyes run the length of her body. God, but she was lovely – her skin smooth and creamy, the lines of her body trim yet rounded. Beneath a tiny waist her hips flared provocatively and her legs were long and shapely. But there was the yellowing shadow of a bruise just below her hip-bone and a cluster of others, splayed in a semi-circle on her thigh. Someone in the not-too-distant past had used her, and used her more roughly than he, judging by those marks. Yet she lay beside him now, sobbing soundlessly into the pillow, and she would not turn her head to look at him.

Irritation spiked his tenderness and he caught her chin between his thumb and fingers turning her head towards him. For a moment her eyes met his and a wave of shock ran through him as he saw the fear naked in them. Then her lashes covered them, lying like soft ravens' wings on her cheeks, with the tears spilling out and running in silent rivers down her face.

'Erin – for the love of God!' He was bewildered now as well as irrationally angry. 'You'll be well paid! What more do you want?'

At his words she writhed like a soul in torture and she covered her mouth with her hands, while the tears ran still faster down her cheeks. He placed a tentative hand on her shoulder but there was no response and with an impatient movement he levered himself up from the bed and reached for the shirt and breeches he had discarded in a heap on the floor.

The girl's sobbing was disconcerting and he turned his back on her while pulling on his clothes. Then he took a handful of guineas from his pouch and set them down on the chest.

At the sound her sobs ceased – it was as if she was holding her breath to listen. A faint ironic smile played about his lips as he imagined her mentally counting her earnings. She was no different to the rest of her kind, then. It was his mistake that he had thought she was. But if she was to make a success of her trade, this was no way to go about it. Had she been warm and affectionate he would have spent the night with her and gladly. But this wailing was more than flesh and blood could stand.

'Goodnight, Erin, and thank you!' he said, with an edge of sarcasm to his voice. Then, with only one backward look at the abject figure on the bed, he left the room.

For a few moments after the slam of the door and the sound of footsteps on the stairs told her he had gone, Erin still lay with her hands pressed over her face.

Holy Mother, was there no end to this horror? When her father had been murdered and she had been raped by the convicts she had thought nothing worse could befall her. But she had been wrong. To be taken in mistake for a strumpet was something so degrading it surpassed even that.

Why did I ever come here? Erin wondered wildly as her sobs subsided enough to give room for conscious thought. Why didn't I realize what would happen? Grianne and even Patrick knew. That was why they were so against it. But perhaps they thought that I would come to it willingly. Surely not even they could have guessed I would be raped so brutally – and by a so-called gentleman.

Hatred rushed through her in a boiling tide, drying her tears. Brett Wilde, officer of the New South Wales Corps, self-styled lord of the manor, farmer and profiteer, had taken her by force just as the grizzled convict in his filthy rags had done. The fact that he had talked of payment and left coins behind made it no different.

As the thought crossed her mind she twisted over onto her knees and crawled to the end of the bed. Yes, there they were, in a shining heap on the unpolished top of the chest, more guineas than she had ever seen at one time. And he had not even bothered to count them!

Her lip quivered at the injustice of it and she longed to brush them roughly from the chest so that they scattered to the four corners of the room. But as she raised her hand to do it she seemed to see the faces of the younger ones, all turned to her, and through the singing of her ears she heard her mother's voice as she had heard it so many times: 'Look after them, Erin. Promise me...'

She bowed her head; the tears began again, falling onto the chest, and instead of scattering the guineas contemptuously as she longed to do she scooped them up.

'I promise, Mama...' It was not like an echo to her. It was real, as real as it had ever been, as though her mother might have been in the room with her, not dead these three years. 'I promise...'

Her gown lay where Brett Wilde had tossed it. She grabbed it up and pulled it over her head but she was shivering now so violently that she found difficulty in fastening it. But she persevered. At the moment there was no clear thought in her head beyond getting out into the fresh evening air – and tidying herself sufficiently so that it would not be apparent to anyone else what had befallen her.

She would die sooner than that! Perhaps by the time she reached home her cheeks would have cooled sufficiently to keep it from the children. If she had been able to conceal it that night in the barn she thought she should be able to manage this, though of course that night their normal faculties of observation had been impaired by fear and grief.

But Alice Simmons was another matter.

At the thought of her, Erin nibbled at her lip in perplexity. Surely Alice must have heard something of what was going on? The footsteps on the stairs had been loud enough to warn her. Then why had she not sent someone up to investigate? It was strange, that. But perhaps there had been no one she could send and she could not climb the stairs herself with her poor broken leg. If that were the case, what would she think of the goingson? Would she blame Erin? Surely she would not condone rape under her roof even if the offender was such an important gentleman as Brett Wilde.

Nervously Erin straightened her gown, smoothing the fabric down over her hips. She combed her hair with her fingers and washed the tearstains from her cheeks as best she could with a handkerchief dipped in the jug of water that stood on the chest. Then, gathering her things together, she started down the stairs.

Voices floated up to her from the rooms below, a blend of ribaldry and conversation punctuated by the chink of glasses, and Erin ignored them. But as she reached the bottom step one voice separated itself from the rest and she drew up, a fresh fit of shivering racking her body.

Brett Wilde! He was still here in the house, blackguard that he was! Had he no decency – no sense of shame? Why, he was in Alice's drawing room if she was not much mistaken and actually talking to Alice!

For a moment she stood undecided. The

84

thought of seeing Brett Wilde so soon was a sickening one. But why *should* she sneak past the room where he was as if she was the one to blame? If he thought he could behave in this way with no repercussions just because of who he was he was much mistaken! She would confront him now and let Alice know the truth of it before he wriggled his way around her and led her to believe it had been very different.

Taking her courage in both hands she crossed the hall. Her slippered feet made no sound on the polished wood floor, though her heart beat so loudly she thought it must announce her presence to everyone in the house. Then she drew up abruptly, hot colour rushing to her cheeks.

They were talking about her! Talking openly about the things that had happened in the room upstairs!

'I'm sorry, Mr Wilde, she's inexperienced, I know.' Alice's voice carried clearly through the half-open door. To Erin's horror she sounded neither shocked nor disgusted, but apologetic. 'She has not been with me long, for I took her on out of pity. You remember the convicts who broke out the night of the big storm? They looted her home and killed her father.'

Erin heard Brett's quick intake of breath and his muttered oath.

'Erin! Of course! I knew I'd heard the name before. She's Paddy Kelly's daughter, is she?'

'Kelly – yes. A rum-soak, God rest his soul, if what I hear is true. But I had high hopes for the girl. With looks like hers she could do well working for me. When she came to me, desperate for money, I took her on at once.'

'She came to you for money?' Brett's voice was thoughtful. 'Why should she do that?'

'Oh, I suppose she knew I was laid up and needed help here.' Alice sounded flustered and Erin guessed she did not want to divulge the real reason – the keg of rum. 'But I thought she knew what that entailed. Surely no lass can be that innocent? And I thought for sure she'd be pleased to accommodate a fine gentleman like yourself.'

'You mean I am the first you sent to her room?' Brett asked harshly.

'Well, yes, but she had to start somewhere!' Alice sounded defensive now.

'And she did not know I was to visit her?' Brett demanded, his voice like thunder.

'No, but ... take no notice of her way, Mr Wilde. She'll be worth the breaking, I assure you...'

All this while Erin had stood almost stunned with disbelieving horror. It couldn't be true! *Alice* had sent Brett Wilde to her room? *Alice* intended her to become ... to become...

Suddenly everything seemed very far away. She could hear the voices still, but they were muffled, as if reaching her through a thick fog. Only Alice's last words echoed and re-echoed in her mind. Worth the breaking! Worth the breaking! Oh dear God, what had she come to!

Not only the voices were muffled now. It had grown dark, too, as if the sun had dropped suddenly behind the mountains. Erin clutched the doorpost for support as her knees gave way

86

beneath her. But it was no good. Her arms were useless, too, and she was falling, falling...

The ground came up to meet her with a rush and then the voices were closer, still muffled, but closer, and there were faces to go with them – Alice's, grown grotesque and ugly, and another, a tanned, lean face bending close to hers – Brett Wilde. She tried to lift herself – anything to escape from him – but she could not move and she felt herself lifted in strong arms. Her head lolled on its useless neck, twisted against his shoulder, and the pungent smell of his tobacco mingled with rum was in her nostrils, making her swoon again. Then the world ceased its jolting and she felt something pressed against her trembling lips.

'Here – drink this. It'll do you good.'

The odour from it was not of rum, and obediently she parted her lips. But as the fiery liquid trickled down her throat it set her choking and she opened her eyes to see Brett Wilde bending over her.

'No!' she gasped, shrinking away, but he eased it to her lips again.

'It's brandy. Just a sip, now, there's a good girl.'

Too weak still to argue, she obeyed, and this time as the liquid slid down she felt warmth beginning to spread through her cold limbs. At once she tried to sit up, but he eased her back, and as her neck encountered cushions she realized she was lying on the couch in Alice's parlour.

'Lie still now,' he ordered her.

'But I must get home! I'm late already. The

87

others...'

'You can go nowhere in this state,' he said firmly. 'Now do as I say and rest awhile. Mistress Alice and I will leave you in peace.'

He moved away out of her line of vision and Alice's face appeared, looking down at her from behind the couch.

'That's right, you rest,' she said, her voice kindly but impatient.

Then she too disappeared and Erin heard the click of the door and knew she was alone. For a moment she lay, while the events of the day tumbled around inside her head. Her body ached from head to foot and the deep burning pain was back between her legs. But it was nothing to the ache within her.

Men! They were hateful animals, all of them, with one thing only on their minds. They would use a woman for their own selfish pleasure with no thought as to her feelings. And when their need was eased and their passion spent they walked away without a backward glance. Yet this was the life Alice Simmons had thought she would be 'broken' to – providing over and over again for these brutes. Dear God forbid that she should come to that!

A shudder ran through her. She couldn't face them again, either of them. Not Alice Simmons, and certainly not that hateful, arrogant Brett Wilde who spent his ill-gotten money on rum, cigars and the women to satisfy his lust. All she wanted now was to return to the peace of Kinvarra and the company of those who knew nothing of her shame.

Carefully she eased herself up to a sitting position. At first the room spun, then it righted itself and she swung her trembling legs to the floor and risked setting her weight on them. Then, gaining confidence, she crossed the room and opened the door.

The passage was deserted. Silently she sped down it, slipping out of the back door of the cottage and around to the stables. Starlight raised his head when he saw her, nuzzling her softly, and she rubbed his nose before hoisting the saddle onto his back.

Why couldn't men be more like horses? she wondered, weak tears threatening once more. Why, it was an insult to a lovely creature like Starlight to describe Brett Wilde and his kind as animals!

She led the pony out of the stable, but as she did so a shout reached her.

'Wait! Where do you think you're going?'

She swung round, heart pumping, to see Brett Wilde coming out of the cottage. Dear God, he's going to try and stop me! she thought wildly.

Quick as a flash she forced her trembling legs to lift her into the saddle.

'Wait!' Brett's voice, heavy with authority, reached her again, but she dug her heels into Starlight's flanks. The pony broke into a trot, but Brett Wilde was running towards her and she had the impression he was about to grab at her reins.

'Giddup, Starlight!' she cried, and as the surprised pony surged forward Brett Wilde was forced to jump clear. As she rounded the corner, Erin saw his horse waiting patiently at the hitching post where he had left it and a new fear filled her. On that great horse he could catch her easily if he'd a mind to. She slowed Starlight and, leaning low, unhitched the great black stallion. For a moment he pawed in surprise but as she pulled on the reins he followed her.

Behind her she heard Brett's angry roar, but as Starlight galloped for the river road the black stallion came with them.

Neck and neck they raced, before the black stallion took the lead and even then he went on with Starlight gamely following. The wind blew Erin's black hair straight back from her face and the exhilaration of the ride added to her sudden sense of triumph.

Brett Wilde would never catch her now! And like as not he would have to walk home to Mia-Mia. That would cool his ardour.

But when at last the black horse stopped to graze and Starlight slowed to a trot, the exhilaration died too. Holy Mother, what was to become of them?

Against her side the golden guineas bumped and chinked, reminding her uncomfortably of the night's work. One resolve emerged crystal clear from the welter of emotions within her.

Somehow she had to keep the family together and to that end she would do everything she had to do. But never, never as long as she lived, would she be placed in the position to submit to the attentions of Brett Wilde and his kind. Never, ever, would she prostitute herself again.

Drawing herself up tight in the saddle she turned Starlight into the drive that led her home.

CHAPTER SIX

During the next weeks as the hot sun of summer cooled gently into autumn Erin had little chance to brood on what had befallen her. There was too much to do at Kinvarra and far too little time to do it. Even if she had not resolved never to go near Blackley's Tower and Alice Simmons again, she thought she would have been forced to give notice at the rum parlour, for without their convict labourers it was impossible to keep pace with all that needed doing at the farm.

For a short while Erin had toyed with the idea of going to Sydney and requesting some more men to be assigned to her but she knew there was little chance of her request being granted. She, a mere girl, could not be given charge of dangerous criminals, and she could certainly not afford to employ an overseer to keep them in order. Why, she doubted if she could afford the food and rum ration for the convicts if she got them.

No, the land was going to have to be allowed to return to its virgin state at least until Patrick was old enough to take charge – if they survived that long – and sooner or later they would all have to hire themselves out to earn enough to keep them alive. But the most pressing problem for the present was looking after their few sad cattle and bringing in the harvest. The grain must not be left to rot in the fields, it was too precious for that. But how to do it – two young women and a boy?

'I can't do it – I know I'd be no use at all!' Grianne wailed and Erin felt the all-too-familiar irritation rising. Grianne had been raised the daughter of a settler just as she had been, yet she still shirked away from the menial tasks, the gritty hard work and the problems as if she were a high-born lady, unwilling to soil her fair hands.

'Perhaps David Percy will send us some help,' she said shortly. 'There are enough of them there.'

But like all the families on the river the Percys were too concerned with getting in their own harvest before it was ruined by the autumn rains to spare any labour.

One afternoon, as all of them, even little Brenna, toiled in the fields under the baking sun there came the sound of horse's hooves on the drive and Erin straightened her aching back to see a wagon approaching, driven by a stocky figure she recognized as Henry Stanton, overseer to Brett Wilde.

Erin's heart missed a beat. What now? she wondered fearfully. Had Brett Wilde decided it was time to claim his dues? It was only what she had been expecting ever since her father's death, for what had happened that night at Alice Simmons's rum parlour had convinced her she could expect no mercy from him. He hadn't known she was no strumpet when he had taken her, she accepted that, but what difference did it make? Even a strumpet was entitled to her feelings and Brett Wilde had allowed her none. He had wanted her and because he had wanted her he had taken her. That was all there was to it. And it would be the same with the land. It was well known the length of the river that Brett Wilde's greed for land was insatiable and where his gain was concerned he would be as ruthless as he had been when his lustful desires had robbed her of what little self-respect the marauding convicts had left her.

In some ways he was even worse than they, she thought. At least they made no pretence at virtue. But Brett Wilde stole and raped under a cloak of respectability.

As the overseer climbed down from the wagon and came towards her she dusted her hands on her skirt and brushed a dark curl away from her sunburned face.

'Yes? What do you want?' she asked shortly.

'Are you Erin Kelly?' His voice was rough and she remembered with a stab of fear that he was a remitted convict.

'I am.'

He acknowledged her with a jerk of his bullet-shaped head.

'I've some stuff here for you.'

She wrinkled her nose in perplexity. 'Stuff? What stuff? I've ordered nothing.'

He shrugged. 'I don't know about that. It's provisions from Mr Wilde.'

'But I can't pay!' Erin protested.

'Mr Wilde said nothing about payment.' The

93

overseer made an impatient gesture towards the wagon. 'Can you send a man to unload it, then I can be on my way.'

Erin laughed. 'A man? I haven't got a man! There are three of us girls and my brother. But it'll be a few years yet before he can be called more than a boy.'

For a moment the overseer seemed nonplussed. Erin saw his eyes go to the field of grain and the narrowed, speculative look that came into them briefly frightened her. Then he turned abruptly towards the wagon.

'I suppose if I'm to get back to Mia-Mia today, I shall have to unload it myself.'

He began to do as he had said and Erin watched in amazement as the pile of provisions on the steps of the veranda grew. Brett Wilde had sent her all this? But why? She had thought her father's credit had been stretched to its limits. Could it be that the profiteer had a spark of decency after all in his black heart? Or did he count it as part-payment for his use of her at Alice Simmons's rum parlour?

At the thought, colour flooded Erin's cheeks and she longed to take the provisions and throw them back into the wagon. She wanted no favours from Brett Wilde. The Holy Mother alone knew how little she wanted them. And yet...

She could no more refuse provisions that would help to keep her brother and sisters from starvation than she could have disregarded the guineas he had left her. Acceptance made a whore of her, she thought, ashamed, but refusal

94

was not a luxury she could afford.

When the overseer had left, Erin returned to the fields wondering what she could tell Patrick and Grianne. But to her surprise they accepted her explanation that the goods had been ordered by her father before his death readily enough. It was as if they were so grateful for the windfall that they deemed it imprudent to question too closely, she thought.

But there were questions next day, however, when, to Erin's utter amazement, the overseer was back once more – this time with six assigned convicts.

'Mr Wilde has sent them to help you with the harvest,' the overseer told her, tight-lipped and clearly disapproving.

At once Erin felt her hackles rising. A helping hand with the harvest was more than she had dared hope for but when it was offered by Brett Wilde she didn't know what to think. She didn't trust him, that much she knew. A man like him would never do anything without an ulterior motive, but not being sure what it was disconcerted her.

Perhaps he wants to keep the land in good shape for when he claims it, she thought. Beyond that, she could not think of a single reason why he should loan her six of his assigned convicts.

'Have you been visiting him on the sly?' Grianne asked unpleasantly, and in spite of her gratitude for the help they offered, Erin could not contain a fresh bout of hatred for Brett Wilde. Perhaps that was what he wanted the district to think – that she was indeed strumpet enough to sell herself in return for assistance. Perhaps he hoped to shame her out of Kinvarra. For she had no doubt that was his ultimate aim.

But for the moment the help was invaluable. The six men were able to do in a day what it would have taken them a week to complete – a back-breaking, wearying week, with one eye on the sky for the clouds that would herald the autumn rains.

And however determined she was – and scornful of Grianne for saying she couldn't do it – Erin was not at all sure she could last out herself.

For some weeks now she had been feeling ill, waking in the mornings as heavy as if she had not slept at all, and when she moved to put her feet to the ground her stomach moved too, filling her with queasiness. Each time it happened she forced herself on, thinking it would ease as the day progressed, and so it did, though it never left her completely and sometimes she would be overtaken by a bout of dizziness that seemed to put her in danger of swooning.

At first she put it down to the shock of all that had happened to her and perhaps an aftermath to fainting that night at Alice Simmons's. But as time went on and the symptoms continued she began to be worried.

What would happen to the others if she were to be ill? she wondered anxiously. For the way she felt seemed to portend something far more serious than the usual minor ailments and she even found herself remembering her mother's last illness and quaking inwardly at the consequences if she, too, should fall victim to the ravages of fever.

But it was not until the harvesting was done and the first cool winds of autumn began to blow down from the mountains that she realized the truth of her condition.

It was the end of a long and wearying day and with the tanks full from the recent rains Erin decided to allow herself the luxury of a bath. She shooed the others off to bed early, pulled the tub into the kitchen, and filled it with the water she had heated on the fire. Then she slipped out of her clothes and stepped gratefully into the soothing water.

For a few moments it seemed care slipped away as she relaxed against the hard rim of the bath. But she roused herself with an effort, taking the cake of scented soap that had arrived along with the provisions Brett Wilde had sent and working a lather from it onto her tired body. As her fingers reached her breasts she winced slightly. My, but she was still tender! Surely the soreness from her rough treatment should have eased by now? Then as she looked down at herself the first tiny shock waves ran through her and her blood seemed to turn to ice in her veins.

Her breasts were not only tender, they were fuller and heavier. And the tips that had been rose pink were darker and more clearly defined. As for her belly, that had always been so smooth and flat, it was curved now to a gently rising mound.

Holy Mary, I believe I am with child, she thought and the sickness rose within her again

97

confirming against all her swiftly found protestations that it was true.

Shaken to the very core she sat stiffly in the tub, no longer making any pretence at washing. She was with child and it had not occurred to her. The month's courses she had missed and put down to shock and overwork. But now there was no disguising it from herself and very soon there would be no way of hiding it from the others, either. Two men had taken her and left their vile seed in her, and the seed from one had taken root and grown. Soon there would be another mouth to feed. Soon everyone would know of her shame.

The water grew cold around her and still Erin sat in the tub like one in a trance. What could she do? To whom could she turn for help? If there had been no one to share the respectable burden of her father's death, it was a certain fact there would be no one willing to help her now. For who would believe her if she told them now that she had been taken against her will? No one – especially since they likely thought the worst of her for working at Alice Simmons's rum parlour.

Oh dear God, what am I to do? she wondered – and the answer came to her in a flash. The one man who had raped her was away and gone, and even if she knew where to find him he would as likely murder her as help her. But the other was still close by. The child she was carrying might not be his, but his guilt was as great. She would go to Brett Wilde and throw herself on his mercy. Much as the idea repelled her, it was the only way.

She pulled herself up from the half-cold water, towelling herself dry with hands that shook and wishing she had been born ugly or deformed instead of beautiful. At least then men would not have desired her. At least then she would have been able to retain her reputation. But it had not been so. Now, for all their sakes, she had to try to talk Brett Wilde into employing her, or helping to support her and the child in some way. Or else, she knew with brooding certainty, ruin faced them all.

The very next day Erin rode to Mia-Mia. As Starlight trotted with her along the river road the sickness was so bad she feared she would have to stop and vomit into the brush at the roadside, but she was determined to keep going as long as possible and by the time she reached the gates of Brett Wilde's mansion it had receded to the ever-present nausea and was almost forgotten in the torrent of nervousness that engulfed her.

Suppose Brett Wilde refused to see her? What then? And even if he did consent, what would she say to him? All the carefully rehearsed speeches that had kept her awake for most of the night had flown now, and her mind was a terrifying blank, empty of all constructive thought.

With determination, however, she turned Starlight into the long drive and trotted towards the grand house that was Mia-Mia.

Although it enjoyed a reputation in the district second to none, Erin had never before seen Mia-Mia except as a quick glimpse of golden stone half-hidden by the orchards that fronted it. The settler whose dream it had been had built it far enough from the river to be out of reach of even the highest of floods, but not wanting to waste the rich river land, he had planted row upon row of fruit trees between house and road.

Now, as she followed the broad drive, Erin saw a low pillared house to which Brett had added a wing on each side, surrounded by the customary veranda and covered by wistaria and creeper. For a moment she hesitated, daunted by the sheer impressive size of it, then, before her courage failed her altogether, she touched Starlight with her heels and trotted on towards the house.

There were convicts working in the orchard harvesting the apples; they watched her with curious and resentful eyes and she averted her gaze and rode on. Close to the house the drive opened out to form a forecourt and Erin slowed Starlight to a walk, wondering which way to go. Then a figure appeared in the doorway at the top of the flight of steps and her already fast-beating heart seemed to drum a tattoo against her ribs.

It was him – Brett Wilde! And he had seen her.

She tightened her grip on Starlight's reins and watched him come down the steps towards her. Today, instead of wearing the open-necked shirt, he was more formally dressed in a cloth coat of soft green, beneath which Erin glimpsed a white waistcoat; his breeches were of finest buckskin and his boots shining black leather. But his clothes altered nothing about him. If anything they accentuated the arrogance of his bearing, and the hard, masculine set of his shoulders and the suggestion of rippling muscles beneath the well-cut cloth was even more disturbing than when they were displayed to view. As for his face, even at this distance Erin fancied she could see the sneer of satisfaction on his sunburned features as he recognized her and hatred for him rose in her in a scalding tide.

Who did he think he was, this English profiteer who had made capital from those worse off than he, and who had used her so disdainfully and with so little regard for her feelings? Oh, if she had a pistol in her hand now she could shoot him without a single qualm. If she hanged for it, it would be worth it just to see that smile wiped from his face once and for all.

He crossed the courtyard towards her and she wondered how even he could be so lacking in shame. He knew now that she had been no strumpet when he had taken her, yet that seemed not to trouble him at all. His cold grey eyes met hers without wavering and as he stopped beside her he adopted a careless stance.

'Good day, Miss Kelly,' he greeted her. 'To what do we owe the honour of this visit?'

She felt the colour beginning to rise in her cheeks and cursed herself for it.

'I have to talk to you, Mr Wilde,' she said with all the dignity she could muster.

His eyebrows arched slightly. 'Really? You have no complaints about the goods I sent you, I hope?'

Her colour rose still further and she hardly knew whether to be more infuriated with herself or with him.

101

'None,' she returned briskly. 'Thank you for your consideration. The provisions were most welcome.'

His eyes appraised her and she thought his expression was faintly amused. Would he be so amused when he had heard what she had to say? she wondered.

'Do not think me rude, Miss Kelly, if I press you as to the nature of your business, but I have to ride to Sydney.' His tone was condescending and again she bristled. It could be his child she was carrying, yet he was attempting to dismiss her as an uninvited visitor. With a small, characteristic movement, she lifted her chin.

'I wished to speak to you in private, Mr Wilde, but if time presses you I'll say what I have to here,' she said firmly, not for one moment betraying the trembling within her. 'You remember, perhaps, the night you called at Alice Simmons's rum parlour? You took your pleasure with me and no doubt thought it ended there. Unfortunately it did not.'

His eyes narrowed and in spite of her nervousness she felt a small quirk of triumph. She had surprised him – he had not expected this. Then he moved impatiently, flicking the riding whip he was carrying against his long muscled thigh.

'Do you mean what I assume you mean, Miss Kelly? That you find yourself in circumstances likely to cause you growing embarrassment during the coming months? Really, I was under the impression ladies of your calling knew better.'

'Oh!' Erin squeaked in outrage. 'Once and for

all, I am not what you think! I was at Alice Simmons's for the purpose of serving customers only. And if you had been less of an animal you would have waited to discover the truth before deflowering me!'

Again his eyes narrowed and her flush deepened. But unrepentant, she held her head high, returning his gaze. Perhaps he had not actually deflowered her, as she had called it, but that made little difference now. But for the convict, his would certainly have been the guilt of taking her virginity – and all against her will.

'What do you want from me?' Brett Wilde asked suddenly.

'What do you think I want? Some security for myself and my child,' Erin returned. 'I'm not asking for charity. But I do need work to enable me to keep my family together. We were in desperate straits before. Now...' Her voice trailed away. He was slapping his thigh again with his riding crop, his face thoughtful.

'You know your father owed me a great deal of money?' His eyes came up to meet hers, a hard, straight look. 'By the time you had worked that off there would be no payment for you for a very long time. No, I don't think the answer lies in my employing you, Miss Kelly.'

'I see.' She drew a harsh breath. 'Then you won't help me.'

A speculative look came into his grey eyes, and the hint of a smile. 'I didn't say that. I have another proposition – a better one, you may think. Mine is a lonely life here, especially since I resigned my commission in the Corps. I would like someone to share it.'

Erin tossed her head so that her dark curls danced angrily.

'Never! I thought I had made it clear I am no whore!'

Her spirited reaction brought the smile to his lips.

'If I thought you were that, I assure you I would not be making this suggestion. I accept now that I was misled by Mistress Simmons. No, my proposal is of a much more permanent nature. I have built an empire here, Miss Kelly, and I have no one to share it with. My suggestion to you is that you should marry me and come to live at Mia-Mia as my wife.'

CHAPTER SEVEN

For a moment the world seemed to tip first to one side and then the other and Erin grasped at Starlight's flowing mane for support.

Had she heard right – Brett Wilde asking her to marry him? It couldn't be true – and yet...

'You seem surprised, Miss Kelly.' Brett's voice was amused. 'But think about it for a moment before you give me an answer. It is a sensible solution for us both, is it not? You are looking for security for yourself and your child. I should like the company and comfort of a pretty woman – and God alone knows there are few enough of them in this place. We would each supply the other's needs admirably, would we not?'

Erin opened her mouth to reply but no sound came out. She was too shocked still – too amazed at his audacity. Didn't he know she hated him? Didn't he know she would die rather than submit to his lust again even once, let alone place herself in the position of having to accept him into her bed every night of her life? Marry him? She would as soon marry a viper!

'You're mocking me,' she managed at last.

He shook his head. 'On the contrary, I was never more serious.'

'And you really think I would marry you, after what you did to me?'

He shrugged. 'Come now, it was not that bad, surely? And what I'm offering you is not inconsiderable. Mia-Mia is quite comfortable and I have convicts to do all the menial work. And soon my new house in Sydney will be completed too. It would not be a bad life, I assure you.'

She lifted her chin. 'The life of a strumpet with a wedding ring to make it respectable! I suppose it would make it easier for you to know you had no need to go out looking for your pleasure – and with no chance of making a mistake and raping a decent girl again – though it doesn't seem to have troubled your conscience overmuch. No, I thank you kindly, Mr Wilde, but I must refuse your offer. I came to ask you for work, and that's all I want.'

'Then I am afraid I must disappoint you.' He smiled coolly.

'But...'

'My offer still stands. Marriage or nothing. Take it or leave it.'

'Oh, I hate you!' she cried, turning Starlight in a tight circle. But his hand on the bridle arrested her.

'Don't be too hasty, Miss Kelly. Stop and think of the alternatives before you dismiss my offer out of hand. It will not be easy for you with another mouth to feed. Before long you will be back at Mistress Simmons's excellent rum parlour begging her to find you work of the more lucrative kind – and your sister with you. You have a sister, do you not? No doubt it will fall to her to sell herself for your crusts while you are heavy with child.'

Erin's hand shot involuntarily to her throat. 'Oh no!' she whispered. 'Not Grianne!'

The cruel grey eyes continued to bore into hers. 'How else will you live? And your creditors cannot be expected to wait forever for their dues. I, myself, have already given you all the leniency I can. Now...'

A small sob escaped her. 'Oh, you wouldn't...'

'My dear Miss Kelly, as you yourself so rightly stated, I am not a charitable institution. I have a business to run, and while I try to aid those who are my friends, I cannot extend credit indefinitely to those who are not.'

The colour drained from her cheeks and it seemed to her suddenly as if the claws of a trap were closing around her. She shook her head from side to side and the dark curls danced on her ashen face.

'I don't understand,' she whispered. 'You're blackmailing me into marrying you, aren't you? But why – why?'

'I told you, I like the idea,' he said coolly. 'Besides...' Her lip was trembling. She caught at it with her teeth. 'Besides what?'

'You tell me you are having my child. I don't want him to grow up in poverty with the stigma of bastard to mar his childhood. Such a beginning can have its effect on a man. And even more than that...' He broke off, a distant look coming into his eyes and he turned for a moment to scan the house, the orchards and the lands beyond, stretching as far as the eye could see. 'I

107

told you I would like a companion here, Miss Kelly, but there is something I want even more than that. I've worked long and hard to make this place what it is. Now, I want an heir, who will grow to love it as I do and take it over when I am too old to bother any more. I want a son, and you can give him to me. He is already there, in your belly. That is why I am encouraging you to accept my offer.'

For a moment Erin did not reply. Breath caught in her throat and she fought the almost hysterical desire to laugh. Brett Wilde was offering her marriage not because he wanted her but because he wanted the child she was carrying. If she accepted, her baby would be born not into poverty but into the new aristocracy of this crazy country where power was all-important and illicit trading bought respectablity as well as comfort. Brett Wilde actually wanted to hand all this to her child because he believed it to be his son. When for all she knew it could be the child of a filthy, unkempt murderer.

'Well?' he pressed her and the laughter bubbled up so she could no longer control it. Oh, but it was rich – rich! She hated him with all her heart and always would. Why, just the sight of his arrogant face was enough to make her boil up inside. But if she was to save herself, her sisters and brother and her unborn child from ruin she had no choice but to accept his offer. And the joke was that he had no idea he might be handing his empire on a plate to the child of a convicted criminal!

The laughter died as suddenly as it had begun

and the tears were there, pricking behind her eyes. She hated Brett Wilde, but she must marry him. And she must keep from him her doubts as to the child's parenthood. If she was to save them all, that must be her secret.

With an effort she controlled the trembling of her lips.

'It's a strange proposal, Mr Wilde,' she said with all the coolness she could muster. 'But I have little choice in the matter. If you are serious, then I accept.'

He smiled, and she saw the triumph sparkling in the grey eyes.

'I assure you I was never more serious in my life,' he told her.

The wedding was arranged with all the speed that Erin's condition necessitated. Brett was insistent upon that.

'I don't want my bride to look in danger of having her child as she stands before the priest at my side,' he said, with a touch of wry humour, and Erin wondered briefly if he might care more for convention than he cared to admit. But she pushed the thought away as quickly as it had come.

Brett Wilde had no conscience about the way he made his profits, why should he have any when it came to allowing the world to know he had planted his seed in his woman before the ring was on her finger? No, she was the one who cared about that, confound it! Why, even now she thought she would die of shame if even her brother or sister should guess the reason behind his proposal. When she had broken the news to them she was careful to avoid their curious questions and gave away only as much as she had to.

Each of them, of course, had reacted to her announcement in their own way. Brenna was so excited she could scarcely contain herself, skipping and squealing with delight and inquiring whether she could be Erin's bridesmaid. Patrick was shocked. His face turned even paler than usual and the haunted look in his eyes told Erin that he was blaming himself yet again for all their misfortunes and for the marriage he shrewdly suspected his sister was being forced into against her will. But Grianne's reaction was the most unexpected.

For a moment she stood staring at Erin with her lip caught tight between her teeth and a look of undisguised envy in her eyes. Then she laughed, a short, mocking laugh that Erin knew so well.

'Brett Wilde! But I thought you hardly knew him! You're a dark horse and no mistake, Erin!'

'I told you I met him at Alice Simmons's place,' Erin said uncomfortably.

'I thought there was something going on when he sent us men to help with the harvest,' Grianne continued. 'It didn't sound like him to do something for us out of the goodness of his heart. How did you get around him, I'd like to know?'

Erin flushed. 'I don't know what you mean, Grianne.'

Grianne laughed again, the undisguised envy sharpening her eyes.

'Oh, come on, Erin, a plum like him doesn't

fall unless you give the tree a little shake,' she remarked knowingly. 'Don't think I blame you, though. I just wish it was me marrying him, that's all.'

Erin's eyes widened in genuine surprise.

'Why should you want to marry Brett Wilde?' she asked. 'You have David, don't you?'

Grianne shrugged her slim shoulders. 'So what? I'd rather have someone like Brett Wilde. David's all right, and he treats me well, I suppose, but he's only a poor farmer and I doubt if he'll ever be more than that.'

'But he loves you!' Erin protested. 'And I thought you loved him!'

Grianne's mouth tightened. 'Love!' she said contemptuously. 'It's only in fairy tales that love stories have happy endings. No, I'd settle for a nice home with servants to look after me any day – and fine clothes and good food. You don't know how lucky you are, Erin.'

Erin turned away, biting back the comments that flew to her lips. How could Grianne say such things! Only because she had not the least idea what she was talking about – praise be! But this was not the time nor the place to tell her so.

'What's to become of the rest of us while you live in splendour at Mia-Mia?' Grianne asked.

With an effort Erin controlled her irritation.

'I've asked Brett if you can all move in with us,' she said evenly. 'In fact I told him you couldn't possibly stay here on your own and I wouldn't marry him unless he made provision for you all.'

'I don't want to go to Mia-Mia,' Patrick said,

111

and Erin's heart sank as she saw the determined expression on his face. 'This is our home. I shall stay here.'

'Please, Patrick, be sensible,' she begged. 'There are too many dangers for you to stay here alone. See what happened when the convicts broke out – that could easily happen again. Or a flood, or a bushfire...'

'But it's our land,' Patrick protested. 'What will happen to it if we go to Mia-Mia? Brett Wilde will take it over, I suppose, and use it to swell his empire.'

'No, it'll still be ours and when you're old enough you can come back and work it,' she promised. 'Now, please, for my sake, agree to come to Mia-Mia.'

'I couldn't stay under the same roof as that man,' Patrick said vehemently, and she caught at his hands.

'I don't think you'd have to for very long. Brett's having a house built in Sydney and his business will keep him there quite a lot of the time. Apart from the labourers there'd only be the overseer at Mia-Mia and as Brett's brother-in-law you'd be treated with respect. Though I dare say you could learn a good deal from Henry Stanton about farming if you'd a mind to listen.'

Patrick nodded miserably. There was really nothing else he could say, though it was no use for him to pretend he liked the arrangement.

'When will the wedding be, Erin?' Brenna asked eagerly. 'Oh, say it's going to be soon! I just can't wait!'

Within her belly Erin felt what might have

been the first fluttering movement of her child. I can't wait, either, she thought, but there was no eagerness in her.

'It'll be as soon as Brett Wilde can arrange for a priest to carry out the ceremony, my sweet,' she promised, and as Brenna clapped her hands together and jumped up and down in delight Erin thought that at least if her sacrifice could save her little sister from the same fate as herself, it would not have been in vain.

The wedding took place on a perfect autumn day when the sky was clear and blue above the eucalypts in spite of a hint of frost in the air.

Father Timothy, the priest, had travelled all the way from Sydney especially to conduct the ceremony and the big drawing room at Mia-Mia seemed to be almost overflowing with guests. The better-off settlers were there, rubbing shoulders with the scarlet jackets of the Corps officers, but few of the humble farmers who Erin knew best had been invited.

Brett had insisted the little family should move into Mia-Mia the day before the ceremony. Though Erin would have preferred to remain at Kinvarra till the last possible moment, he was firm on that point. She could not arrive for her wedding spattered with mud from the track.

It wouldn't do for me to show myself up in front of his fine friends, I suppose, Erin thought miserably, and her glimpse of life as it was to be did nothing to cheer her. Hard and frugal though her existence at Kinvarra might be, at least she could be herself. After today that identity would

113

disappear and she would become Mrs Brett Wilde of Mia-Mia.

On the morning of the wedding, however, she was forced to admit that it did have its compensations. Two convict women brought water for her bath, then left her to soak in its scented luxury. Perhaps Brett had not wanted them to notice her condition, she thought, resting her back against the rim of the tub and letting her eyes roam the length of her body from the swollen breasts with their dark tips to the mound beneath them. But after a while they returned, averting their eyes tactfully as they towelled her dry and rubbed oil into her skin, especially where it was stretched taut over her belly. They fetched the wedding dress that Brett had bought for her with a great deal of rum – a gown of Chinese silk, more delicate than anything Erin had ever seen, much less owned. As they slipped it over her head it slithered down to caress her still-damp skin and briefly Erin revelled in its luxury. Then they were seating her before a mirror, combing the tangles from her dark hair and smiling at her reflection, and suddenly the nausea returned to choke her.

This should be the happiest day of her life, she thought, remembering with a rush of sadness all her childhood dreams of the day when she would be a bride. Instead it was one of the most wretched.

Reflected in the mirror she could see the big bed and the sight of it added to her nausea. Tonight she would have to share it with Brett Wilde. Tonight and tomorrow and every night for the rest of her life if he chose. And he would choose. An animal like him would be insatiable. That much he had proved already.

The door opened and Brenna came skipping in, all dressed for the occasion in a gown of pink silk. As she saw the happiness shining out of the child's face Erin felt a momentary stab of gratitude that he had done this for her. Then, once more, the bitter resentment clouded in. It wasn't likely he'd done it for Brenna. More likely it was to create a good impression on his important guests. It would not look good, after all, for Brett Wilde's future sister-in-law to appear in a shabby gown.

Through the open door, Erin saw a figure in the red jacket of a Corps officer crossing the landing and her heart jumped into her mouth for she knew the moment had come. The officer was Arthur Gill, who had been one of Brett's brother officers and who had agreed to give her away since Patrick, her only living relative, was still too young to do the job.

She rose, taking one last look at herself in the mirror before crossing the room to take his arm. His eyes appraised her but they did not linger and Erin sighed with relief. The high-waisted gown was a good disguise for her swelling belly. Perhaps not too many of those gathered in the drawing room would be aware of her condition.

Holding her head high she walked beside Arthur down the broad staircase and the guests assembled below craned their necks to catch their first glimpse of Brett Wilde's bride. Few of them knew her; there was little exchange between the rich and the poor. But for the most part they were surprised with his choice of wife and the speed with which the wedding had been arranged, particularly as Brett had spoken so often about an English girl to whom he was betrothed.

But still, this Erin Kelly was certainly very beautiful, with her glossy dark curls tumbling about the ivory silk of her gown and her eyes huge and blue in her pale face.

On Arthur's arm, Erin walked between them looking neither to left nor right. They were just a blur to her, a blur of faces and murmuring voices and conflicting perfumes – rum, tobacco smoke and expensive oils and scents from the East. Only one person in the room was real – the man who stood waiting for her, his head turned to look at her. Above his frilled shirt and silk cravat his face was still tanned from the summer sun – not even the winter months would muddy that – and there were still sun-bleached streaks in his thick brown hair. But it was his eyes that Erin could not draw her gaze away from – those sharp grey eyes that could be at once amused and hypnotic, and which she felt missed nothing – nothing. They were raking her, those eyes, taking in every detail of her from the top of her head to the toes of her slippered feet, and lingering briefly on the rounded swelling between her narrow hip bones. Then, with a small satisfied smile he turned back to the priest and before Erin had time for more thought the wedding service had begun.

How she stood there while the vows were

116

made she was never afterwards to be quite sure. More than once the nausea rose to threaten her but she closed her eyes, gritted her teeth and hung on. As if from a long way off she heard Brett's voice, low and firm, and then more surprising, her own, repeating the words that Father Timothy fed to her. Then, just when she felt she could endure no more, a handful of words separated themselves from the others:

'You may kiss the bride.'

She swayed slightly as he turned to her and the lean brown hands gripped her arms. She smelled the cigar smoke on his breath as he bent his head to hers and the sickness turned in her stomach once more. She gasped, a small intake of breath, but he seemed not to hear. His lips covered hers, drinking deeply, while his hands held her firmly against his long, hard body. Instinctively she sensed his hunger for her and everything within her cried out against it. He was showing everyone in the room that she was his, not only in name, but in the flesh too. Shamed, yet not wishing to do anything to draw attention to the fact that she was a most unwilling bride, she remained passive beneath his kiss while his lips probed hers and his strong hands held her rounded belly hard against his flat, muscled one. The room began to spin around her again, but just as she feared she would swoon he released her, holding her away, and she opened her eyes to see him looking down at her with a mixture of triumph and desire.

Her heart was pumping like a frightened bird. Holy Mother, it was done now! she thought.

There could be no going back.

Just as she thought her fears would overwhelm her, hubbub broke loose. Brenna ran to her, catching at her skirts and hugging her, Grianne, the envy still shining in her eyes, was kissing her cheek, and the congregation crowded around, chattering, laughing and offering their congratulations. Then Brett's hand was beneath her elbow, ushering her between the people to the dining room where the wedding breakfast had been laid out – two tables groaning beneath the weight of more food than Erin had ever seen.

''Twould keep us fed for a year,' Patrick murmured, filling his plate with cold kangaroo meat and all the delicious accompaniments.

There was wine, too, enough to make some of the guests merry, but it only made Erin's head spin again. She had slept little last night and she expected to sleep even less tonight and the weight on her eyelids seemed to be pressing down relentlessly.

When Brett was engaged in a joke with some of his friends and Erin was left alone, it occurred to her that no one might miss her if she slipped away for a few moments. A quick look round assured her that Patrick was still eating hungrily and all Grianne's attention was given to flirting with a handsome, scarlet-jacketed young soldier. As for Brenna, she was nowhere to be seen.

Quietly Erin made her way to the door and no one attempted to delay her. Into the hallway she went, stopping to draw a breath of pure relief to be away from the mass of bodies in the dining room, and up the stairs.

The room that had been allocated to her was just as she had left it except that the tub of water had been taken away and a nightgown of softest silk had been laid out on the bed. When she saw it, a small sob caught in Erin's throat. Tonight she would have to wear it when she submitted to Brett Wilde's desires. There could be no escape. But for now the weight of sleep that was on her eyelids could no longer be denied. Her pregnancy, the wine, and the sleepless nights had combined with the strain of the occasion to brew too strong a drug. Erin pushed the door closed behind her, slipped out of her wedding gown, and lay down on the bed. Beneath her cheek the counterpane was soft and silky, quite different from the rough homespun one in her room at Kinvarra. Gratefully she closed her eyes and almost at once the world receded. While the river folks celebrated her wedding in the room below, Erin slept.

A hand upon her shoulder brought her sharply back to awareness and she opened her eyes to see Brett Wilde bending over her. His face was close to hers, very brown above the brilliant white of his frilled shirt, and at the neck, where a button was unfastened, she saw the crisp brown hair curling out. A small cry of shock rose involuntarily to her lips and her body seemed to freeze, lying rigid and immobile upon the silken counterpane.

'Erin – are you all right?' His voice was rough and she guessed he was angry with her for creeping away from the wedding celebrations.

She nodded, though the shock of her awaken-

119

ing had made her teeth begin to chatter. 'Yes.'

He stretched out a lean, sunburned hand; mesmerized she watched as it came close to her face, brushing the dark curls from her forehead and tracing the line of her jaw till it reached her chin.

'You're sure you're not ill?'

She shook her head, confused. His fingers were gentle on her face and the expression in his eyes was stirring a chord deep within her. That look – why, if she had not known better she might almost have thought it was tender – the look she had seen in her father's eyes when she had hurt herself as a child and he had kissed away the tears...

'I was just tired,' she murmured.

'I'm not surprised.' His fingers moved on, outlining the curve of her mouth and parting her lips slightly before fanning out onto her cheeks and running along her cheekbones where her lashes lay in a soft sooty sweep. Slowly he bent his head to hers, gently touching with his lips where his fingers had touched. She lay inert while he kissed her eyes, her cheeks and her lips, breath suspended while a strange, half-forgotten longing gnawed at her. His lips moved down her throat, planting kisses in the hollows at its base and her skin prickled oddly beneath them. Then his fingers brushed the swell of her breasts above the lowcut neck of her chemise and the pleasurable sensation was immediately suffused with dread.

Memories of those other nights and the hands that had torn roughly at her soft skin came rushing in, blurred together, and she jerked away

120

from him, her body tense, her mouth tight closed.

'Erin, don't turn from me!' His voice was ragged. 'It'll be all right now, you'll see. Just let me teach you, love, how it can be...'

At his words, her eyes opened wide in disbelief and horror. Did he intend to take her now? Was this why he had come looking for her, to claim his rights as a husband? She had known she must submit tonight and she had been preparing herself for that. But she had not expected him to want her now! And oh, she was not ready for him, in any way...

'Couldn't you wait?' she burst out. 'Do you have to take me like a rutting boar at the first opportunity?'

She felt him flinch and her fear took a new, sharp edge. She shouldn't have said it, she knew. She was, after all, his wife...

She cast a sidelong, nervous look at him and her throat seemed to close up. There was no tenderness in his look now. How could she ever have thought there was? There was only fury – and lust – narrowing his eyes and lending a dangerous curl to his lips.

'I can see I will have to teach you the hard way,' he snarled. 'But I will ride you, milady, have no fear on that score.'

With one careless movement he ripped the chemise from her body, leaving her exposed and trembling. Then he straightened, divesting himself of breeches and boots before lowering himself to the bed beside her. His two hands caught her shoulders, forcing her down into the deep, downy mattress and his body covered hers with all the lazy power of the tiger.

His ruffled shirt front scratched the soft flesh of her nude bosom and the hard, driving strength of his manhood was hot between her legs. She twisted beneath him, wifely duty forgotten as the memories of rape spun at her in a nightmarish kaleidoscope.

'No!' she screamed. 'No! No!'

At once his hand covered her mouth, his fingers brutal on the soft skin he had so recently caressed.

'Quiet! Do you want the whole house to hear you?'

She arched her body, pummelling at his back with her fists, and as she did so he drove into her. This time there was no pain, but the breath left her in a rush and all the humiliation came flooding back. She lay beneath him tense but subdued while the tears welled up in her eyes and she sobbed softly in time with the rhythmic working of his body.

At last it was over. One moment he was thrusting deep within her, the next he was still, and though his weight still ground her into the mattress, his lips found hers, covering them with some semblance of the tenderness he had shown earlier, while his hands gently brushed the tangled hair from her face.

For some reason the irony of this incensed her even more than his enforced love-making and she twisted her head away violently.

'I hope you're satisfied!' Her voice was sharp with the bitterness that came from knowing she must submit to him over and over again. 'How shameful, not to be able to wait for even a few hours!'

She felt him stiffen. 'You're my wife now, Erin,' he said softly. 'I wanted to show you the way it could be. But if you fight both me and yourself there can be no pleasure for either of us.'

Her lips trembled but she turned the threatening sob into a harsh laugh.

'Pleasure? Let me remind you, Brett, that I married you against my will. You blackmailed me for your own ends and you left me no choice. But don't expect me to welcome you into my bed as if I were a loving bride. And don't expect your son to be born unscathed, either, if you continue to use me this way while I carry him in my body!'

His face darkened. He rolled away from her, levering himself to his feet, and she knew that one of her barbs, at least, had gone home.

'Just remember I hate you for what you've done to me, Brett Wilde!' she cried.

The tears were beginning in earnest now. They blurred her eyes and she turned her face away into the pillow so that he should not see them. Her head was singing so loudly she scarcely heard him recovering his clothes and it was only when she heard the click of the door that she turned quickly over. The room was empty and she was alone. And as the loneliness crept like a cold shadow into her heart she turned her face once more to the pillow and wept.

CHAPTER EIGHT

As the door closed behind him Brett Wilde stood for a moment undecided on the landing.

From the storey below he could hear the merriment and chatter of his guests and he knew he should return to entertain them. But at present he could think of nothing but the girl he had left sobbing in his bed, the girl who these few hours since had become his wife, and on whom he had forced himself yet again.

Why had he done it? he wondered bitterly, cursing himself for his lack of self-control. Why hadn't he wooed her gently, the way he'd intended? She'd looked so lovely and desirable lying there, it was true, that his senses had been stirred unbearably. And when she had turned on him with her viperish tongue it was as if something had exploded within him. But that was no excuse. It wasn't that he hadn't had a woman for a long while – he had. He had recently been in Sydney on business and there was no shortage of attractive young ladies there only too eager to please the rich and powerful Brett Wilde. Yet even when he had been with them he had found his thoughts returning to the Irish-born lass he had taken at Mistress Simmons's rum parlour in mistake for a strumpet. Even before he had known she was bearing his child he had been unable to get her out of his mind. Wherever he had looked it had seemed she was there, and that was strange, since it should be Therese who occupied his thoughts, Therese with her golden hair and her aristocratic ways and the beauty that had held him captive for more years than he cared to remember.

He stood for a moment at the landing window, letting his eyes roam across the vast expanse of his land. All this he had done for Therese. For five years he had worked and gambled and connived, thinking of nothing except that the faster he could make his fortune the sooner she would join him. It was, he knew, his only chance with her, though she had said she loved him. For Therese was the daughter of an English earl, while he...

With an impatient movement Brett selected a cigar from the box on the landing table and lit it with a taper. He did not want to think about his own background. It did not matter now. Here, on the river, he was Brett Wilde of Mia-Mia, disliked and feared, perhaps, by those with less than he, but respected and envied too. And if Therese would never now come to join him and share the empire he had built for her, so be it. The girl in his bed was now his wife and soon she would bear him a son and heir.

Drawing deeply on his cigar, Brett let his mind wander back to the first time he had seen her at Alice Simmons's rum parlour. Even then, when he had thought she was a strumpet, he had been struck by her beauty and the pride of her bear-

125

ing, and he had known that here was a girl who could make him forget, for a while at least, the accursed news he had received that day from England. Such was the impression she had made on him that the following week he had returned to Blackley's Tower to seek her out. In spite of her protestations he had been of the opinion that now she had discovered the easy money that was to be made from whoring she would continue to ply that trade. And he was surprised and a little sorry when Alice Simmons told him she had not seen the girl since that night. The discovery that she certainly was no strumpet had prompted him to send a wagonload of supplies and when Henry Stanton had returned with the information that the four Kellys were attempting to bring in their harvest alone he had instructed that half a dozen convict labourers should be sent over to assist.

'Damn it, Stanton, we can spare them for a day or two!' he had snapped irritably when the overseer had rewarded him with a searching look, and he had scarcely stopped to ponder his motives in the matter.

It was only when he had seen her again that he had realized how she had occupied his thoughts, and when she had told him she was carrying his child he had acted with the same swift decisiveness that had helped him make his fortune.

His hopes for a future with Therese were gone now. They had died the day she married an English lord. But this girl, this strangely haunting girl who was such a compelling blend of contrasts and contradictions, would give Mia-

Mia the heirs it needed. As for the rest...

With an abrupt movement, Brett ground out his cigar into a silver dish that graced the landing. As usual, he had got what he wanted. Erin Kelly was his wife. And downstairs in the drawing room thirty guests were likely wondering what had become of the bride and groom.

Straightening the crumpled frill of his shirt, Brett went down the stairs to play host once more.

It was sundown when the last of the guests finally departed. As she stood with Brett on the verandah to watch them go Erin felt that the last of her freedom was going with them.

With the celebrations completed there was nothing left now but her life with him, nothing but endless days under the reproachful eyes of his servants and nights when she must submit to him again and again.

Why, already he had shown his uncontrollable lust. She shivered as she remembered the way he had taken her, half-asleep as she had been, while the wedding guests revelled below them. If there had been any doubts in her mind before, there were none now. He was an animal, pure and simple, no better than a stud bull or a wild stallion with the scent of a mare in his nostrils.

She shivered again, and his hand dropped around her shoulders, making her tense.

'Are you cold?' he asked roughly. 'You'd better get back inside. That gown is too thin for these autumn winds.'

She lifted her chin. How hypocritical he was!

Here, within the view of others, he could be solicitous of her welfare, protective even. But as soon as they were alone...

'I'm all right,' she said sharply.

She felt him stiffen slightly and triumph stabbed at her that she had seen through his veneer and he knew that she had. Then he pushed at the door, holding it open for her and standing back himself.

'You go on in. Don't think me rude, but I like to smoke a last cigar before I retire, and have a look around my estate to ensure everything is as it should be.'

She nodded. 'Please, do as you always do,' she said, but perversely even this irritated her. Surely he could at least have come in and talked to her a little, tried to get to know her, instead of treating her only as a legalized whore. How could he expect her to respond to his love-making when there was such a lack of not only love, but companionship too? Did he intend to continue in this way?

She went into the hall and as she crossed it something pink between the banisters at the top of the stairs caught her eye. It was Brenna, fallen fast asleep in the place she had chosen to watch the departing guests.

Smiling to herself, Erin climbed the stairs to reach her. She had thought Grianne would put her little sister to bed tonight, but clearly she was too occupied on business of her own. She dropped to her knees beside the child, slipping her arms beneath and around her, and she was about to lift her when a voice from the hall below

128

arrested her.

'Erin – don't! Not in your condition!'

Startled she looked down through the banisters to see Brett looking up at her.

'I'll put her to bed. You mustn't strain yourself.' He took the stairs two at a time, lifting Brenna with ease and holding her firmly against his broad chest.

'I thought ... I thought you were going to smoke your cigar and take a tour of the estate,' Erin faltered.

He did not answer, giving all his attention to the sleeping child in his arms. Along the landing he carried her and into the room that had been allocated to her. Then he set her down on the bed and turned to Erin.

'I'll send one of the convict women to undress her.'

'No!' Erin said sharply. 'I'd rather see to her myself.'

His eyes narrowed. 'You shouldn't be doing menial tasks.'

'It's not menial!' she returned shortly. 'She's my sister and she's not very old. She'd be frightened out of her wits to wake in a strange place all alone with one of those women.'

Brett's eyebrow raised slightly. 'You don't want to stay with her all night, do you?'

'No, don't worry, Grianne will be with her then,' Erin said with a hint of sarcasm.

He nodded abruptly. 'As you like. Just as long as you remember you are mistress here now and that is the way I would like you to behave.'

With that he left the room and Erin stared after

129

him for a moment, amazed by his arrogance. Did he expect her to neglect her brother and sisters now she was mistress of Mia-Mia? If he did, he was going to have a fight on his hands and no mistake! Tears of regret for having been forced into marrying such a heartless monster stung her eyes, but impatiently she brushed them away, bending over the sleeping child and easing the pink gown over her head. So childishly defenceless she looked lying there that all Erin's tenderest instincts were aroused. If she could keep Brenna as innocent as she was and protect her from hardship, then whatever she had to do she would do it. What happened to her didn't matter much any more.

As she lifted Brenna enough to wriggle her into her nightgown the little girl stirred, murmuring something and twisting her arms round Erin's neck, but Erin gently disentangled them, straightening the sheets about the small, round body. Then she bent to blow out the candle that stood on the chest beside the bed.

'Good night, my love,' she whispered. 'Sweet dreams.'

'Sweet dreams,' came back the sleepy reply, and Erin's lips twisted sadly at the irony.

Oh, her dreams would likely be anything but sweet!

Closing Brenna's door after her, she went along the landing to the room she was to share with Brett. She would retire now, she decided, rather than look for Patrick and Grianne to wish them good night. She did not think she could face their knowing looks just now, and she wanted time to prepare herself for the ordeal ahead of her.

She went into the room, leaving the door ajar behind her, and crossed to the window. Then she caught her breath.

This room faced the opposite way to her old room at Kinvarra. That had looked down the avenue of eucalypts and mimosa towards the river. But this room was at the rear of Mia-Mia, and from this window she could see the full extent of the property. So still it seemed now beneath the deep violet of the sky, with none of the ever-present dangers showing their claws to detract from the beauty and the peace. So still and so vast – more land than she had ever dreamed of owning as she helped work the small grant at Kinvarra.

What would you think of this if you knew, Father? she wondered silently. Your grandson the heir to all this!

But there was no reply even inside her head; just the empty ache of wishing, even now, that it could be different. Once, she had shared love, if only for a little while, and though that had not stood the test, perhaps in time there would have been someone else to fill her with dreams. Now that could never be.

She turned away abruptly, back to the room with its rich and ornate furnishings, bought from the foreign traders as proof of his success, and the emptiness rose to choke her.

With rough fingers she unfastened her wedding gown, letting it slip to the ground, and her chemise with it. In the mirror her reflection

131

danced up to meet her – the breasts more volup-
tuous still as the pregnancy advanced, the stomach high and rounded, legs long and slender as
ever – and she twisted away, reaching for the
nightgown put ready for her on the bed and
pulling it on to hide the proof of her temptation
for men. How she hated her body for what it had
brought her! And how she hated the evidence
that she was carrying the child of one or the
other hateful unions!

Someone had laid out her toilet items on the
dressing table – the tortoiseshell brush and
matching comb that had been her mother's and
which the convicts had somehow missed when
they looted Kinvarra. She sank down onto the
small stool that stood before the dressing table
tugging at her tangled black curls with the brush
in an effort to make them conform. To her
surprise she realized that in spite of the daringly
cut neckline of her nightgown, which exposed
most of her breasts to view, in the candlelight
her face looked almost as innocent as Brenna's.
And after all that had happened to her, too!

So engrossed was she in her toilet she did not
near the door open softly and it was with a shock
that she suddenly became aware she was no
longer alone. There was another figure reflected
behind hers in the mirror – a tall, unsmiling
figure in frilled shirt and buckskin breeches
whose eyes seemed to burn into hers.

Something strangely painful twisted deep
within her as those reflected eyes held hers, and
for a moment breath seemed suspended in her
throat.

132

'Brett!' she said shakily. 'I didn't hear you come in.'

He placed his hands on her shoulders, bending his face close to hers, and every nerve in her body began to tingle in anticipation of what was to come. Already with his breath warm on her cheek she could imagine his greedy hands tearing at the fine cloth of her nightgown, and she held herself tensed in readiness.

But to her surprise he only pulled the nightgown higher over her breasts.

'If you do not wish to tempt me, you must learn not to display yourself so enticingly.' There was a harsh note in his voice and in the candlelight his grey eyes were veiled and unreadable.

The brush almost fell from her fingers. She tightened her grasp upon it.

'I don't understand you, Brett.'

His fingers were still biting into her shoulders, holding the nightgown high to conceal all but the slimmest ridge of her neck.

'I'm sorry. How can I make myself clearer? If you wish me to leave you in peace you must not flaunt your undoubted charms. It is too much to expect of me, my sweet.'

Her eyes widened. He didn't mean, surely, what she thought he meant? That he did not, after all, intend to sleep with her this night? But why, after all he had done to her, should he suddenly shrink from upsetting her? What hypocritical game was he playing now?

'You mean you do not wish to take me again?' she burst out before she could stop herself, and to her utter chagrin he threw back his head and laughed at her.

'Don't sound so pained, my love. You made it plain enough that was how it was to be.'

His laughter irritated her. What he had done to her was certainly no laughing matter. And she was oddly hurt that he could dismiss it – and her – so lightly.

'I'm surprised you show so much concern for my feelings all of a sudden!' she flared.

His laughter stopped abruptly.

'Don't flatter yourself,' he returned harshly. 'It's not you I'm concerned about. It's my son.'

He released her shoulders, turning away, and she watched him cross to the door, hot colour rising in her cheeks.

'Where are you going?' she asked foolishly.

He stopped in the doorway, looking back at her, and there was a sardonic curl to his mouth.

'I'll sleep in my dressing room. It's comfortable enough. And you will be able to get the good night's rest a woman with child should. Good night, my sweet.'

Then, before she could reply, he was gone. She stared for a moment at the closed door, her mouth dropping open with surprise. Then she crossed to the bed, climbed in, and pulled the covers up to her chin.

In spite of her relief, there was a strange, indefinable emptiness inside her. This was what she had wanted, wasn't it – to be left alone? But that didn't stop the strange ache of rejection that niggled within her. She didn't want Brett, it was true, but to have him turn his back on her without a second glance now that she was his wife was somehow deeply hurtful, and she found herself remembering Alistair Percy who had left her for the daughter of a Paramatta trader.

'What's wrong with me?' she wondered, raising herself on one elbow to blow out the candle beside the bed.

And although no answer came to her, it was a long time before Erin slept.

CHAPTER NINE

A few weeks after the wedding Brett's house in Sydney was completed, and he was anxious to move in right away.

'I've much to attend to as regards my business that can be better done if I'm close at hand,' he told Erin, and her heart sank like a stone.

She had known the time was coming when he would take her away from the river, but oh! how little she wanted to go! Unhappy though she was with her situation as mistress of Mia-Mia, at least it was peaceful here and familiar, and she could still take Starlight for a canter and forget all her troubles for a little while. But Sydney would be all strangeness and bustle, her brother and sisters would not be there, and she would have no one but Brett, who seemed now not to care a fig for her.

Since their marriage night he had not once attempted to touch her, or share her bed, and oddly she did not know whether to be glad or sorry.

Oh, she did not want his attentions, to be sure, but the hurt she had felt that night remained and grew a little with each rejection of her. And of those, there were plenty.

It was not only that he did not attempt to make

use of his husband's rights. He hardly seemed aware she existed at all. In the mornings he was always up with first light and often she awoke from the heavy slumber that preceded the continuing nausea to hear the hooves of his horse, Jack, galloping away from the stables. Then, he was usually away all day, and when he did return in the evening he was more often than not engrossed in conversation with Henry Stanton, his overseer, on some problem concerning the running of the property.

Erin did not like Henry Stanton, and because she did not like him she resented his intrusion. He seemed to assume so much and even she, a small settler, would not have cared for a former convict to take such a lot upon himself in her business. But Brett seemed not to mind. He treated him more as an equal than a servant, though to the convict labourers on the estate and the women who worked in the house he could be as haughty and dictatorial as any lord of the manor.

It was a puzzle Erin could not fathom, though she had plenty of time on her hands to try.

Never, she thought, in all her life had she been so idle. And never had she been less content. Mia-Mia had been organized to run without a mistress and she was needed as little here as a nun in a rum parlour.

Her days she spent at the sort of pastimes she had never had time for before – working at a tapestry and some fine needlepoint – but she was not used to such fine work and she soon lost interest when the stitches came repeatedly too large. Tired of feeling utterly useless she went to the kitchen to engage in baking, which she loved, but the convict women working there soon made it plain she was encroaching on their preserve and to save face she was forced to withdraw.

The only things now she seemed to be good for were teaching Brenna her lessons and exercising Starlight and Bess.

Grianne, on the other hand, seemed delighted with her opportunity to live the life of a lady of leisure. If Erin suggested going to Kinvarra to keep the house in order she generally turned up her nose, so that Erin either went alone or with Patrick, and she hardly ever seemed to go to visit the Percys any more.

'You're neglecting David shamefully,' Erin reproached her one day, but Grianne only shrugged.

'Surely he doesn't expect me to run after him? If he wants to see me, he can always come here.'

'He's likely too shy for that,' Erin returned. 'This is not Kinvarra, after all, and he no doubt feels he'd be intruding upon Brett Wilde.'

But Grianne refused to bother her head.

'That's hardly my fault,' she said airily. 'If he wants me, he knows where to find me.'

Erin said nothing, but she thought her sister might live to rue the day she had treated David with such high-handed carelessness. David Percy was a nice enough lad and he clearly thought the world of Grianne. But seeing the life Brett Wilde lived at Mia-Mia had had its effect on the younger girl – a fact that was demonstrated once again when Erin broke the news to her that she and Brett were leaving for Sydney.

'Oh, Erin, couldn't I come with you?' Grianne asked, her eyes shining with excitement.

'Come with us? Whatever for?' Erin returned in surprise.

'Because I'd love to live in Sydney! Isn't that reason enough?' Grianne cried.

Erin bit her lip. 'I don't know what Brett would say. And besides ... what about Patrick and Brenna? Brenna's far better being here, on the river, but she needs someone to look after her.'

'She'd have Patrick, and there are plenty of servants. Oh, please, Erin, won't you ask him?' Grianne begged.

'But what would you do in Sydney?' Erin persisted.

Grianne's eyes narrowed speculatively. 'I'm sure I'd find plenty to do – and interesting people to meet, too! Just think, I might find a rich husband as you did!'

So that was it! Now that she had sampled the life of a lady, a hard-working farmer like David Percy was not good enough for her.

'Don't be foolish, Grianne,' Erin told her sharply. 'Settle for someone who loves you.'

'Love?' Grianne stretched like a kitten in sunshine. 'Why do you think only poor folk can love? I'm sure I could be far happier with a rich man.'

Sickened, Erin turned away. There were times when Grianne talked like a common whore.

'You don't know what you're saying!' she

139

snapped.

Grianne tossed her head angrily.

'Oh, I might have known you wouldn't agree. You're afraid I'll do as well as you and that wouldn't suit you, would it? You want to be the lady – and what's more, you want to make a martyr of yourself. You know if I had a rich husband too I'd soon discover for myself it's not the torture you try to make out?'

Although Erin was stung by the injustice of Grianne's remarks, she said nothing. There was no point in reasoning with Grianne when she was in this mood. But that night when Brett came in from the property she managed to catch him alone and ask if he would have any objection to Grianne accompanying them to Sydney.

Surprised, Brett looked up from the ledgers he was checking. Then his eyes came to rest on Erin's stomach, more prominent with every passing day, and he nodded.

'You want your sister with you. Yes, I can understand that.'

Beneath the folds of her dress, Erin crossed her fingers tightly. If that was what he chose to believe was behind her request, so be it. At least it would save her having to go into embarrassing explanations.

'I would feel happier if I had her there,' she agreed.

'Then she'd better come,' Brett said shortly, bending his head over his ledgers once more, and Erin felt another stab of the hurt she could barely understand.

He had acceded to her request, hadn't he? So

what more did she want? Surely she was not still hankering after the kind of treatment she had experienced so briefly from Alistair Percy? If so, she was more foolish and romantic than she had thought. Brett Wilde was not the man to make a fuss of a woman, except when he had his sights set on his own lustful ends. And in any case, he had made it plain enough that he had married her for one reason only – because she could give him the heir he wanted so much. But what would he think if he knew that the child she carried might not be his at all?

She put her head to one side, watching him as he worked. Supposing she was to tell him now – in the same matter-of-fact way she had asked for her sister to go to Sydney with her? That would make him look at her, to be sure! His ledgers and business accounts would be forgotten then. After his neglect of her these past weeks it was a temptation that was difficult to resist. But even as the thought crossed her mind she knew she would not dare to do it. What Brett's reaction would be she was almost afraid to imagine, but he would certainly be angry as well as disappointed. Why, he might even turn them all out of the house, lock, stock and barrel, and she could not risk that. Besides...

A small, treacherous ache niggled inside her and for the first time she acknowledged the truth. She did not want her baby to have been fathered by the filthy, lice-ridden convict, and to admit aloud that it might be was to make it more real, more possible. Arrogant and hateful Brett might be, but he was not odious as the convict had been. And though the way he had acquired his empire might at times have been doubtful, at least he was no common criminal. No, if she had a choice there was no doubt but that she hoped it was Brett's seed that had united with her own and if for one moment she had thought otherwise it was only for spite at the man who seemed to have everything she and her family did not and who had forced her against her will into a marriage she did not want. It was her consolation to know that in her keeping was the one thing that could pierce his armour and dent that infuriating self-confidence of his – the trump card that might, in the end, mean she had compromised the powerful, quick-witted master of Mia-Mia.

Sydney was everything Erin had been afraid it would be – brash, rowdy and crowded. The streets that would be thick with dust in summer were now a mud-bath, and the seas that washed the harbour were thick and treacly beneath the leaden skies.

The house, too, she disliked. It was too grand by half for her taste and filled with treasures Brett had bought as evidence of his position in the town. From the first moment she set foot in it she was longing to be back at Mia-Mia, or better still, Kinvarra, where the friendly mimosa and eucalypts stood sentinel and she was not afraid of breaking some precious piece each time she flicked around.

Brett's store, in fact, was the only place in Sydney that she cared for and both she and

Grianne were fascinated by the assortment of goods that were gathered together under one roof. There were all the ordinary, everyday items, it was true, such as candles and cooking pots, but there were also luxurious things that the girls had never seen before – or not that they could remember – silks and spices, cobweb-fine shawls and sandalwood – and they could hardly keep away from the place. Brett raised no objection to their going there. If anything he was amused by their interest and Erin liked to think that perhaps she could be of some help when she got to know more about the stock and the book-keeping.

One winter's day when the cold wind off the sea was making her shiver in spite of the warm gowns Brett had bought for her, Erin was alone in the store. She had come in with Brett and Grianne, but Brett had left on business, Grianne had decided to take a walk down to the harbour to see a ship that was coming in, and Andrew Pitman, who managed the store for Brett, was anxious to slip home for a few minutes to see how his wife, who had just given birth to their first child, was faring.

'Could you manage without me for half an hour, do you think, Mrs Wilde?' he asked.

Erin nodded at once. In her condition she had every sympathy with Mrs Pitman and besides she was thrilled by the prospect of managing the store all alone for a short while. When Andrew had put on his top coat and gone she stood looking around her proudly, running her fingers over the kegs of molasses and the sacks of flour, rearranging this length of cambric and that basket of candles. The store was not busy today – Andrew would never have left her if it had been – and she served two or three customers, her customers, her confidence growing all the while.

It was in a small lull that the New South Wales Corps officer came into the store. Erin could tell at once both from his uniform and his bearing that he was of high rank – higher than Brett had been before he resigned his commission – and for some reason her throat seemed to close up with nervousness. This man had likely been Brett's superior – he would now be most critical of the enterprise that had tempted the junior officer away from the regiment and curious to see how well it was run.

For a few moments he strode around the store, picking up some items and poking others, and Erin's nervousness increased so that by the time he approached her to ask about a gift suitable for a lady she was almost overcome with confusion.

'What kind of lady?' she inquired, eager to help constructively and she was horrified when he threw back his head and laughed at her.

'I'm sorry...' The quick colour flooded her cheeks. 'I didn't mean...'

Like many others before him, Major Allen was beguiled by the pink cheeks and the way the dark lashes fluttered down to kiss them. His narrowed eyes took on a glint of interest and his fleshy lips curled slightly above the heavy paunch of chins.

'What kind of lady? Oh, a pretty one, my dear.

Though perhaps not quite so pretty as you.'

Her colour deepened. She turned quickly away to hide it.

'We've perfume – shawls – and some beautiful jewellery that came in on the last trader.'

She bent to reach the cases beneath the counter in which the precious jewellery was kept out of reach of thieving hands, unaware of the enticing picture she presented with her rounded breasts partially exposed beneath the dipping neckline of her gown.

'Perhaps she would like these ear-rings,' she suggested. 'Or this necklace – see, it's one of the finest we've ever had. 'Twould grace any lady's throat.'

He nodded and while his thick fingers tested the strength of the chain and the weight of the jewel suspended on it his eyes were still on the fullness of Erin's breasts.

'Yes, the necklace is indeed a fine one. But I am only a mere man. I know nothing about these things,' he murmured.

'Oh, I'm sure that's not true!' Erin protested. 'Not only would the lady be delighted with it, I'm sure when you see her wearing it you will know without doubt you made the correct choice.'

His eyes narrowed, sliding upwards from Erin's breasts to her full red lips, then down once more to the slender arch of her neck.

'Perhaps ... oh, no, 'twould be too much to ask...'

'What?' Erin asked, mystified, but still eager to please.

145

'Oh...' He gave a little laugh. 'I was wondering if perhaps *you* would be so kind as to put the necklace on yourself – just so as to allow me to see the way 'twould look. But I realize...'

'Well, of course I will!' Erin exclaimed, relieved to find his request such a simple one. 'Though I feel sure your lady will be wearing it with a gown more glamorous than my workaday winter one!'

He did not reply and she lifted the necklace to her throat. The heavy jewel fell temptingly into the valley between her breasts but for the life of her she could not make the fastening, hampered as she was by the sweep of her long, dark hair.

'Let me help you.' Major Allen slipped nimbly between the bins of flour and the huge yellow cheeses to come around to her side of the counter. Gratefully she turned her back on him, presenting him with the two ends of the chain.

He took them, moving the weight of her hair to one side and fastening the clasp with ease. But he did not move away and as she tried to turn to show him the full beauty of the necklace his hands slid down her smooth shoulders, holding her fast.

'Would that the lady for whom it is intended had such a pretty neck,' he murmured, his lips close to her ear.

At his words and touch Erin froze. Her instinct was to turn and slap him full in his podgy, self-satisfied face, but he was a customer – a good one – and a former superior officer of Brett's into the bargain. If she was to retain her dignity and the good name of Brett's stores, she must handle this with decorum.

'I'm sure you don't mean that, Sir,' she began, but he only laughed playfully.

'Indeed I do, my sweet. Do you not know how you tempt a man?'

The full, rubbery lips sought the softness of her throat and as she felt their moist touch she squirmed inwardly. Then the plump hands slid down her arms to turn her towards him and as she caught sight of the leering lust in his small, bright eyes and the uncontrollable quiver in his lips an uprush of panic threatened to choke her. That look of desire was unmistakable! Oh, sweet Jesu, surely history was not about to repeat itself again!

'How dare you!' she gasped, trying to push herself free. But the Major's strength was treble her own. He held her easily, smiling down at her, and all the while the lust burned in his eyes.

'Come, my dear, one kiss and I'll buy the necklace and the ear-rings too...'

His face came closer to hers, blotting out the light, and she turned her head away. She'd heave on his lips – she knew she would! Then, just as she expected to feel them on her cheek, the Major stiffened, raising his head as if he had seen something she had not. As his grip on her arms relaxed she managed to half-turn, following his eyes, and her heart rose in her throat like a plum-stone.

Brett! And a Brett whose face was contorted with anger!

Before either she or the startled Major could move he was across the store, knocking aside the

147

kegs and sacks that stood in his way. She cringed as she saw his arm come up and a gasp escaped her as he struck the Major full in the face with the back of his hand. The older man staggered backwards, releasing her abruptly, and with a sob she halffell against a sack of flour, sitting into it as it moulded beneath her weight.

The Major, regaining his balance with surprising agility, was backing across the store, one hand pressed to his stinging mouth, and Brett, his hands become fists, followed him.

'You lecherous bastard!' he threw at him, his voice low with fury. 'You've deserved that from many a husband, and how often I've longed to do it when I served under you!'

Above his hand the Major's eyes were wide with outrage. 'I'll see you pay for that, Wilde,' he grated.

Brett followed him threateningly, hands on buckskin-clad hips.

'You've no redress with me now, *Sir*,' he stated sarcastically. 'Now get out of my store before I throw you out!'

With all the dignity he could muster, the Major dusted down his uniform while heading for the door.

'I'm going. But don't think you've heard the last of this, Wilde! You have not!'

His shaking hand found the door and pulled it open. As he went into the street, Brett kicked it to after him so that it closed with a bang fit to shatter the glass and turned on Erin.

'As for you, Madam, I am speechless!' he threw at her furiously. 'But I tell you here and

148

now, I won't stand for my wife acting like a common whore!'

Tears of shock were stinging Erin's eyes.

'I wasn't!' she protested. 'I was only showing him a necklace at his request. He wanted to see what it looked like on a lady's neck, and I was unable to fasten it. Then he ... he tried to kiss me...'

Brett's mouth curled cruelly. 'Luckily for you, milady, I know Major Allen of old. He has cuckolded half the officers under his command – or attempted to. But without encouragement his advances would not get him very far.'

'I didn't encourage him!' Erin cried, stung by the unfairness of his allegations.

'Maybe not. But you, my dear, tempt without realizing it.' With an impatient sweep of his hand he indicated the neckline of her gown with the swell of her breasts above it, and the rounded body, still lovely even now it was grown larger with child. 'It was the same when you were at Mistress Simmons's rum parlour. Your behaviour and the look of you invite, whether you mean them to or not. Why, they are the causes of your being here now! And after what happened, I should have thought you would have learned your lesson.'

'Oh!' she cried. She was white-faced now and trembling, quite unable to think of a thing to say in her own defence.

'Well, that's it!' Brett continued angrily. 'I won't have this sort of thing happening in my store to my wife. Why, when the story gets around that you are an easy catch, every love-

149

starved man in town will be queuing for your attentions.'

'How dare you!' she managed, and his eyes, snapping grey fire, held hers.

'I am your husband, remember, and the father of your child. If you can't control youself then I must do it for you. You are not to come here again, flaunting yourself. You will remain at home and occupy yourself as a good wife should.'

'Wife?' she cried. 'Wife? What do you want with a wife? You never so much as touch me!'

As soon as the words were out she could have bitten off her tongue, but his expression was as cold and hard as ever.

'That, I understood you to say, was in the interests of the well-being of my child,' he grated. 'Now get your things together. I'm taking you home. And you won't be coming here again.'

Too frightened to disobey she reached for her cape. Through tear-blurred eyes she saw Grianne's shawl hanging on the peg beside it.

'What about Grianne?' she asked in a shaking voice. 'Is she not to come here either?'

His lips tightened. 'Grianne can do as she likes. She is not my responsibility. You are.'

'I see,' she whispered. 'You mean I am to be your prisoner.'

He swung around. For a second she caught the strangest expression in his eyes – something she might almost have taken for raw hurt if she had not known better. Then his lips twisted sardonically.

'I mean, my dear, that you are my wife,' he

150

informed her. 'And right this minute I am taking you home where you belong.'

'But the store – there's no one here to mind it,' she faltered.

'No. And that blackguard Pitman will pay for his absence when he returns with half a week's salary.'

'Oh no!' she cried. 'Brett, you can't! His wife has just had a child!'

'That's his problem, not mine,' Brett returned tightly. 'By the time I've finished with him he'll think himself lucky not to be out of a job altogether. Now get your things. I'm locking up the store and taking you home at once.'

Trembling, she slipped into her cape. As God was her witness, she had done nothing wrong, but she was to pay for the Major's lechery by forfeiting her freedom. How hard Brett was, and how unfair! And yet...

For just a second a tiny speck of hope brightened her world. For Brett to get so angry must mean surely that he cared just a little about her?

But even as that thought crossed her mind it was snuffed out. Brett was angry because he was jealous of his reputation in the town. Though he had taken her for a whore he did not want others to, now that she was his wife and would soon be the mother of his child. That was all there was to it. Brett Wilde cared for nothing but his lands and his position. It was the way he was and nothing would change that.

Blinking away the tears, she lifted her head high and went past him through the open door.

CHAPTER TEN

Now that she was no longer allowed to go to the store, the days in Sydney crawled by even more slowly and Erin thought she would go mad with frustration. There was nothing to do either in the new house or outside it, for like Mia-Mia it ran like clockwork under the care of the hired hands and assigned convicts, and she no longer even had the company of Grianne, who still went to the store as often as she could.

'If only I'd been there instead of you!' Grianne had said enviously to Erin when she heard the story of Major Allen's advances. 'If I had been I might have my future settled by now, with a high-ranking officer of the Corps begging for my favours.'

'Major Allen has a wife already,' Erin said shortly. 'All he wants from his women is a little distraction.'

'But you said he was buying the necklace for a lady,' Grianne argued. 'I wouldn't mind someone buying a necklace for me.'

'And it seems to me you don't much care what you have to do to get it!' Erin retorted.

Grianne smirked, her eyes going to the bulge of Erin's stomach. 'There's nothing very unusual in that, is there? Don't let's be coy, Erin. I can count, you know, and if you think you can fool me into believing that baby you're expecting is a result of your wedding night, you'd better think again.'

Quick colour rose in Erin's cheeks and she gaped at her sister, lost for words.

Grianne laughed shortly. 'Oh, don't look so horrified, Erin. I must admit you certainly knew how to choose. Besides his money and position, Brett is a very attractive man. I suppose with a few luxuries to smooth the way, one can get used to most things, but I'd still prefer to see Brett's face on the pillow next to mine than a great lump of lard like the Major's.'

Quickly Erin turned away. Grianne laughed again, thinking she had shocked her sister, but Erin did nothing to enlighten her as to the real cause of her discomfort. Grianne could think what she liked – she probably would – but at least she did not know the truth – that although she had now been a wife for several months Erin did not wake to see anyone's face on the pillow beside her. To admit that her husband did not want to share her bed would be a terrible admission of defeat, however little she wanted it herself.

How, Erin wondered for the hundredth time, could he be so cold and remote? Oh, he had made it plain enough he had married her only because he wanted an heir, and the baby she was carrying was all that mattered to him. But once upon a time he had thought her attractive enough to bed her. Now it seemed he could hardly bear the strain of being in the same room with her for any longer than he could help.

What will happen when the baby is born? Erin wondered, and a small chill of foreboding rushed in to follow the thought. Once she had provided Brett with his heir, would he have any further use for her? Or would he install a nursemaid to look after the baby and turn her out, lock, stock and barrel?

It was the first time such a thing had occurred to her, but suddenly it seemed frighteningly possible. A nursemaid would, after all, be easier for him to handle. He could give his orders as to how the child was to be brought up and she would obey. And because he had married Erin and given the baby a legitimate name, he would have the right. As to how he treated his wife, no one in this brash new country would care very much. It would be a nine-days' wonder, no more, for folk were too concerned with scratching a living themselves to worry about others.

As the picture formed within her mind, Erin began to tremble. The Holy Mother alone knew how little she had wanted to bear a child under these circumstances. As little as she had wanted an enforced marriage with Brett Wilde. But it would be too cruel now if she was parted from that child.

'Yes, if I were you I'd be a lot nicer to Brett than you are.' Grianne's mocking voice cut into her thoughts. 'If you don't want him to look elsewhere, that is. For if I'm not mistaken, there are plenty who would be ready and willing to take your place.'

Yourself included, Erin thought wryly, but it

154

was a passing notion only.

There was something in what Grianne said, after all. Perhaps she should try to please Brett at least a little. The thought of being chained to him for the rest of her life was bad enough. But to be turned out, leaving her baby behind to be raised by the man she hated, was infinitely worse.

That night, however, when Brett returned home, he had news for her.

'I'm afraid I must leave you lonely for a while,' he told her, lighting a cigar. 'I'm going to sail to Van Diemen's Land tomorrow.'

'Van Diemen's Land?' she repcated, surprised. 'Why should you go there?'

Behind the haze of cigar smoke his eyes were veiled.

'Governor King is setting up a new penal colony there and I have a chance to visit it,' he replied vaguely.

'But why should you want to visit a penal colony?' she persisted, unable to contain her curiosity.

He threw back his head and laughed. 'I can see you won't be satisfied with anything less than the truth,' he said wryly. 'Very well, I'll give it to you. I have the opportunity of purchasing a small trading vessel and if you stop to think about that for a moment you will see what it could mean. With my own ship I should no longer be dependent upon the traders. I could obtain what cargoes I chose – and not be forced into paying exorbitant prices for them. But before chancing a small fortune on the purchase I wish to be sure the vessel is seaworthy. Hence a voyage to Van Diemen's Land – not too near, not too far – but probably far enough to learn if the *Amber Fawn* as she is called will stay afloat.'

A tiny chill of fear ran down Erin's spine.

'But supposing she *won't* stay afloat?' she burst out. 'Isn't it a bit risky to go yourself?'

Around his cigar butt Brett's mouth twisted in amusement.

'Not concerned for me, surely, my dear?' he murmured. 'How very unlike you!'

Confused, she turned away. Oh, why did he have to twist everything? He really was the most insufferable of men!

'I'm sure I'm not in the least concerned for you!' she snapped before she could stop herself. 'Don't they say the devil takes care of his own? No, it's just that I wouldn't like to see you lose everything at the bottom of the ocean.'

He ground his cigar out and although his face was set his voice was light – teasing, almost.

'That's more like the Erin I know and love,' he murmured. Then, before she could recover from her surprise, he went on matter-of-factly. 'You'll be well taken care of, have no fear of that. I wouldn't want my son to be born a pauper, any more than I would want him born with the stigma of illegitimacy. I know too much about both states to be able to countenance that.'

'*You* do?' she queried in surprise. 'But how?'

A faint smile touched his lips and he rested his long, buckskin-clad thighs against the rim of the table.

'You married me knowing very little about me,

156

my sweet,' he said, his amused grey eyes never leaving her rapt face. 'I was not always the wealthy landowner you know. I can well remember the times when I was hungry and scorned back in the old country.'

'Tell me,' she urged.

He shrugged his broad shoulders. 'There's little enough to tell. My mother was an actress – not a very good one, I'm afraid – who had run away from a respectable family to join a travelling company. I don't know who my father was. She never would tell me. He might have been a fellow traveller, or he might have been a duke. Not even that would surprise me. She was a fine-looking woman and she could charm the birds off the trees.'

'Where is she now?' Erin asked.

'Dead, these many years.' The grey eyes were clouded now like mist over the harbour. 'When she died, my grandfather claimed me. She had disgraced him and he had sworn to have no more to do with her as long as she lived. But when she was dead he would not see me starve. He gave me a home, grew quite fond of me, I think. But oh! the barbs I endured from the other boys! Safe in their own tidy lives, they always loved to remind me that I was different. Many was the fight I had with those who called my mother a whore. But what they dared not say to my face they still said behind my back. And I was an embarrassment to my grandfather, too – a constant reminder of how my mother had disgraced him. When I was old enough he set me up in life – obtained for me a commission with the New

South Wales Corps, and he was glad enough to see me go. So, you see, until I came here, Erin, I had nothing – not even a name I could call my own. But I've changed all that.'

There was a lump in her throat. As he had spoken she had somehow been able to see the boy he had been very clearly and she was suddenly overcome by a pressing urge to take those strong brown hands in hers and tell him that whatever he had been, whatever he had endured, now he was Brett Wilde of Mia-Mia.

But she could not bring herself to touch him. Although there was a warmth within her that was almost painful in its intensity, she knew she could not.

'So that's why you've built yourself such an empire here,' she murmured. 'To satisfy your need to be someone.'

The grey eyes snapped. It was as if a shutter had come down and all the distance was there between them once more.

'That – and other things,' he said, straightening abruptly. 'And now, Erin, if you will excuse me, I have a great deal of paperwork to attend to.'

His tone hurt her oddly. For a moment she had felt closer to him than ever before. Now, with those few cool words, it was all gone. He didn't want her. That was plain. But why did it suddenly matter more than it had done?

Tears of despair stung her eyes, though she barely understood why they had come. To hide them, she lifted her chin and turned away.

'In that case I won't take up any more of your

time,' she said sharply.

With a swish of her skirts she flounced out of the room, and as the door closed after her, Brett crossed to pour himself a glass of rum and drink deeply of the burning liquid.

Why had he told her all that? he asked himself as the spirit seared his stomach. Why had he confessed to being less than he would have New South Wales society believe? Because, for a short while, he had actually believed she was interested, not in his wealth, not in his position, but in him and all he had once been.

But of course he had been wrong, just as he had been wrong about Therese. Women were all the same, damn them – caring only for what a man could give them. Why should he have imagined for a moment that this raven-haired strumpet who had persuaded him to get her with child was any different? And why, knowing that, did he still want her every time he looked at her?

He did not know. But if anything could rid him of the notions that were blinding his heart to the truth of the matter, a voyage to Van Diemen's Land might be the cure.

Tomorrow he would sail on the dawn tide.

Next morning when Erin awoke Brett had already left. It was a crisp winter's day and she stood for a while at her window that overlooked the bay, watching the white cats' paws on the murky grey depths and thinking how fathomless it looked. Then, sighing, she turned away, smoothing her skirts over her rounded belly.

Oh, but if it hadn't been for her fears for the

159

future she would be longing for the day when she was rid of this weighty burden! The nausea had gone now, it was true, but she still did not feel truly well and that, too, worried her. Superstitious it might be, but she couldn't help wondering if it might mean the baby was forming from the convict's seed, for if it had been a love child, surely it would have lain more easily within her? And the more trouble it gave her, the more odious the parentage...

Quickly she pushed the thought away. It didn't bear thinking about and she wouldn't waste energy on it. But it persisted, none the less, all the more because she had nothing else with which to occupy her mind.

What *could* she do to pass the time? she wondered. She had proved she was not much of a needlewoman and though she had persisted until her fingers were sore the tapestry she had begun had not progressed much. And whenever she went to the kitchen the convict women who worked there took umbrage, asking what was wrong with their cooking that she should want to take it over. But what else was there that a lady could do – especially a lady in her condition...

Except learn to play the piano! It came to her suddenly, in a flash of inspiration, and she wondered why she had not thought of it before. There was a piano in the drawing room, a beautiful instrument that was Brett's pride and joy because shipping a piano from England was a risky business. Most people in the colony who had tried to bring one in hand found it had arrived like so much matchwood. But typically enough, Brett's had not, and it stood like a spoil of war in a most conspicuous place for visitors to admire.

Why had she not thought of it before? Erin wondered as she hurried excitedly to the drawing room. Perhaps because she would have been almost afraid to touch it with Brett in the house. If she had had any knowledge of music it would have been different, but she didn't. She was a complete beginner and she would be bound to make some horrible noises with the beautiful instrument before she was able to make music.

But with Brett away and no one to hear her fumblings perhaps she could make some progress.

She lifted the lid, touching the ivory keys with half-afraid fingers and listening with delight to the sound they made. To her they sounded like bells, clear and sweet, and growing bolder she explored them. For how long she experimented she did not know, so entranced was she, and when she did break off it was because she was interrupted by a small sound in the doorway.

Swinging round on the stool she was surprised to see one of the convict women standing there. In her hand she held a cleaning cloth but it was clear to Erin she was not dusting, but watching and listening to her childish fumblings.

'What do you want?' she asked, shamed into sharpness.

Lucy Slack, the convict woman, flushed dully.

'I'm sorry, ma'am, I didn't mean to disturb you. It's just that that piano has stood here untouched for so long I never thought I'd hear

161

anybody play upon it.'

Erin laughed softly. 'I wouldn't call it playing, exactly. I was just tinkling, that's all. And I don't suppose I'll ever learn, either, much as I'd like to, with no one to teach me.'

The convict woman took a step into the room, twisting the cleaning cloth between her red, puffy hands.

'I could teach you.' There was an eager note in her voice and Erin looked at her in surprise.

'You?'

'Yes, I used to play back home, though I haven't touched a keyboard now in years. Oh, you'll likely think it an intrusion on my part, but...'

'No, of course not,' Erin said quickly. 'Play something for me, won't you?'

'Oh, but...' Lucy Slack looked critically at her now-mishapen hands but there was no mistaking the look of longing in her faded eyes.

'Please!' Erin begged. 'I'm sure it'll soon come back to you.'

Hesitantly Lucy Slack approached the piano and took Erin's place on the brocaded stool. Then, slowly and with great care, she began to play. Her puffy fingers looked awkward on the keys but as she gained confidence the music swelled out, making Erin catch her breath at the beauty of it.

When at last she finished and made to rise Erin touched her arm.

'That was beautiful. Where did you learn to play like that?'

Lucy's lips twisted with sad humour.

162

'My father was a music master. He taught some of the finest families in the town where we lived. But he was a gambler and when he fell from grace, so did we all.'

'Then you – you really could teach me?' Erin asked eagerly.

'I said so, didn't I?' the woman returned dourly.

'And when could we begin?' Erin persisted. It was only when Lucy laughed bitterly that the truth came home to Erin. She was mistress here. This woman might be the expert in her field but it was for Erin to command her.

'Now, perhaps?' she suggested, not finding the sensation of power to her liking and wondering in passing how Brett could ever find it agreeable.

'If you say so, Mrs Wilde,' the woman acquiesced.

That lesson was the first of many and soon Erin knew she had found a cure for her boredom and frustration. The fingers that had been so clumsy with the tapestry needle took to the keys naturally and even the dour Lucy was forced to admit Erin had talent.

'Practice makes perfect,' she would say when Erin fumbled in her scales or the first elementary tunes, and heaven only knew, she had plenty of practice. Two, and sometimes three, times in the day she would retire to the drawing room to go through the exercises Lucy had set her and both pupil and teacher were delighted with her progress.

Besides the pleasure that came from learning to play, Erin couldn't help thinking it would be an asset for her in Brett's eyes. It was, after all, the accomplishment of a lady, and there were few enough people here in New South Wales who could call themselves musicians. If she could provide some genteel diversion when Brett entertained, surely it would weigh with him? Eagerly she awaited his return when she would be able to prove to him that in this, at least, she was able to conduct herself as a lady.

The days passed, each one greyer and more wintry than the last, with no hint yet of the coming of spring, and Erin began to be anxious.

Surely Brett should have returned by now? When she was not practising on the piano she took to standing at her window looking down at the bay. Ships came and went and though she was forced to admit she would not know the *Amber Fawn* if it sailed in under her very nose, she watched all the same. But Brett did not come and a dull fear began to creep through her veins. Suppose the ship was not seaworthy? Suppose it had gone down in the grey waters when there was no help on hand? Even at this distance the white-topped waves looked evil and hungry; close to they must be big enough to swallow a small vessel whole.

She stood at the window, her hands pressed against the bulge of her stomach, while the nightmarish pictures danced before her eyes. Was her baby to be born fatherless after all? What would become of them? Oh, she could imagine the speed with which the vultures would

164

move in on Brett's empire! For all his grand talk of her being 'taken care of' they would tear it to pieces about her ears, making this claim and that, and before she could turn around, she would be left with nothing. And besides...

Unwilling though she was to admit it, she did not like to think of Brett going to a watery grave. Arrogant he might be, and a profiteer to boot, but she could not wish such a death upon her husband in the prime of his life.

As the days became weeks the dark fear grew within her. No news was good news, she supposed, and yet somehow it was beginning to be impossible to imagine him ever returning.

One night Erin was woken from sleep by the clamour of a storm. The wind was howling about the house and the rain lashed angrily at the windows.

She lay for a few minutes listening to it and her blood seemed to turn to ice within her veins. Sweet Jesus, if the storm was bad enough to waken her here, on land, what was it like at sea? And Brett, if his ship had not already foundered, must be out in it.

With an effort she hauled herself from bed and crossed the room to the window. Through the scudding rain she could see the devil's horses in the bay, white in the light of the fitful moon, though she knew close to they would be a muddy yellow, flecked with flotsam and jetsam – the remains, perhaps, of some poor craft that had foundered and smashed to pieces on the high seas.

She shivered suddenly, and like one in a dream

crossed to the chest where her possessions were kept. The top drawer she slid open, fumbling inside in the darkness until her fingers encountered her rosary beads and drew them out.

When her mother had been alive the rosary had been used often, but of late Erin had neglected it. Whatever her conscience had told her, there had been no time for rosaries in the busy years when she had cared for the family, and since all that had befallen them in the way of trouble, Erin's faith had been sorely tried.

'What's the use?' she had thought, when she thought about it at all. Her mother had been a good Catholic and it had not saved her.

Now, however, she twisted the well-worn beads between her fingers, searching for the first, the 'Our Father', and the familiar words came tumbling out. She did not even stop to think it was strange she was praying for Brett, whom she hated. She only knew that if there was anything she could do to bring him safe home, she must do it.

The night wore on as Erin stood at the window numbering her rosary beads, and when dawn began to break and the wind dropped a little she was too exhausted to feel anything but despair. For a while she crept back to bed but sleep would not come and eventually, when she thought she could safely do it without waking the whole of the house, Erin went down to the drawing room and the piano.

It was the only way she knew of soothing her jangling nerves, and as she began haltingly to play through the tunes Lucy was teaching her, some of the tension seemed to fly away on the sweet notes.

For how long she played she did not know, but suddenly she was interrupted by the sound of the door opening behind her. She swung round on the stool and her heart seemed almost to stop beating.

'Brett!' she whispered, hardly able to believe she was not dreaming.

He stood for a moment in the doorway, rain dripping down his neck from his wind-blown hair, and foolish tears of relief sprang to her eyes.

'Oh, Brett, thank God!' she sobbed. But he did not return her welcome. Instead his face darkened like a thunder cloud while his eyes sparked like grey flints.

'What do you think you are doing?' he demanded.

She stared, shocked. 'What do you mean?'

'The piano – you'll ruin it!'

'I – I'm sorry!' she gasped, confused by his anger. 'I didn't think I was doing any harm.'

'You shouldn't meddle with things that don't belong to you,' he snapped. 'Don't you know its value?'

Trembling, she snapped the lid down over the keys. Oh, how hateful he was!

'I can never do anything right in your eyes, can I?' she cried. 'And to think I've been worried about you! I don't know why I was bothered. As soon as you come through the door you turn on me. Why, Brett Wilde, I believe you hate me as much as I hate you!'

167

She saw his face change, saw him take a pace towards her; but she side-stepped nimbly to avoid him.

'Don't touch me!' she grated.

'Don't worry, I wasn't going to. That's one thing at least we seem to have agreed on.' His tone was sarcastic and it brought the tears to her eyes. She turned away quickly so that he should not see them and with head held high and shoulders rigid she made for the door. His low, bitter laugh followed her but she did not turn, swishing out with all the dignity she could muster.

Then she stopped dead in her tracks. Grianne was in the hall, standing right outside the door. And Erin knew she could not have avoided overhearing everything she and Brett had said.

'Grianne...' she faltered. 'How long have you been there?'

Grianne's lips curved slowly and a triumphant gleam came into her clear blue eyes.

'Long enough,' she murmured. 'But don't worry, Erin, your secret is safe with me.'

Then with a long and meaningful glance over her shoulder towards the drawing room and Brett, she turned and swept away along the hall leaving Erin to stare after her in horror.

CHAPTER ELEVEN

As the voices of the two girls died away across the hall Brett stood for a moment longer in the drawing room, his hands balled to tight fists at his sides.

Dear God in heaven, he had almost struck her! And why? Because she had said she hated him. Well, he had always known that. It was nothing new. And what else could he expect when he spoke to her as he had done? He had not meant to do it. He didn't know now what had possessed him to greet her so. During the last storm-tossed days of the voyage he had had plenty of time for thinking, and a great deal of it had been about Erin. Again and again he had seen her pale oval face with its frame of glossy dark curls and the blue eyes that were so misted and deep – it had seemed to be there in the frothy waves and the heavy skies, haunting him as it had from the first time he had set eyes on her. He had made up his mind that when he came home he would woo her – try to make something of the marriage which was, as yet, nothing but a mockery. They couldn't, after all, go on this way all their lives, he had reasoned. It didn't hold out much prospect of happiness for either of them and little future for their child. No, he would try to make

169

her forget how they had begun, he had decided.

As he had climbed the hill from the harbour there had been eagerness in his step, weary and spray-soaked though he was. And then what had he done but snap at her the moment he came through the door! No wonder she said she hated him.

It had been hearing her play the piano that had done it, of course – Therese's piano that had never been touched since it had arrived from England. As he had crossed the hall and heard it tinkling it had been like hearing an echo of the past and when he had opened the door and seen her sitting there he had hit out blindly. And why? Because she was not Therese?

Damn Therese! he thought irritably. Would she never let him go?

He turned abruptly and went into the now-empty hall calling for Georgeson, his manservant. He was cold, he was hungry, he was wet. But more than anything he wanted a good hot bath.

He strode up the stairs, his long, muscled legs taking them two at a time with ease. The door to the bedroom he should share with Erin stood ajar and automatically he pushed it open. Then he stopped, the breath coming hard in his throat.

Erin was sitting half-dressed on the bed. He had not noticed in the confusion downstairs that she was still in her night attire, but now she was clearly preparing herself for the day.

Her back was turned towards him, slender and creamy, with her hair tumbling unchecked over her shoulders. The curve of one glorious breast was visible, but nothing of her swollen belly, and she looked as delectable and young as he had ever seen her.

Desire twisted within him, desire so fierce it rocked him on his heels, and he longed to touch that smooth, creamy skin with his hands and his mouth, tasting its sweetness and feeling the soft, full curves moulding to his hard chest. An ache of fire seared his loins as his body remembered the glory of her and he wanted nothing but to crush her beneath him, discovering again each hill and hollow until at last he possessed her...

As if his gaze had drawn her to awareness she turned suddenly, her hands flying protectively to cover her breasts, and he saw the fear flare in her eyes.

At once desire became anger. Why, she looked like an animal waiting to be slaughtered! They had that same look of blind terror when they had the smell of blood in their nostrils. Yet she was his wife and all he wanted was to make love to her.

'Don't worry,' he spat harshly. 'I already said I wouldn't touch you, and though you may find it hard to believe, I'm a man of my word.'

She did not answer, only sitting mutely with her arms wound tightly around her and her blue eyes wide behind the black fringe of her lashes, and he swung abruptly round on his heel.

Damn her, too! Damn all women! His estate he could run without ever doubting himself, taking decisions as and when he needed to and never looking back to regret them. His convicts he controlled with the iron hand necessary to keep dangerous men in their place, and the traders with whom he dealt knew him as a man to drive a hard bargain and one whom they would try to cheat only at their peril. Even when he had been a young officer in the New South Wales Corps he had known how to get the better of the most seasoned soldiers under his command.

But this slip of a girl, who had no more experience of life than what she had gleaned on a small farm on the banks of a half-settled river, could get under his skin and make a callow boy of him.

He flung into his dressing room, pulling off his wet coat and boots and shouting again for Georgeson.

Better to keep women in their place, he reasoned. Erin was his wife and would give him the heirs to whom he could pass on Mia-Mia. But for pleasure it was best to think no further than the strumpets who frequented the harbour. They were well versed enough to know how to please a man and satisfy his body.

As to his heart – that was something best ignored.

The days after Brett's return were strange ones to Erin. Never, she thought, had her emotions been in such a state of confusion, for she felt all the while as if she stood on the edge of a precipice uncertain which way to jump.

The hours still dragged, all the more now that she was no longer able to practise on the piano, yet she doubted she would have been able to concentrate even on that. All the time there was a waiting in her – and not only waiting for the arrival of the baby. For some reason she was anxious to see Brett and restless when he was out of the house. Yet when he returned she felt perversely unable to face him, and would retire to her room, pacing the floor while her cheeks burned and the baby shifted uncomfortably within her.

So much for the serenity of motherhood! she thought wryly as a faint picture flashed into her mind of her own mother when Brenna had been on the way. Erin had been little more than a child herself but she could remember the warm glow that had seemed to surround Mama – and the way she had still found room on her lap for the little ones even when the bulge threatened to squeeze them out.

But it had been different for her, Erin thought. Brenna had been conceived in love, a wanted babe, while with her it was very different and for all she knew it could be the fruit of an evil murderer and rapist that grew within her. And if it was, what heritage would have passed into its veins? Dear Holy Mary, was it possible the child would grow up like the man who had fathered him?

The thought was nightmare enough to wake her at dead of night when she lay alone in the bed that had been made for two. She lay with her fists pressed against her tight-closed eyes until the horror began to pass and then the whole of her skin began to crawl with some strange, restless need.

Slowly she pushed back the covers and swung her legs over the edge of the bed. The floor felt cold to her bare feet but she wriggled her toes and put her weight on them, crossing to the window that overlooked the harbour.

It was a clear, cold night and the velvet dark was studded with stars, but she was reminded of the night of the storm when she had stood here looking out and worrying about Brett.

Why did I do it? she asked herself.

Since his return he had been no different to the way he had been before – even tonight he had gone out after dinner and she had been left to come to bed alone. Her only consolation was that Grianne had been out too, visiting some people she had met at the store, and so had not been here to witness his neglect of her. Since she had overheard their quarrel and learned more about their relationship than pleased Erin, she had been extra sensitive about what her sister saw and heard.

Where did he go? she wondered. He never troubled himself to explain his movements to her and she could not bring herself to ask. At first she had assumed it was business, but now she was beginning to be less sure. Could it be, perhaps, that he went to visit some woman or other? It puzzled her that he never tried to take advantage of his husband's rights, especially since she had learned to her cost of his lusty appetite, and if he had a strumpet somewhere in town it would explain why he no longer wanted her.

For some reason the thought made her skin prickle all the more and something strangely painful twisted within her. Was he home now, she wondered – or was he still out, passing the night heaven only knew how?

She moved away from the window, crossing the room on silent feet and carefully opening the door that connected the bedroom with his dressing room where he slept, giving the excuse to the servants that it would be more comfortable for both of them until after the baby was born.

Although the night outside had been dark, his room was darker and it was a moment before her eyes adjusted sufficiently to make out the form beneath the blankets. But she knew at once by his even breathing that he was there.

'He sleeps like a child without a care in the world,' she thought, and somehow the thought only added to her loneliness.

For a few seconds longer she stood there, looking at the long frame and remembering, for some reason, the first time she had seen him at Alice Simmons's rum parlour. How little she had guessed then how their futures were to be entwined! A lump came into her throat and she turned away, closing the door and retreating into her bedroom.

She still felt restless and the big bed had never looked less inviting. She took her wrap and once again crossed to the window, settling herself down on the wide sill with her knees drawn up as far as the bulk of her stomach allowed, and her head resting on her arms.

It was chilly here. In spite of her wrap the cold had begun to get to her and she shivered a little but she did not move. Anything was preferable

175

to the warm, crawling sensation that came when she lay sleepless beneath the cloying bedclothes, and she liked the look of the stars in the velvet dark.

For a long while, it seemed, she sat there, growing steadily colder and more cramped, yet at the same time becoming drowsy until at last the heavy kiss of sleep could no longer be denied. The room drifted away from her and she felt as if she was merging with the night and the stars. Then, as if through a feather pillow, she felt a touch upon her and she shifted restlessly.

'Don't!' she whispered. 'Leave me alone.'

'You can't stay here. You'll catch your death of cold.'

The voice took her by surprise; in spite of the touch she hadn't realized there was anyone in the room with her. But her eyes were still too heavy to open. She felt drugged, the way she had felt as a child when she had had toothache and her mother had given her more laudanum than was wise.

As if through a haze she was aware of arms about her, strong arms, and as they lifted her she made no protest. It was Brett, she knew, carrying her as he had carried Brenna on the night of their wedding, but she could not be bothered to complain. She let her head rest against his broad shoulder, turning her face into him so that she smelled the faintly salt tang of his skin, and realizing dimly that he was naked, from the waist up at least. But even that did not disturb her.

She felt safe for once in her life, safer than she

176

had felt since she was a child, though had she known the tumult that was rocking him, she would have been awake in a second.

'Here, this is where you should be.'

Gently he laid her down upon the bed, calling up every ounce of self-control to keep himself from throwing himself down onto her lovely, drowsy body and possessing her.

'It's a good thing I found you, isn't it?' he continued hoarsely. 'Who knows what fever might have overtaken you by morning if I had not.'

She opened her eyes for a moment. Above her the hard lines of his face were muzzed by their closeness to her eyes, and she smiled sleepily.

He bent close to her, pulling the covers over her and pressing his lips briefly to her forehead. A warmth began where his lips had touched, spreading through her veins until the whole of her body glowed with it.

It was still warming her when sleep claimed her once again.

It was day when she awoke, a bright, cold, winter's day. When she opened her eyes the warmth was still there, making happiness sing in her. To begin with she could not remember why.

Then memory returned and some of the magic faded. Had Brett really found her sleeping in the window sill last night? Or had she stumbled back to bed herself and simply dreamed that he had carried her in his arms like a drowsy child? She could not be sure. But even if it had been a dream, the feeling of safety had spilled over into wakefulness and she lay a little longer luxuriating in it.

Perhaps if she was really to make an effort there was hope for her and Brett. Once, he had found her attractive. And who knew, he might find the state of affairs between them as miserable as she did, though he had a different way of showing it.

With renewed determination she slid her legs over the edge of the bed. As she drew her nightgown over her head the cold made her shiver and she realized how foolish she had been to sit so long in the window last night.

Brett had been right. She could easily have caught a chill, and in her condition it might turn to fever. She shivered again and this time it had nothing to do with the cold. She had seen at first hand what fever could do.

She took a warm woollen gown from her wardrobe, holding it against her before the mirror. The blue of its fabric reflected her eyes and though its neckline was cut more for warmth than seduction she knew it had the advantage of helping to disguise her bulging stomach. She slipped it on, catching her curls at the back of her head with a matching ribbon so that they cascaded to her shoulders in a flattering switch, and smiling at her reflection. She looked more rested than at any time since she came to Sydney, her eyes bright and her cheeks pink, and she squeezed them between her finger and thumb, pinching extra colour into them.

If Brett was still at home she wanted to look good for him. And she had a feeling he was still at home...

178

At last she was ready. She went along the narrow landing, past the window with yet another view of the harbour, to the head of the stairs. It wasn't an imposing staircase. Unlike the one at Mia-Mia that swept grandly into the hall below, this one clung to the side of the house, taking up as little space as possible, and it was almost hidden from most of the downstairs rooms of the house. Erin was halfway down when she heard voices and stopped, looking over the shiny wooden banister. That sounded like Grianne's high-pitched giggle, though it was unusual for her to be up so early. And the low-throated chuckle, although she had heard it seldom enough in their married life must, without a doubt, belong to Brett!

As soon as she leaned over the banister she saw them – or rather she saw their reflection, for they were in the drawing room whose door was immediately opposite the staircase, and although they themselves were out of sight the mirror that hung on the wall facing the door threw their images directly at her. They were standing close together and Grianne, her hand on Brett's arm, was laughing up at him.

'Well, I declare, Brett Wilde, I'd never have thought it of you!' Grianne's voice carried clearly through the open door and Erin's hands tightened on the banister.

The little minx! What was she up to? Usually she hardly spoke a word to Brett, but now she was flirting shamelessly. And more than that – Brett appeared to be enjoying it!

As she watched he threw back his head and

laughed, then bent close to whisper something in Grianne's ear, and Erin stared, unable to believe her eyes. This wasn't like the Brett she knew. Did he always behave this way when he and Grianne were alone? Why, they looked almost intimate, the two of them...

As the thought crossed her mind she caught her breath, her hand flying to her mouth. She had wondered earlier if Brett might have a lover – someone to whom he went for the comforts he never sought from her. Supposing it was *Grianne* he had turned to – *Grianne* who gave him what she did not!

The sickness that had been so much better these last weeks returned with a rush, and Erin twisted away violently so that the mirror images disappeared from view, running back up the stairs to her room, slamming the door behind her and leaning her shoulders against it.

It couldn't be – she wouldn't believe it! Determined as Grianne might be to do well for herself, she wouldn't stoop to trying to steal her own sister's husband.

Yet Erin had seen her with her own eyes, laughing, flirting, touching his arm. And besides...

Unwillingly Erin found herself remembering that while Brett had stopped her going to the store, he still allowed Grianne to go there as often as she pleased. He had said it was because he had no responsibility for her, but now Erin wondered if there was another, more sinister, reason.

And did it stop there? Why, last night when

Brett had been out on so-called 'business' Grianne had been missing too, supposedly visiting people she had met at the store. But might that just have been a cover? Could it be that the two of them had met secretly somewhere?

Sudden tears pricked at Erin's eyes and she covered her face with her hands. Just a few minutes ago she had been so happy because of her half-memory of Brett's tender care of her last night. Now she remembered only his warnings of fever and it came to her that once again it had been only the baby he was concerned about, not her at all. 'Perhaps he was afraid that if I became ill he might lose his son and heir,' she thought, and the desolation within her began to turn to anger. It was, after all, no more than she had come to expect of him – selfish to the last. Oh, how she hated him! And as for Grianne...

She won't get away with it! Erin decided. I won't be made a fool of in my own house!

It was bad enough to think of Brett going into Sydney to find his pleasure, but for her own sister to offer it to him under her very nose was quite insupportable.

She straightened up, brushing the tears from her eyes with the back of her hand. Why should she skulk up here as if she was the one at fault? She would go down right away and have it out with Grianne.

She dabbed cold water from the basin onto her cheeks and tidied the curls around her face. Then, with chin held high, she marched downstairs again.

No voices rose to greet her this time and the drawing room, when she peeked into it, was empty.

She found Grianne in the dining room drinking coffee from the elegant cups Brett had obtained from the last trader to dock in Sydney harbour. There was a smug expression on her face that made Erin's blood boil, and as the girls' eyes met Erin fancied she saw the hint of amused challenge in the sharp blue.

'Well, well, Erin, you're up bright and early for someone in your condition,' Grianne drawled.

'Yes, and I was up earlier than you anticipated, too,' Erin returned shortly. 'Since you expect me to lay abed I suppose you thought you could take the opportunity to make up to Brett and get away with it.'

Grianne's eyes narrowed. For a second Erin saw an expression of surprise cross her Dresden-doll features. Then the half-smile curled her lips again.

'I don't know what you mean, Erin.'

'Oh yes you do!' Erin snapped. 'You were in the drawing room with him, flirting shamelessly. I know you've made up your mind to leave poor David Percy and find yourself a rich husband, but kindly remember Brett is already spoken for.'

As she spoke Grianne's eyes were growing steadily wider. Then, quite suddenly, she tossed her head and laughed scornfully.

'It's not the happiest of marriages, though, is it? Or do my eyes and ears deceive me? No,

182

from what I've seen, Erin, Brett is ripe for a little pleasurable dalliance, and if you don't give him what he wants you must expect others to step into your shoes. If it wasn't me it would be someone else. So we might as well keep it in the family, don't you think?'

Erin stared at her, speechless with horror. Had she no shame at all?

'How dare you, Grianne!' she cried angrily. 'How dare you say such things! You're a guest in this house, remember, and though you're my own sister, I won't stand for it!'

Grianne laughed again. The colour was high in her cheeks, making her eyes sparkle dangerously.

'Oh, Erin, you really are a caution. The house belongs to Brett, not you, and I'm his guest, not yours. That means I shall stay just as long as he wants me here and since he seems to enjoy my company, I think that will be quite a long time. No, whoever leaves, I don't think it will be me!'

'You seem to forget that I am his wife!' Erin said, controlling her voice with difficulty.

Grianne reached unhurriedly for the delicate coffee pot to pour herself another cup of coffee and above it her cool eyes met Erin's furious ones.

'In some respects, Erin, I find that very difficult to believe,' she murmured.

Erin's hands flew to her flaming cheeks. So Grianne knew! But how? From things she had overheard? Or from what Brett had told her? Humiliation washed over Erin, but somehow she managed to keep her head erect and her voice, when it came, was so steady it surprised even her.

'Is that so, Grianne? Then let me remind you of one thing – I am going to have his baby,' she said.

With all the coolness she could muster she turned and walked from the room.

It was only when she was alone once more in the privacy of her bedroom that she allowed the tears to come, and when they started it seemed to her that they would never stop.

Holy Mother, was there no end to the indignities she was forced to endure? she wondered as the tears cascaded down her cheeks. How could she go on with the life that had been forced upon her? But go on she must. It was the only way for all of them.

CHAPTER TWELVE

Slowly, so slowly, winter began to give way to spring. The winds that blew down from the mountains were still chill, but the days grew steadily longer and warmer and the first tender sprouts that would in time become a blaze of yellow could be seen on the mimosa trees.

Erin saw them and thought with longing of Kinvarra. But she kept her thoughts to herself, though at times she thought she would die of homesickness for the river and for those she had left behind.

Since the day of their quarrel, she and Grianne had never again raised the subject of Grianne's dalliance with Brett, though it was still a sharp pain within Erin's heart even when her conscious mind was otherwise occupied.

But she said nothing. There was no point. She could get nowhere with Grianne, it was obvious – she had become utterly shameless in her quest for wealth and station. As for Brett, if he knew that she knew it would only add to her humiliation.

One day when there was the first hint of real warmth in the sun, Henry Stanton, Brett's overseer from Mia-Mia, rode into Sydney.

Erin was pleased to see him. Though she had

no liking for the dour man who had once been a transported convict she was anxious for news from the river and she ran eagerly down the stairs, dropping the tapestry she had once again been struggling with to pass the time.

He stood in the hall, talking to Brett, a thickset figure whose rugged, homespun appearance immediately marked him out as a river-dweller among the Sydney folk she had mingled with these last weeks, and the rush of familiarity made her feel warmer towards him than she had ever felt before.

Her pleasure in seeing him, however, was to be short lived.

'How are Brenna and Patrick?' she asked eagerly. 'Have they been well? Did they send any messages?'

Henry Stanton's brow seemed to drop, settling his face into its usual attitude of disapproval.

'They've been well enough,' he conceded. 'Young Brenna's a bundle of mischief, but the women have been able to handle her, and I think they're fond of her in their way. But the boy...' His voice tailed away meaningfully.

'Patrick? What's wrong with Patrick?' Erin asked sharply.

Henry Stanton's eyes slithered to Brett, who was standing, hands on buckskin-clad hips, listening to what he had to say.

'Go on, Stanton,' Brett prompted him. 'My wife wants to know about her brother – and so do I.'

There was the faintest warning note in his voice and Erin felt a small chill run through her.

She hoped Patrick had not done anything to make Brett angry. But whatever it was, she had to know.

'Well, if you must know, he tried to run away,' Stanton told them. 'The weather was bad and the young fool didn't get far. We found him and brought him back. But it meant taking the men from their other work for a day and risking losing them in the forest, so I promise you, Mr Wilde, I did my best to ensure he doesn't attempt a madcap caper like that again.'

'What do you mean?' Erin asked.

The overseer chewed on his stump of Bengal twist, looking at Brett out of the corner of his eye.

'I thrashed him, like I'd have thrashed one of the men if he'd tried the same.'

'Oh, how dare you!' Erin squealed in outrage. 'You had no right to do that! He's not one of your convicts!' She turned to Brett for support, but she found none.

'He'd every right,' Brett said flatly. 'Mr Stanton is in charge of Mia-Mia in my absence, and if Patrick put our men at risk, he had to be taught a lesson.'

'Not that way!' Erin flared. 'If he ran away there must have been a reason. Didn't you bother to find out what it was?'

The overseer shrugged. 'I don't have time to go into things like that.'

'But you found time to thrash him!' Erin returned furiously.

'And he also found time to search for him and bring him back safely,' Brett interposed harshly.

187

'Just remember that, Erin. And remember too that Patrick and Brenna are at Mia-Mia at your request. If you don't care for their treatment they are free to go back to Kinvarra at any time you choose.'

'Oh!' Erin gasped, stung, for there was no answer she could give Brett. He was right, of course. She had requested him to take care of her young brother and sister and if Patrick behaved badly then he had to be disciplined.

But to have it pointed out to her in no uncertain terms in front of a hired employee was yet another humiliation.

'Is he all right now?' she asked, swallowing her anger with difficulty.

'I suppose so,' the overseer muttered off-handedly. 'He doesn't do much, perhaps that's his way.'

'What do you mean?' Erin queried.

'I've done my best to find him work to do and teach him something about farming, but it's the devil's own job to get him up off his backside,' Stanton replied coolly.

Erin bit her lip. It certainly was not Patrick's way to be lazy. He was a dreamer, yes, who was happy to spend long hours by himself. But he had worked very hard for her at Kinvarra, doing all she asked him and more.

Of course, it had been different there. Kinvarra was their own farm, and he had been working for the good of the family. Now, perhaps, he felt there was no point in making an effort, when the land he was expected to work was Brett's, and there were as many convicts and hired hands as necessary to do the job. She could understand that point of view now that she came to think about it, but it worried her all the same. For it must mean that Patrick was very resentful – and very unhappy. And it was her doing.

When Brett and Henry Stanton retired to the room Brett used as an office to talk business, she remained in the drawing room, deep in thought.

Patrick had never wanted to go to Mia-Mia and perhaps she had been wrong to tell him he must, just as she had been wrong to allow Grianne to come to Sydney where there was far more opportunity for her to behave like a shameless strumpet. All in all, marrying Brett had not brought the family the benefits she had expected, and although it was too late now to change that, maybe she could improve matters by returning as far as possible to the way of life they had known before their world had turned topsy-turvy.

'I'm doing no good here,' thought Erin. 'I'm going crazy because I have nothing to do. But if I was to return to Mia-Mia perhaps I could encourage Patrick to go to Kinvarra to keep things in order. And besides...'

Her eyes narrowed thoughtfully and she chewed on her lip. If she was not here it would be improper for Grianne to remain. And once back out of harm's way on the river perhaps she would give up the crazy notion of finding herself a rich husband at all costs and settle down with David Percy, who loved her.

Yes, she would raise the subject with Brett at the first opportunity, Erin decided. And perhaps when Henry Stanton returned to Mia-Mia she and Grianne could go with him.

All day Brett was closeted with the overseer and Erin's impatience grew. Were they never going to emerge from the office? Once, when a pot of fresh coffee was taken in, she glimpsed them bent over sheaves of papers and she guessed they were not only working on the accounts of Mia-Mia over the past year, but also planning the coming one.

Restlessly she paced the floor. Just why she was completely unable to keep still today she did not know. Perhaps it was thinking of going back to the river that filled her with this strange, crawling energy – or perhaps it was the niggling discomfort in the hollow of her back. Pregnancy was really becoming wearisome, she decided, shifting her weight from one foot to the other with no appreciable improvement in her comfort. But it would not seem nearly so bad back in the quiet reaches of the river with Patrick's industry to encourage and little Brenna to cheer her when she was down.

Brett and Henry Stanton came straight from their consultations to dinner, not bothering to change, and her unasked question burned on Erin's lips as they ate so that she simply could not manage to do justice to the meal, delicious as it was. And afterwards, to her annoyance, they retired yet again, taking their brandies with them.

'Henry wants to leave tomorrow,' Brett explained as he excused the pair of them. 'He cannot leave Mia-Mia for more than one night.'

'Surely there must be someone else there you can trust?' Erin muttered with a hint of sarcasm, but Brett seemed oblivious to her meaning and she was forced to wait yet again for her opportunity.

If Henry Stanton was returning to Mia-Mia tomorrow, then there was no time to be wasted if she was to go with him, she thought impatiently.

For once the evening hours flew by. The time came when Erin usually retired and still Brett and Henry Stanton were closeted behind the heavy door.

What could she do? Erin wondered desperately. It would do no good at all to knock on the door and ask Brett if she could speak with him. He would only be annoyed by the interruption. But how much longer would it be before the pair of them emerged?

When Grianne came to bid her a good night there was a curious look in her blue eyes and Erin decided that to avoid speculation on all sides she would do best to wait for Brett in her room. She climbed the stairs, hoping against hope it was the last night she would spend in this hateful house for some time to come, and went into her bedroom. Then she sat down fully clothed on the bed to wait.

The clock ticked by the long minutes and the niggle of discomfort in Erin's back grew more insistent. But still she sat and at last, just when she had begun to think that Brett and Henry Stanton would be talking all night, she heard voices on the stairs. The door across the hall where Stanton was to sleep banged shut and a moment later she heard movement in Brett's dressing room.

Nervous after all the waiting, she stood up and crossed the room on legs that had grown stiff and cramped. Then she tapped on the door and waited.

'Erin?' Brett sounded surprised and tentatively she turned the ornate handle and pushed at the door. It swung open and she saw that Brett was halfway across the room to meet her. He had begun to undress ready for bed – his cravat hung loosely around his neck and his ruffled shirt was unfastened to the waist, revealing the matt of curly hair that covered his broad chest.

'What's wrong?' he asked sharply.

She took a deep breath, suppressing the desire to giggle hysterically.

'Nothing. It's just that I wanted to talk to you, Brett.'

He jerked off his cravat, throwing it down onto his dressing table.

'Won't it wait until morning? I've had a long day, and you look as though you need your rest.'

'No, it won't wait,' she said swiftly. 'Henry Stanton is going back to Mia-Mia tomorrow, isn't he? Well, I wanted to ask you if I could go with him.'

Brett's head came up with a jerk and his grey eyes narrowed.

'Why?' he asked shortly.

'Because ... oh, it's plain I'm needed there,' Erin explained. 'After what Mr Stanton said I'm worried out of my mind about Patrick and I'd like to go home and see what's wrong. There

192

may be something I can do to improve matters.'

Brett turned away for a moment, taking up his jacket from where it lay carelessly across the bed and hanging it in his wardrobe. When he faced her again his eyes were veiled and unreadable.

'It was tactless of Henry to worry you, but I honestly don't think you need upset yourself about it,' he said smoothly.

'I can't help worrying...' she began, but he continued as if he had not heard her.

'Everything is being well taken care of, I'm sure.'

'Yes – by thrashings!' Erin burst out before she could stop herself. 'That's not the way to deal with a boy like Patrick. Oh Brett, I know him, you don't. He's sensitive, a dreamer. He would never give anyone a moment's trouble unless something was very wrong.'

Brett did not reply, and gathering her courage she ran on. 'Let me go, please! It's not as if I'm needed here. There's nothing to keep me.'

She saw his face change from puzzled surprise to a strange, shut-in look. If she hadn't known better she might almost have thought she had hurt him.

'I'm sorry, Erin,' he said briefly. 'I understand your concern for your brother and I sympathize. But I'm afraid I can't hear of your leaving Sydney just now.'

Her heart sank like a stone.

'But why?' she whispered. 'He is my brother, Brett.'

His lips tightened. 'And you are my wife.'

193

Tears pricked behind her eyes. Wife! What sort of a wife was she? He had no need of her at all. Not as housekeeper, or companion or lover. But Patrick needed her, and Brenna. And even, in her own way, Grianne needed her.

'Brett, I beg you,' she pleaded. 'They're all alone – I'm all they have. When my mother died I promised her I would take care of them. And they're children still!'

Brett's eyes held hers for a moment, then he lowered himself to the edge of the bed and began to pull off his boots. The silence seemed to go on forever and in it Erin thought she could hear the beating of her own heart. Had he conceded her argument? Would he let her go?

She stood knotting her fingers nervously together while he pulled off both boots and set them aside. Then he looked up at her and to her dismay she saw that his expression was as wry and set as ever.

'How can I make you see you have other duties now, Erin?' he asked softly. 'Your concern for your brother and sisters is commendable, but they are, I repeat, well taken care of. Your more pressing responsibility now is to your new family.'

'But why – you don't want me any more than I want you!' she burst out.

A muscle in his cheek tightened.

'There is another who needs your attention far more than your brother and sisters,' he said coldly.

Her hands flew to her stomach.

'You mean my baby? Well, of course I

wouldn't do anything to neglect it! Do you think I'm inhuman?'

'No, just thoughtless.' He stood up, towering above her, to pull his shirt out of his breeches and unbutton it completely. The casual way he was dismissing her request while continuing to prepare himself for bed infuriated her.

'What a thing to accuse me of!' she cried. 'Why should it be detrimental to my baby to return to Mia-Mia?'

His face was wooden and expressionless.

'The journey wouldn't do you any good for one thing. Even at this time of year the roads are rutted enough to give you a good jolting. And in any case, I'd prefer you to remain in Sydney until the baby is born. Mia-Mia is all very well, but it's a long way from civilization if anything should go wrong.'

'That's rubbish!' Erin flared, ignoring the little stab of fear that twisted within her at his words. 'Plenty of babies are born on the river and it's a chance I'm willing to take.'

'But I am not,' Brett said coldly. 'It's my son's safety we're discussing, Erin, and the sooner you realize I won't do anything to jeopardize that, the sooner we can both get some sleep.'

She caught her breath, staring at him for a moment as startled as if he had struck her. How arrogant he was! How utterly, selfishly, sure of himself! Well, he'd made himself plain now, and no mistake. She was of no interest to him except as a body to breed his heir. If he had been concerned about her safety as well as the baby's it might have been different. But he wasn't.

'All you care about is the baby, isn't it?' she choked out. 'I've always known that, of course.'

He was half in and half out of his shirt and she saw his rippling muscles freeze.

'Erin...' There was a ragged note in his voice but she did not hear it. The tears were singing too loudly in her ears.

'Suppose I was to tell you something, Brett,' she ran on, the words tumbling out one on top of the other. 'Suppose I was to tell you that the baby I'm carrying might not be yours at all? Now what would you say to that?'

For a split second there was complete and utter silence in the room. It was as if it had been frozen, suspended in time. Then Brett moved. With a long stride he reached her, his hands shooting out to grip her arms and hold her pinioned like a helpless bird in a snare.

'What did you say?' His voice was low, yet the undertones were such that the very air seemed to reverberate with it.

She began to tremble – her arms where he held them, her legs, her lips. But somehow she kept her head erect.

'Oh Brett, you should see your face!' she said with a little laugh. 'I've really shocked you now, haven't I?'

His fingers bit into her arms like ribs of steel.

'What did you mean – the baby might not be mine?' he demanded.

She wriggled in an attempt to free herself.

'You're hurting me, Brett. Let me go!'

'Not until I have the truth out of you.' He shook her so that her head jerked back on her neck. 'Why might the baby not be mine, Erin? Answer me!'

'Because ... oh, I don't know! I was only making it up!' she faltered, frightened suddenly by the intensity of his anger. But it was too late now for pretence.

'Don't lie to me!' he thundered, shaking her again until her teeth chattered. 'Whose baby are you carrying? Answer me, Erin!'

'I can't!' she sobbed. 'Not like this!'

'Whose?'

'I don't know – there was a convict – the night of the break-out – he raped me ... Oh, Brett, please...'

'A convict? Dear God in heaven, what do you mean, a convict?'

'I told you – one of those who broke out! I tried to shoot him and he raped me!'

'God's truth!' He threw her aside so roughly that she half-fell onto his narrow bed, but he did not look at her. She lay cowering while he paced the room and returned to stand over her. 'You whore!' he spat at her.

'No!' she whispered. 'I didn't – I wouldn't! He took me by force, I swear it!'

'You told me I was the first!' he thundered. 'You came to me begging for help because you said I had given you a child! You said nothing of this. You tricked me, Erin, into marrying you!'

'No!' She twisted her head from side to side, desperately trying to remember just how it had been. 'It wasn't like that! Oh please, listen to me, Brett!'

'And how many more have there been?' he

demanded. 'How many more scum might be the father of the child you wished to pass off as mine?'

'None!' she sobbed. 'I tried to tell you, Brett, but you didn't want to know. You were so besotted with the idea of your precious heir. But it might be yours, anyway. You raped me too, remember!'

He bent over her and she shrank away from the blind fury in his eyes.

'It had better be mine. For your sake and the baby's, it had better be, Madam.'

'But how will you know?' she whispered. 'How will we ever know?'

Brett's lip curled. 'Oh, I shall know all right, Erin. Have no fear of that. Look!' He straightened up, pulling his shirt right off and turning his back on her. 'See?' With his left forefinger he indicated a spot just below his right shoulder blade. 'Have I not showed you my birthmark? All the male members of my family have it, and so far as I know always have had. They call it the lucky horseshoe, though what luck it has ever brought to any of us I don't know. It's a curse, more like. But if the child is mine, the mark will be there. If not...'

In the candlelight the mark glowed a dull red and Erin seemed unable to tear her eyes away from it. Holy Mother, suppose her child was born without it? Would it brand him the son of an evil murderer? Wasn't it possible he could still be Brett's child – the first of a generation to be missed by the mark? But Brett would never believe it, never accept him as his own. And supposing the child was a girl – what then? Would Brett disown her – throw her out? It was no more than she deserved. He had every right to be angry. She had deceived him. But oh, she hadn't meant to! Why, she'd never even wanted to become his wife...

A sob caught in her throat and somehow she rolled away along the bed, scrambling to her feet and pushing past him. The door to her room was still ajar but she did not make for it. It was still too close to him and she wanted to get away – right away. She wrenched open the dressing room door and ran onto the landing, plunging down the stairs without a thought for her safety. Near the bottom her ankle twisted and she almost fell.

'Erin! For God's sake!' Brett thundered behind her, but still she ran on.

She reached the door and as she fumbled with the heavy bolts she heard him pounding down the stairs after her. In a panic she tugged at them. They gave and a blast of cold night air hit her as the door swung open beneath her anxious hands. Still she had no thought in her head but to get away – away from his accusations and his anger, away from the house where she had been so unhappy.

She never even saw the first of the steps that were cut into the path leading down to the rough road, although she had gone down it many times since coming to Sydney. By the time she remembered it was there, it was too late. She screamed as she catapulted forward, grabbing wildly for the handrail Brett had had installed, but it was no use. She fell headlong, hitting the ground, with a great, bone-shuddering crash that seemed to dull her senses. For a moment in time it seemed she lay there, hurting all over. Then, through the mists, she heard Brett's voice, still angry, still raw:

'Little fool! What do you think you're doing?'

She opened her mouth to answer, but no sound came except a gasp of pain and shock. She felt his arms go round her, lifting her gently to a sitting position and suddenly the pain was moving, localizing. It was no longer all over. It was in her back, where it had been bothering her all day. Only now it was worse, much worse...

The gasp became a scream as the pain crushed her, filling every corner of her mind so that there was no room left for thought. But as it faded a little, easing back into the nagging ache, she knew.

'Oh Brett!' she whispered, half in panic, 'Brett, I think it's started! I think I'm going to have my baby!'

He did not reply. But without more ado he scooped her gently up into his arms and carried her back into the house.

CHAPTER THIRTEEN

As he swept up the stairs with Erin in his arms it seemed to Brett that the whole house was already awake. Grianne was leaning over the banisters, a candle lighting up the curiosity in her face, and the door to Henry Stanton's room was ajar, with Henry peering out to see what was going on.

Brett shouted to him to knock up one of the hired servants to go for the doctor and kicked open the door to Erin's room. Then he laid her gently down on the bed, kneeling beside her to brush the tangled hair from her face.

'Don't worry, Stamforth will be here soon,' he said, naming the doctor he had already briefed to attend Erin, and hoping, though he did not say so, that the man had not had too heavy a time the night before. Stamforth was a good doctor – or so those who had engaged his services said – but he was also too fond of his rum either for his own good or the good of his patients.

'Dear God in heaven let her be all right!' he prayed silently, looking down at Erin's face, white as death in the candlelight. What had possessed her to go running out of the house like that in her condition? Even at the height of their quarrel it had never occurred to him she would do anything so foolish! And now...

He saw her face screw up as another pain began and he raced to the door, roaring again for the servant who was to fetch the doctor.

'Where is he, damn him? What does he think I'm paying him for?'

His eye fell on Grianne, still hovering on the landing with her candle, and he caught roughly at her arm, pulling her into the room.

'You're a woman. Erin wanted you here. What do you know about birthing babies?'

Grianne looked at her sister with frightened eyes. She had been awakened by all the uproar, though she had no idea what had been going on.

'Nothing,' she admitted in a shaking voice. 'I was only a child when Brenna was born. And there weren't any more babies in our family.'

Brett swore again. 'Perhaps one of the convict women knows what to do. Go and wake them – go on!'

Grianne shrank back nervously. The convicts lived in the attics at the top of the house and she never went up there. But Brett in this mood was more frightening than any convict.

'Go on – what are you waiting for?' he demanded, and Grianne turned and scuttled out of the room. A few minutes later she was back with a sleepy-looking Lucy Slack who was tying a wrap around her nightgown as she came.

'What's going on then?' she asked sullenly, and Brett indicated the bed.

'Your mistress is having her baby. Can you help until Dr Stamforth gets here?'

Lucy bent over the bed, prodding at Erin with

202

her gnarled fingers.

'She'll be hours yet,' she sneered. 'First babies don't come just like that, you know.'

Beneath her hands Erin twisted uncomfortably and Brett swore.

'What do you mean, hours?'

Lucy shrugged. 'Noon at least. Longer if t'aint lying right. If you don't believe me, Dr Stamforth'll tell you the same. Now, you just try to relax, Ma'am,' she said to Erin. 'Let your body do its own work and save your strength. You'll need it before this day is out.'

'Hell's teeth!' Brett straightened, hating the feeling of helplessness which was new to him. Most situations he could control, or at least have his say in. This was completely beyond him.

Before long Henry Stanton returned with Dr Stamforth and when the latter had examined Erin he confirmed what Lucy Slack had said.

'I might as well go home and finish out my sleep,' he muttered irritably, but Brett would have none of it.

'You'll do nothing of the sort, man. I've paid for you to attend my wife and I want you here in case anything should go wrong.'

Stamforth cast him a disparaging look.

'Why should it? She's as strong as a young mare.'

'But she is not a mare. She's my wife,' Brett returned. 'I want the best of attention for her and the child, Stamforth. I told you that.'

'Of course, of course, the baby's your first, is it not? Your son and heir, I think you said,' Stamforth muttered, and Brett turned away, saying nothing.

Strange the way this had affected him. Such a short time ago, when she had told him the baby she was carrying might not be his, he had been so stunned and so angry he could have strangled her with his bare hands. But since she had fallen down the steps he had not given it a thought. It wasn't that it had ceased to matter. Her deception was a knife-thrust in his heart and just what he would do if the child was not his he did not know. But for the moment it had shrunk to un-importance and there was no time to worry about anything except Erin's welfare.

And so it was throughout the long day. Never, in the whole of his life, could Brett remember feeling so helpless, never so beset by nameless fears. As soon as Dr Stamforth had woken up enough to accept the fact that Brett was deter-mined not to allow him to return home until the baby had been safely delivered, he took control, providing Lucy Slack with a long list of things he would want and shooing Brett out of the room.

'Husbands are more bother than they're worth,' he asserted. 'I'm sure you can find some-thing better to do with your time than wearing out the floorboards here – like adding a bit more value to the business you're building up for the scrap that's causing all the trouble.'

At his words, Brett's lips tightened a shade, but he did as the doctor bid without comment. It was good to be away from the cloistering atmos-phere in the bedroom and he thought that once he could no longer hear the bouts of harsh breathing that warned at regular intervals of Erin's pains he would be content to leave her in the capable hands of the doctor and convict women and find something to occupy his mind. But that was less easy than he had imagined.

Wherever he went in the house his thoughts went with him and no matter what he tried to do he kept seeing her deathly-white face surrounded by the tumble of her dark hair.

What would he do, he asked himself, if anything happened to her?

Swiftly he pushed the thought away. Nothing would happen to her. As Dr Stamforth had said she was young and strong. But for all that...

'It's my fault she's lying there now,' thought Brett. Whether or not it was he who had brought her to bed, it was certainly because of him that she had fallen down the steps. If she should have injured herself in some way and brought about complications he would have to blame himself. Though surely no one could expect a man to react any differently to revelations such as Erin had made this night.

Dawn broke and the pale light of a spring morning warmed the house. In the dining room Henry Stanton made a good breakfast in spite of his disturbed night, but Brett could manage only to wash down some scalding coffee and light up the first cigar of the day. He felt more like rum than coffee were the truth to be known, and with an oath he gave way to the inclination, liberally lacing the cup with it.

Henry Stanton was to start back for Mia-Mia as soon as his horse was saddled and Brett knew there were last-minute things he had intended to tell him, but try as he might he could not concentrate his mind on business. It was impossible to think of anything for two minutes at a stretch without being distracted by wondering what was happening upstairs.

As noon approached Brett became restless. Lucy Slack had prophesied this was the time when some news could be expected. But there was no sound from upstairs. He found Grianne, hovering nervously in the passageway, and asked her to find out what was going on. But when she returned her expression was sober. Things were not progressing as fast as the doctor had hoped. There was no sign yet that the birth was imminent.

'What does the fool think he's playing at?' Brett asked furiously, pouring himself another glass of rum from the crystal decanter and downing it in one great gulp. 'Isn't there anything he can do for her?'

Grianne shook her head and the frightened expression on her face fuelled his anger.

'Much good you are, too, Madam!' he threw at her. 'Isn't that the reason you're here – because Erin wanted your support when the time came?'

Grianne's lip trembled and she caught at his arm.

'Oh, don't be cross with me, Brett!' she simpered. 'I'm so worried about her, I'm going plum' crazy!'

Brett shot her a quick look of surprise and caught the sly slither of her eyes as she watched for his reaction.

'I don't believe you've a thought in your head for her!' he snapped. 'She may be your sister, but there's only one person you're concerned about. Yourself.'

'Oh! Is that so?' Grianne's blue eyes began to spit fire. 'Then let me tell you something, Brett Wilde. It's no good for you to play the distraught husband to me because I know different. You and Erin are at daggers drawn, aren't you? And you don't give a fig about what happens to her as long as you get your precious son!'

For a second fury flared in Brett's face, then he slammed his glass down and turned sharply away. Just at present he couldn't trust himself to answer Grianne. He would deal with her later. For the moment he could think of nothing but Erin.

He went into the hall and took the stairs two at a time. The bedroom door was closed but he could hear the sound of voices from within, and at all-too-frequent intervals that awful, gasping breathing. He was standing in a daze, wondering whether to knock or go right in, when the door suddenly burst open and Lucy Slack emerged carrying the china water jug.

'What the hell is going on in there?' he demanded, his voice slightly slurred from all the rum he had consumed.

Lucy shot him a sharp look.

'We need more water for dabbing her brow. She's in a fever, poor lamb.'

He snatched the jug from her.

'I'll get it. Go back and stay with your mistress.'

She stared in amazement as he disappeared back down the stairway. Then, a few minutes later he was back, the jug filled with fresh cool water. The door now stood ajar; with a purpose this time he kicked it open and went in.

The scene that met his eyes made him stop short in his tracks. The doctor stood beside the bed, sleeves rolled up to elbows, while Lucy Slack bent over the bedhead affixing what looked like a strip of pillowcase to the rail. But it was to Erin that his eyes were drawn. She lay half-covered by a clean white sheet that exposed her slim shoulders bare of any nightgown. But she was a very different Erin to the one he had left those few hours before. Her hair was now not only tangled but matted and damp with perspiration, her eyes were half-closed and her face, though pale, was also moist and twisted into an expression of agony. As he watched he saw her body writhe beneath the sheet and her head turn and twist on the pillow.

Lucy bent over, catching at her hands and fastening them onto the strip of pillow case.

'Here you are, lovey. Pull on this. 'Twill help you.'

But only a weak moan escaped Erin's lips.

Brett thrust the jug of water towards Dr Stamforth and sprang to the bed, going down on his knees beside it and taking her hand in his. At once her fingers gripped it, squeezing so tightly he thought she would crush his bones. Then, as the pain eased, her eyes opened again, focusing mistily on his face.

'Brett!' she whispered.

'I'm here, love,' he said softly, then turned to look over his shoulder in helpless anger at Dr Stamforth. 'Surely there's something you can do, man?'

'I'm doing all I can,' the doctor replied impatiently. 'And you'd be better out of the way as I told you.'

His words seemed to penetrate Erin's haze and her fingers tightened once more on Brett's hand.

'No – don't go! Please, Brett!' she murmured urgently.

'It's all right, I won't,' he promised her and with an abrupt movement the doctor set the water jug Brett had thrust at him down on the floor beside the bed.

'Well, if you must stay, at least do something useful,' he ordered. 'Sponge her face and hands and try to keep her cool. And if you panic, I'll have you out of here in a minute. I don't care who you are, in the sick room, *I'm* the one in charge.'

Brett ignored him, taking the sponge and doing as he was bid. Beneath his fingers Erin's face burned, but as he squeezed the cool water onto her forehead she opened her eyes again.

'How much longer, Brett?' she asked softly.

'Not much longer, sweet, I'll see to that,' he murmured, as if for all his inexperience he and not Stamforth was the doctor.

The slow hours of afternoon ticked by and the sun was low in the sky when Grianne, still hovering anxiously at the foot of the stairs, heard a whoop fit to wake the dead. She jumped

209

nervously as the bedroom door flew open, her hands going to her throat. This last quarter of an hour her sister's moans had been audible even downstairs and a few minutes ago a piercing scream, followed by silence, had turned her blood to ice.

Now as she saw Brett emerge from the bedroom and come to the head of the stairs her heart pumped furiously. But as he approached her, taking the stairs two at a time in his usual impatient way, she knew at once that it was over – and that all was well with Erin.

'What is it – a boy or a girl?' she cried eagerly.

Brett swung her up into his arms, swizzing her round so that her feet left the ground.

'A boy! And after all that time! Dear God, I'd no idea!'

Grianne laughed, her usual self-assurance returning as fear was chased out.

'Men! What do you know about it? You take your pleasure and you have no thought for what you're letting us in for.'

She felt him stiffen and dimly she was aware that it was her words that had brought about the change in him. He set her down abruptly and the darkening of his face made her wonder yet again about the man her sister had married. Holy Saint Teresa, he could change in a minute! A chameleon was more predictable than he! Why, only a moment ago he had been overjoyed at the birth of his son and now, without warning, one of his black moods had descended again. Perhaps after all Erin was right to be less than enthusiastic about being married to such a man. Handsome he might be, and rich, but there was something to be said for a husband whose temper was a little more even.

'There's no need to take offence,' she teased. 'If your son grows up to be as dashing as you I'm sure he, too, will find some girl willing to go through hell for him.'

But he was not listening to her. Without another word he turned on his heel and slammed out of the house.

After the first cries of her son disturbed the stillness of the early evening Erin lapsed into a heavy slumber which lasted, almost uninterrupted, until the soft dawn light warmed her room.

She lay for a moment luxuriating in the smoothness of her freshly laundered sheets and wondering at how much pain could be diminished so quickly to little more than a sore discomfort. Then she eased herself up on the pillows, looking around for her son.

It was a boy – that much she remembered from the twilight world where she had languished before sleep claimed her, and briefly Lucy had placed him in her arms. She had a misty memory of warmth and firmness but not even his proximity had been able to keep her awake, and now...

Where was he? wondered Erin, a moment's panic assailing her. There had been nothing but pleasure in Lucy's voice as she had relayed the information to Erin, and Dr Stamforth had not said anything either. But supposing something had gone wrong afterwards, while she was asleep.

211

As she pushed herself up higher on the pillows the door opened and Lucy Slack came in. She was beaming with all the pride of her new-found status as a nursemaid and in her arms was a small, tightly wrapped bundle.

Erin's face lit up. She stretched out her arms and Lucy placed the baby in them, a little screwed-up scrap with flattened ears and a dented forehead. Erin's smile faltered and she looked up at Lucy in alarm. But the woman only beamed still.

'He's a bonny boy, Ma'am, have no fear. And those dents will go in a few days. They're only there because he took such a long time to get born.'

Erin nodded, relieved. Oh, but he was so small and perfect, with his cap of dark hair and his eyes big and blue beneath the dented forehead! As she took him his mouth opened like a baby bird waiting to be fed and Lucy stepped forward, taking it upon herself to unfasten the neck of Erin's nightgown.

'Give him the breast, Ma'am. The sooner the better, I always say.'

Erin looked quickly around, overcome by sudden modesty.

'Brett...'

'Oh, it's a shame he had to leave early this morning, so it is!' Lucy remarked, misunderstanding Erin's meaning. 'I made so bold as to tell him so, too. "I'd have thought you could forget your business for one day now you've a brand new son to admire," I said. But there was no moving him. He said he had to go.'

Erin said nothing but her heart sank a little with disappointment. Yesterday there had been a bond between them – even in her twilight world she had felt it. Brett had been there just when she needed him most and she would have thought that what they had shared would bring them closer together. But it had not been enough to keep him from his business. As always that had come first, before his wife and child.

As the thought crossed her mind Erin stiffened suddenly and all her most nightmarish fears came flooding back. *Was* her baby Brett's son? Or was he the child of a convicted criminal? He looked so sweetly innocent lying there, his small button mouth sealed contentedly around her nipple so that shivering sensations ran through her body. He must be Brett's! Oh Holy Mother, he must be! But not until she saw the horseshoe mark on his shoulder would she know for sure. And if it was not there...

She shifted the baby slightly against her breast. He was so tightly wrapped up it was impossible to see anything but his small, down-covered head. And yesterday by the time he had been born she had been in no state to take notice of such a thing, though Dr Stamforth had held him up before her, stark naked.

'Though I don't believe I ever saw his back,' she thought. It was his face and his stomach that had been towards her. But Brett had been behind him. Brett would have seen!

At the thought her stomach seemed to fall away. Brett would have seen. Brett would have looked at once for the proof, or otherwise, of his

213

parenthood. And Brett, in spite of all his solicitous concern for her yesterday, was not here now. He had left, too early to even bid her good morning – on business. Dear God in heaven, did it mean that there was no horseshoe mark, and he was disowning the babe who lay in her arms?

Erin was trembling now, so violently it seemed the very bed rocked. Oh sweet Jesus, it could not be! Her baby the child of a rapist and murderer! It was more than she could bear – and not only because it would mean the end of her marriage to Brett. No, it was more, much more, than that. His heritage would be sullied and stained, with the blood of a villain in his veins. Sweet and innocent as he was now, dearly as she loved him already, she would kill him before she would allow him to grow to a monstrous replica of the man who had taken her so vilely beside the body of her dead father.

But first she must know the truth.

With clumsy fingers she fumbled for the tucked-in end of the wrapper, lifting the small firm body to find it. Then, her heart beating a sickening tattoo against her ribs, she began to unwind it.

His hands she freed first, looking in awe and wonder at the tiny, perfectly formed fingers, each tipped with a pearly nail. But after a brief pause she continued to unwind the wrapper until two small feet were also exposed and there was only a loose gown covering him.

The baby's mouth was still tightly fastened to her nipple. With shaking hands that were not yet used to handling such a small scrap anyway she lifted him, easing him away from her breast. He let out an indignant wail, but she persisted. She had to know. And she had to know now – before Lucy Slack returned.

Carefully she sat him up, supporting the downy head with the palm of her hand while she tipped him forward. Then with her heart in her mouth she eased away the loose neck of the gown.

Her first view was of a smooth white shoulder and a sob rose in her throat. Then, as her fingers tightened on his body, a fold of loose skin shifted and she saw it.

A mark, fiery red against the pale skin! And as she eagerly stretched it out she saw it in its entirety and the sob escaped from her lips. But now it was a sob of joy and pure relief.

The horseshoe mark! Brett's horseshoe mark! He was indeed Brett's son!

Happiness flooded her so that for the moment all else ceased to be of importance.

He was Brett's son – Brett's heir. And more than that he was hers – her own dear babe. Nothing could alter that now. Nothing could take it from her. Satisfied she lay him back again, and as his mouth fastened at once to her breast, it seemed to Erin that the whole world lay here, in her arms.

CHAPTER FOURTEEN

Brett was away for two days – two days that floated by for Erin on gossamer wings. She dozed, she woke, she fed her little son, and all the while waited on hand and foot by Lucy and the other women who were overjoyed at being involved in the welfare of the new arrival. It was a strange, unreal world into which people floated like silver-grey ghosts – Grianne, eyeing the baby with a mixture of distaste and awe; Dr Stamforth, whose repeated calls set her imagining something was wrong until he explained he was here by prior arrangement with Brett; even a stream of callers who did business at the store looking in to offer their congratulations and take a peek at the heir to the Wilde empire.

These Erin did not care for; though they treated her with exaggerated friendliness she had the uncomfortable feeling that those who had been at their wedding had told the others of their doubts about her and accordingly she could not feel relaxed with them. Compared with the river folk she thought most of them a scheming lot, concerned only with improving their status in Sydney and conscious that, as a man of such substance, Brett was not to be ignored.

And they did tire her so! Never in her life, she

thought, had she felt so weary lying abed and doing nothing!

On the second afternoon, the wives of two of Brett's former colleagues in the New South Wales Corps called and had hardly left when Lucy popped her head around the door to ask if she could show in Mrs Fanny Hubbard and her daughter Isobel.

Mrs Hubbard Erin particularly disliked – as wife of one of the town's principal traders she fancied herself a cut above everyone else. And Isobel was a plain, skinny girl who had not been able to attract a husband in spite of being sixteen years old and one of the few single women in the colony. Mrs Hubbard had always treated Erin with barely veiled dislike and Erin suspected she had been responsible for scuttling the woman's hopes of arranging a match with Brett.

Today, however, she followed Lucy into the room with the minimum of propriety, gushing at Erin as if the two had been bosom friends.

'A son! My dear Erin, how like Mr Wilde he is! Can you not see the likeness at once? Say you agree with me, Isobel!'

The girl's thin lips twitched but she said nothing and Fanny Hubbard gushed on.

'A bonny babe indeed! What is he to be called? Might we have the honour of knowing?'

Erin shifted on the pillows. The movement was a great effort.

'Brett and I haven't yet had the chance to decide on a name.'

'Oh come, you're teasing me!' the older woman pressed her. 'You must have some idea! All parents talk about such things – if the child is a wanted one, that is.'

A small chord of pain stirred deep within Erin. There had been too many doubts in the last months to be dispelled so quickly.

'We've talked, of course,' she said defensively.

'And what were the favourites – oh, let us into the secret!' Fanny persisted with forced gaiety. 'Just a little hint, Erin, I beg of you!'

Erin swallowed. It was plain the woman would go on and on like a dog with a bone until she said something. And oh, she would give anything just to shut her up and have her go and leave her in peace.

'My father's name was Patrick,' she said wearily.

'Oh – and you will call him Patrick too! How sweet!' the woman crowed.

'No, I don't think so. My brother is called Patrick also – it would be too confusing. Maybe his second name, William...'

'William. William Wilde,' Fanny repeated, rolling it around on her tongue. 'It sounds well enough. But there must be a second name, too. One that gives a ring to it. You're Irish, aren't you, by birth? Then why not Sean? Or perhaps a name from the Good Book – Abel, perhaps, or Jeremiah. Now that sounds impressive indeed! Jeremiah William! A fine name.'

'I thank you for your interest, but when I need your assistance in naming my son, I'll let you know.'

At the deep voice from the bedroom door they all jumped; none of them had heard Brett approaching up the stairs.

'Why, Mr Wilde! I was only trying to be helpful,' Fanny Hubbard simpered. 'Erin was just telling me the child was to be called William after her father and I thought perhaps as the son of such an important family the name needed a little embellishment to distinguish it.'

Brett came right into the room. In his buckskin breeches with his shirt open at the neck he looked tall and strong and almost as strikingly casual as he looked back at Mia-Mia.

'I wasn't aware that we had decided upon a name,' he said smoothly.

Erin flushed, afraid he would think her over-presumptuous.

'I never said we had, Brett! Mrs Hubbard misunderstood me...' she began, but Brett went on.

'However, I'm sure anything Erin chooses will be very suitable. She is, after all, the baby's mother.'

'Well of course!' Fanny Hubbard agreed hastily. 'And a beautiful picture the two of them make, too. You said the very same thing, didn't you, Isobel?' she added pushing Isobel forward.

But Brett was looking at Erin, noticing the pallor of her face and the way her head sagged back against the pillows no matter how she tried to keep it erect.

'I think it's time you were leaving,' he said shortly.

Fanny Hubbard's eyes widened. 'But we've only just arrived, Mr Wilde! We...'

'And I'm sure you would not wish to outstay your welcome,' Brett continued sweetly, holding the door open.

The woman's face registered utter amazement and umbrage.

'Well!' she expostulated. 'If that's the way you feel, we'll bid you good afternoon! Come, Isobel!'

With heads erect, bristling with indignation, the two left the room and the picture of injured innocence they made was so complete that Erin could not help smiling.

'Oh Brett, you shouldn't have done that!' she protested as the door closed after them. 'You've offended them mortally, and you can't afford to make enemies.'

'Enemies? Those two? Pooh!' Brett said rudely. 'They'll be fawning around again in next to no time, mark my words. And if they hadn't the sense to see that you're in no fit state for visitors, then it was my duty to point it out to them.'

'Oh, I'm all right,' Erin murmured, without much conviction. Then, as she remembered the awkward moment when Fanny had presented Brett with his son's names as a *fait accompli*, she went on. 'And I didn't tell them what the baby was to be called, truly I didn't! And Jeremiah was entirely her idea, though I did mention my father's second name was William.'

Brett dropped to his haunches beside the bed, taking her hand in his.

'And would you like to call the baby after him?'

'I would – but it's your decision, Brett.'

He smiled, his grey eyes softening.

220

'I think William is a fine name. What's more, it happened to be the given name of my grand-father.'

'Oh!' Warmth suffused her, driving out the tiredness. 'Then you mean...'

'We'll call him William – with no other names to confuse the issue. What's the point? He won't need them. Our son will be so special, Erin, that he will stand by that alone. And however many more there may be of the same name there will never be any doubts but that he is *the* William Wilde.'

She smiled. Her hand in his felt good.

'Brett...' she murmured sleepily.

He straightened up, looking down at her.

'I'm going now. I'll send Lucy in for William.'

'No – don't go!' she tried to say. There were so many things she wanted to tell him, so much she wanted to ask. But she could not form the words and she felt the sense of loss as he went away from her.

'Get some rest, my sweet,' he said. Then the door had closed after him and he had gone.

Why didn't he stay with me? Erin wondered drowsily. Then her eyes became too heavy to prop open any longer and once again she slept.

As the days passed and she grew stronger Erin found she had plenty of time on her hands for thinking.

William was a good baby, crying only when he was hungry, and as soon as Erin had satisfied his needs he fell asleep again or lay gazing content-edly at nothing. And when he did get a crying fit,

221

Lucy was always on hand to take charge of him, rocking him in her arms and cooing at him with a warmth that never failed in its purpose.

As for the stream of visitors, they no longer came – Brett had put a stop to that – and Grianne ventured into the bedroom but seldom. Erin wondered if she might be upset at the words that had passed between them and hoped that the opportunity to put things right would soon present itself.

But most of all her thoughts were with Brett.

It was a strange thing, she thought, that even though she had entered upon this marriage with such reluctance she should now be giving so much time to devising ways to improve it and make it work.

Perhaps it was the fact that William was now here, a living, breathing babe who needed a secure and loving home. Motherhood could bring about devastating changes in a woman, she was sure. But in moments of honesty with herself she knew it was more than that.

Briefly – oh, so briefly – she had caught glimpses of another side of Brett – a man as different from the hard-hearted profiteer as could be – and she had begun to see how it would be to be loved by him. It was too much to hope for, of course, that he should love her. He had married her because she was bearing his son and heir and for no other reason. But maybe, just maybe, they could build some kind of relationship if they took the trouble. Maybe at least they could behave like man and wife in some respects – giving and receiving companionship, comforting one another in hard times, and sharing a marriage bed. Much as she had disliked her previous encounters with the process of mating there were times when she looked at Brett and wished it were not so. His broad shoulders and long, hard thighs evoked a response in her that unwillingly reminded her of the times he had possessed her, and a treacherous desire to feel his lips on hers had niggled deep within her.

It was humiliating, too, to think that he went elsewhere for his satisfaction – especially if the somewhere else he went was to Grianne. But Erin had taken careful note and had not seen a repeat of the scene she had witnessed between them. Grianne no longer hung about where Brett was and he seemed almost to ignore her.

But for all that there must be a lady somewhere in Sydney who knew that all was not as it should be between man and wife. A man like Brett, with healthy appetites, could not surely be living like a monk. And much as it went against the grain, Erin discovered that she actually minded.

'No relationship can ever exist between us until we share a bed,' she thought, looking at the large, empty expanse beside her. 'We cannot hope to build a framework for our life together until our heads lie on the same pillows and our bodies are covered by the same sheets. And until he takes me again, and properly consummates this marriage that knew only one brief, snatched union – and that before the ink on the marriage lines was dry!'

As she remembered that occasion something

sharp and sweet, but disturbing, twisted inside her and she pressed the bedclothes firmly around her stomach, arresting the sensation. Clearly her insides were still upset from childbirth. If she was to make her plans lucidly she must ignore them.

But how to ask Brett to move back into her bed without appearing either too forward or too affectionate? She did not know. She could only, she thought, wait and see what happened and take any opportunity that offered. There was no other way.

For two days it played on her mind, making her awkward with him when he came into the room to see William. She was as shy as a young girl with her first beau, she thought, shyer than she could ever remember being with Alistair if it came to that – and Brett was her husband and the father of her child, who had sat with her, if she remembered rightly, until the very moment of birth.

It could be that, of course, that added to her awkwardness, for she could never remember a time with Alistair when her voice came out sounding short when she intended it to be sweet, or when she turned away with abruptness that bordered on the rude rather than let him see a flush of colour in her cheeks. And there was her fear too that he would think she had read too much into his concern for her on the day that William had been born. She would die rather than that he should think that when she knew very well it had been the baby's safety which had given him such cause for concern.

One evening, however, Brett came in later than usual. Business had delayed him at the store, and she was giving William the last feed that would, she hoped, take him well into the night, when she heard Brett's step on the stairs.

At once she clamped William closer to her. Strange how defensive it made her that he should find her with the baby at her breast! Then, as he came into the room, she looked up shyly, smiling at him over the baby's head.

Brett crossed to the bed, bending to drop a kiss on her forehead before flinging himself into the chair that stood beside the bed, and stretching his legs out before him with a sigh.

'You're late tonight,' she ventured.

'Yes, a shipment of goods arrived just when I was about to leave,' he explained. 'I wanted to examine it right away and it's as well I did. Most of the stuff was damaged by salt water. But they'd have tried to fob it off on me if they could.'

She smiled. 'Still the same Brett. The man who can pull a fast deal on you has yet to come to this new country, I believe.'

'You're wrong,' he said and when she looked up with a questioning, defensive expression in her eyes, he went on. 'The man who can pull a fast deal on me has yet to be born! But then, I have much more to work for now, haven't I? So much more to make me determined to succeed – and succeed handsomely.'

She followed his eyes to William and illogically felt a small barb of hurt. She should be glad he wanted to succeed for her son – she *was* glad.

But, oh, it would have been nice if he had wanted, just a little, to succeed for her.

To cover her thoughts she said quickly, 'He's doing well, isn't he? I'm sure he's grown already, though Lucy would no doubt say I'm imagining it.'

Brett's eyes rested thoughtfully on his son.

'Lucy's been good to you, hasn't she? Stamforth said her help was invaluable at the birth and from what little I've seen it appears she does far more than anyone could expect of her in the line of duty.'

'Oh, she does!' Erin returned eagerly. 'She always has! Why, it was she who taught me to play...' She broke off, hot colour flooding her cheeks as she remembered the disastrous consequences of that particular venture of Lucy Slack's.

Brett shifted a little in his chair, settling himself more comfortably.

'Erin – about the piano. Perhaps I was a little hasty that day when I returned. I was cold, wet and tired – though I know that's no excuse – and I was taken by surprise to find you trying to play upon it. But I've decided if you could take proper lessons so that you do not deafen us all with a lot of horrible discords, I've no objection to you using it.'

'Oh, thank you, Brett!' she cried in surprise. 'But Lucy *is* a proper teacher. She tells me her father taught some of the grandest families in the town where they lived.'

Brett laughed. 'It seems Lucy Slack is full of surprises. I think I shall have to speak to the

Governor about her when next I see him. If ever a convict deserved to have her sentence remitted, I believe it's Lucy.'

Erin wriggled up against the pillows, pleased, and eased William from her nipple without even thinking about Brett sitting beside the bed. It was only when she had covered one naked breast and was about to bare the other that she looked up and saw him watching her. Her fingers froze and the colour rose once again in her cheeks.

'Oh – I – I'm sorry...' she murmured foolishly, protecting her breast with her forearm though William began to whimper softly with impatience to resume his supper.

Brett's lips tightened a shade and his eyes slid away from her.

'I'm the one to apologize. You clearly wish to be alone.'

'No – not really. It's just that...' she broke off, flustered. How could she explain to him the choking embarrassment that had coursed through her to think he had looked on her breasts, swollen with the milk to feed his baby? It was stupid, ridiculous, that there should be this restraint between husband and wife.

He made to move and she reached out and caught at his wrist. Beneath her fingers it was strong and sinewy.

'Brett – don't go!' she murmured.

He seemed to freeze and her eyes followed her fingers, noticing the tiny golden hairs that were still bronzed from the summer which now seemed so long gone, and the veins that stood out in ridges along the back of his hand.

A strange, unfamiliar desire began running through her, tugging at the same sweet secret depths that William's gummy mouth, drawing on her breasts, seemed to reach. She shivered at its intensity and shyly she let her eyes roam slowly over his hand again, past her restraining fingers and the frilled cuff of his shirt, and up his thick muscled forearm, covered now by fine linen. The tiniest move and her eyes were dwelling on the breadth of his chest, hesitating at the carelessly opened neck of his shirt and sliding on upwards to his face.

In the soft candlelight his lips were full and sensuous; she remembered too clearly for comfort how they had felt on her own. If it had not been for that jutting jaw and nose they would have dominated his face. Or would they? Unwilling now, like a moth mesmerized by a lamp, she found herself meeting his eyes. They were narrowed and almost hidden in shadow, and yet still they drew her, the piercing grey seeming to have become liquid silver.

She caught her breath and the tremor that ran through her transmitted itself through her fingers to him. She felt the answering spark with every nerve in her body and suddenly her fear was wondering joy.

'Don't go, Brett, please!' she said again, and it was as if the words released a dozen others and a dozen more, all locked inside her. 'I've been thinking, it's foolish for you to sleep on that hard, narrow old bed in your dressing room. I wouldn't mind if you were to come here and sleep with me. I don't take up so much space as I did...'

He did not reply and her voice tailed away. Why was he looking at her like that – so intently, and yet...

'Brett?' she whispered.

He drew a harsh, shuddering breath, his hand beneath her fingers grasping at the bedcovers.

Dear God in heaven but she was enough to tempt a man, lying there so lovely! She had always been beautiful, but since the baby had been born there was another quality added to her loveliness – a delicate translucence that came from the tired shadows remaining still under her eyes and the way her pale skin stretched across her cheek bones, and yet something else besides – for all the fragility, a glow of warm fulfilment.

It seemed to him that she had grown more desirable with every day that had passed since she had borne his child. Or was that in his mind only? He had not thought of Therese in days now – maybe even weeks – and he did not think he would ever think of her in terms of love again. This woman had filled every corner of his mind – and yes, of his heart, too.

He could not imagine why he had not loved her on sight – though on reflection, perhaps he had. Why else should he have sought her out again at Alice Simmons's, even though he had not found her? Why else should he have felt such responsibility towards her that he had sent her goods and men to help with the harvest even though he scarcely knew her? And above all, why had he insisted on marrying her when she

229

had come to him for assistance? He had told himself – and her – that it was because she was carrying his son. Now he was not sure that had been the whole reason.

His mind ran back to the day when William was born – the long, never-ending day when he had watched her in agony and been helpless to do anything for her. It had been only hours after she had told him the child might not be his; hours after she had brought the world tumbling about his ears. If he had married her only for the child, he should have hated her then, but he had not. Shocked and angry though he was, his only concern had been for her – more so, perhaps, now that he was aware that the child she was bringing so painfully into the world might not be his.

As he had sat beside her that day there had been a depth of feeling within him that he had never experienced for Therese, and he had vowed that if she was spared to him he would do everything in his power to make her happy, whether the baby was his or not.

But it had been his. William was unmistakably branded with the mark that had run through his family for generations, and once more he had held the world in the palm of his hand. Since that day his enthusiasm for work had been fired again and he had moved mountains in his efforts to make his business empire more secure for what had suddenly become his family – working from morning till night. But still he had not dared hope she would come to him yet. That, he had thought, would be a long, hard road – and a lonely one. But now...

His eyes softened as he looked at her, her hair as black as ravens' wings spread across the pillow, her rosy lips parted. The tip of her breast was hidden by the baby's suckling mouth, but its soft, creamy curve was as enticing as ever and it was easy for him to picture the delicate lines of her body beneath the sheet – the hips, rounded, but too narrow for ease of childbearing, her stomach, grown flat once more, her long, slender legs. The imagining started a fire within him.

Oh, how his body ached for her! It was so long since he had had a woman – longer than he could ever remember since growing to manhood. But he had not wanted one. The appetite she stirred in him disappeared when he was faced with any other but her. He had tried visiting his favourite places in Sydney, but the moment he walked through the doors his appetite left him, though he had found the girls there a welcome relief when his dreams had been of Therese.

As for Grianne – he could have had her, he supposed. There had been a look in her eyes when she teased him that told him so. But Grianne he wanted least of all. With her dark hair and blue eyes she reminded him too much of Erin – and she was Erin's sister, in any case, and he would not dream of humiliating his wife so.

No, he might as well admit the truth. There was no one he wanted but Erin. And he wanted her with every fibre of his being – wanted her far too much to be able to lie beside her in the bed and not take her. When her every touch was like a firebrand on his skin, when her nearness set his senses reeling, how could he control his desire? Even now when their only contact was her fingers on his wrist the recollection of her sweet flesh against his was a tinderbox to fire his passion and he wanted nothing more than to possess her as he had possessed her before. Only this time he would take her with gentleness, drawing her along with him on the upward path to the heights that he was sure she had never yet discovered, sharing the delights of love.

But it was too soon. Stamforth had not minced his words on that score. In his blunt fashion he had told Brett there must be no intimacy yet awhile. Erin's fragile state of health would not permit it.

He moved his hand abruptly beneath hers, wishing there was some way he could explain, yet afraid for her to know what was in his mind. Perhaps indeed she meant him only to share the bed, not realizing that the temptation would be torture for his yearning body. He had no wish to frighten her again.

''Twould be best for me to stay where I am for the present,' he said and even to his own ears his voice sounded harsh and ill-tempered. It was the strength of desire within him, he supposed, but he could not tell her that.

'Oh, would it?' she asked, her voice rising.

He ignored the demands of his own body.

'Yes.'

He bent over to kiss her forehead and the scent of her hair made his senses swim so that it was nothing but a relief when she turned away.

232

'Get some rest, sweet,' he said gently. 'You need it. I'll send Lucy in for the child.'

He moved away and she saw him leave the room as if through a mist. The tears burned behind her eyes, the back of her throat ached unbearably and sense of desolation within her was so complete she might have been nothing but an empty shell.

So it was true – he did only want her for her baby. If ever she had had doubts, now there could be none. For a few glorious moments she had imagined that they were sharing some special togetherness and she had offered him an olive branch with foolish eagerness. But he had rejected it.

The hot tears came to blind her, burning her eyes and running in rivers down her cheeks to splash disconsolately onto William's small, un-suspecting head.

She had asked him to share her bed and he had refused. She would not ask again.

CHAPTER FIFTEEN

During the days that followed Erin scarcely saw Brett and it seemed to her he was avoiding her. When he did come into her room there was a constraint between them and she felt sure it was William he came to see, so quickly did he remove himself from her vicinity.

Sometimes he joked with her, though, and one day he again mentioned the piano, suggesting that when she was fit to rise from her bed she should begin her lessons, but she thought he was probably trying to distract her from the fact that all his interest was in William, and the emptiness still ached deep within her.

William was a joy, of course. Every day, it seemed to her, there was something new to notice about him, and she loved holding him close, smelling the sweet baby scent of him and feeling his smooth, damp skin beneath her cheek. But she would be glad when she could get up and about again. And on that score Dr Stamforth was being as stubborn as an old mule.

'If you set foot to the ground yet I won't be responsible for you,' he told her sternly when she asked, yet again, to be allowed out of bed.

'But I feel so well – never better!' she protested, wriggling her toes in impatience. 'I'm not tired now – at least, only sometimes, and I could easily sit down and rest if I needed to.'

But Dr Stamforth only clicked his teeth at her and shook his head. 'It's more than my reputation's worth to allow it. Why, if harm came to you, your good husband would never forgive me, and my future here would be worth less than a field of rotted wheat.'

At his words Erin turned her head away so he should not see the tears gathering in her eyes. They came too easily these days, those foolish tears. And always when she was reminded of how little Brett cared for her.

'Why, if only Dr Stamforth were to know the truth, he would realize it would be nothing but a relief to Brett to be rid of me!' she thought and although she knew in her heart it was an exaggeration that did not seem to help.

'Now, now, my dear. It's natural you should be emotional after the birth of a child,' Dr Stamforth said now, leaning over to pat her hand, and Erin nodded wordlessly.

Thanks be at least that he did *not* know the truth! If he had done she did not think she could bear the shame!

But as soon as he had left, she made up her mind. These ready tears were an annoyance to someone as strong willed as she was – perhaps they would flow less easily if she had something to occupy herself. And how could it possibly hurt her to get up for just a little while? The good doctor was probably only being stuffy and over-cautious. And she could not bear to remain in bed a moment longer.

235

The house was quiet now, with William sleeping peacefully in his cradle, and she pushed aside the covers and slid her legs over the edge of the bed. If she could get into her clothes, everyone would be able to see how fit she was, she thought.

But as her legs took her weight, she was astonished at how weak they felt, and the blood seemed to sing loudly in her ears. Gripping her lip tightly between her teeth, she struggled on, but in the centre of the floor she stopped, alarmed.

Surely the chest with her clothes on it had never been this far away before? But no one could have moved it without her seeing. And it had looked no different when she had been in bed...

She took another step, but her knees were so wobbly they would no longer support her and it seemed the floor was moving with a swaying motion like the sea. For some reason it took her back to the voyage she had made with her parents all those years ago from Ireland, halfway across the world to the new country.

Before her misted eyes she seemed to see the ghostly figures from the past. 'Father...' she heard herself whisper, and then the floor was coming up to meet her, not in a rush, but slowly, relentlessly...

'Erin! Dear God in heaven, what do you think you are doing!'

Brett's voice seemed to be coming from a long way off, and she was vaguely surprised when she felt his arms around her, lifting her as easily as if she were a child and carrying her back to the bed. 'Foolish girl! Are you trying to kill yourself?'

The pillow was behind her head and her eyes came into focus to see him bending over her. He looked cool and angry, but his arms felt good around her and she turned instinctively towards him.

'Brett...' she whispered faintly.

'What were you thinking of?' he asked again, as if he had not heard her, and as he moved away she was overwhelmed by a sense of loss.

'I wanted to get up,' she whispered weakly. 'I'm so tired of lying here, Brett.'

'You're too impatient,' he said shortly. 'I don't think you realize, my love, how ill you've been.'

'But people have babies all the time,' she argued.

'And most of them have them a great deal more easily than you did. Now, promise me, Erin, that you'll be good and not do anything foolish again. If I hadn't come in, heaven only knows how long you would have lain there. And I'm not going to be around for the next few weeks to keep an eye on you. The *Amber Fawn* is making her first voyage for me and I want to go with her.'

'But why?' she cried.

'I'm not happy that the crew I've engaged are competent to bargain for me. I know I can't always travel, and I must engage someone to trade for me, but there's too much at stake this time to entrust the task to an untried man. I'll be away for a few weeks only, but I want your

237

word, Erin, that you'll do as Dr Stamforth tells you.'

She could not answer. Her throat was full. She hated it here – hated it – and without Brett it would be unbearable. The weak tears welled up again in her eyes and though she despised herself for them she was quite unable to hold them back.

'Erin? What is it? What's wrong, love?' Brett was beside her again in a moment. He hated to see her cry, yet his heart leaped treacherously within him. Was it possible she cared enough that she was crying to see him go?

She swallowed hard, catching her lip between her teeth.

'I'm sorry. I know I'm being silly. Only...'

'Only what?'

'I'm so homesick for the river, Brett. And if you're not going to be here, surely it wouldn't make the slightest difference where I am? I know I can't travel just yet, but when Dr Stamforth says I'm fit ... oh, please, could I go back to Mia-Mia?'

At her words his heart sank like a stone. So much for his conceited assumption it might be him she was lonely for! But if she wanted so badly to go back to Mia-Mia then it would be cruel of him to prevent her.

He straightened, looking down at her. She was just a shadow of her old self, pale and fragile with dark shadows beneath her blue eyes. But she had never stirred his blood more than she did at that moment.

'Very well,' he said gruffly. 'If that's what you

want, I have no objection. Provided, of course, that Stamforth has given his approval – for both you and the baby.'

She nodded. 'Thank you, Brett,' she whispered.

But the tears still stung her eyes and the emptiness still ached within her. He had said she could go home – the very thing she had longed for. Yet, perversely, the fact that he had acceded so quickly to her request stung painfully. He did not, then, mind that she would not be here on his return. It did not trouble him one jot. And why should it?

'One other thing – make certain that Henry Stanton comes down himself to escort you,' Brett continued smoothly. 'Foolhardy you might be, my love, but I don't want to expose my son to the dangers of the river road without a man to look after him. Do you understand?'

'Yes,' Erin murmured, turning away.

Oh yes, she understood very well!

Three weeks later Dr Stamforth pronounced Erin fit to travel, and arrangements were made for Henry Stanton to come to Sydney so as to escort her back to Mia-Mia.

'I don't want to go – I'd much prefer to stay here in Sydney!' Grianne said, and Erin could not find the strength to argue with her. If he wanted her out of the house, Brett would no doubt deal with the matter when he got home. If he didn't...

It was a bright, shimmery day when Henry arrived in the wagon to drive her up river and she settled herself with William in the rear seat, prepared to enjoy every moment of the journey.

But before they had gone too far clouds obscured the sun and Henry urged the horse forward.

'Looks like the rains are going to begin afore long,' he said in his short way.

Erin said nothing, but she tucked William more tightly into the crook of her arm. She hated the spring rains, when the deluge fell day after day until the ground was sodden and the river rose to a swirling brown torrent. There would be no fear of flooding at Mia-Mia, thanks be, as there had been at Kinvarra – sensibly it had been built well above the reach of even the fiercest flood, and the fields where the spring crops were planted were above the house. But that did nothing to allay the fear that troubled her when she thought about it, for her fears were imprinted too deeply within her from the years when she had been the daughter of a poor settler.

Even now she could remember too clearly for comfort the first time she had seen the river in flood – the way it had suddenly shown a side to its nature that was full of menace – and she had stood on a high point on the bank, clutching her father's hand and watching it rush by below, carrying with it all the flotsam and jetsam it had accumulated along its raging course – branches of trees, the carcasses of animals caught unawares, even a few sticks of furniture.

Though it was the same almost every year, she had never become used to it. It was like seeing a good friend suddenly become a dangerous

240

enemy that could destroy everything within its path, she thought. But to say so to Henry Stanton would sound foolish and fanciful. A man such as he would never understand.

Beneath Henry's urging the horse surged forward and the rain was still no more than the first threatening drops when they reached the gates of Mia-Mia. As the wagon turned into the drive Erin could hardly contain her longing to see Patrick and Brenna again, and before they had gone far the front door flew open and her little sister appeared, running to meet them so eagerly that Erin was afraid she might run beneath the horse's hooves.

'Brenna – steady!' she warned, but as soon as the wagon came to rest the child clambered in, throwing herself at Erin and almost suffocating William.

'Oh Erin, Erin, I've missed you so!'

'And I've missed you too, darling. But don't squash your poor nephew! Look, what do you think of him?'

'Oh!' Brenna cried, enraptured. 'Oh Erin, he's just beautiful! Can I hold him – please?'

Erin freed an arm to give Brenna a huge hug.

'Presently!' she laughed. 'Give us time to catch our breath!'

'I'd get indoors if I was you, before the storm breaks,' Henry advised.

With the baby in her arms, Erin rose awkwardly and climbed down from the wagon. Already, she thought, she was missing Lucy Slack's assistance and she wished she had thought to ask Brett before he left if Lucy could come to Mia-

Mia with her. Lucy had been upset at the parting, too, and Erin doubted whether anyone at Mia-Mia knew as much as she did about babies. However, there would be plenty of time for her to join them as William's nurse when Brett got back from his voyage, and for the moment Erin did not intend to let anything mar her home-coming.

'Where's Patrick?' she asked Brenna when they reached the veranda with no sign of her brother.

Brenna shrugged her shoulders gaily.

'I couldn't say. He goes off by himself a lot.'

'He hasn't run away again, has he?' Erin asked in alarm.

'No, I don't think so. Though he says he's going to,' Brenna told her matter-of-factly. 'And he promised to take me with him, too.'

Erin swung round.

'What?' When did he tell you that, Brenna?'

'He says it all the time,' Brenna supplied. 'I don't know if he will, though. Mr Stanton was very cross with him last time. He took the strap to him.'

'Yes, I heard about that,' Erin returned grimly, but Brenna's fleeting attention had wandered. All she was interested in at present was baby William, who seemed to her better than any new toy. Happily, she danced on into the house in front of Erin.

'Come on! Come inside, *please*!' she begged and, laughing, Erin put her worries aside and followed.

* * *

242

The rains came in earnest, pouring relentlessly from a leaden sky, and there was a feel of damp everywhere. Erin worried ceaselessly about whether William's sheets were properly dried, and wished again and again that she had thought to ask to bring Lucy Slack with her. None of the convict women here at Mia-Mia seemed to know the first thing about babies, though they all tried to improve their status in the household by vying for the position of nursemaid.

One afternoon, when she had been back three days, Erin managed to snatch a quiet moment to talk to Patrick, and knowing that, dreamy as he was, it was no use to beat about the bush, she immediately raised the subject of his running away.

'Why did you do it, Patrick?' she asked gently. 'What good did you think it would do?'

Patrick shrugged unhappily. 'I didn't mean to cause trouble, Erin. But I thought if I could find work somewhere I could support us and we wouldn't have to be dependent on Brett Wilde any more.'

Erin bit her lip.

'I know how you feel, Patrick, but there's no need for you to, really,' she said softly. 'He's my husband, remember, and he's quite happy to provide for you, Brenna and Grianne until you're older. Why, I thought you understood, if you would only learn from Henry Stanton, you would be able to take on Kinvarra later on. With some labourers to help you it would soon be a profitable farm again. But you can't do that unless you learn how.'

Patrick did not look at her, but she could see the unhappiness in his face.

'What is it, Patrick?' she asked.

'I don't feel like a farmer,' he replied slowly. 'I don't want to farm Kinvarra, or anywhere else.'

'But I thought you loved it!' she protested.

He kicked at the leg of the chair. 'I do. I loved it as my home, when we were all there. But I wouldn't know where to begin working the land, however hard I studied Henry Stanton's lessons – and he's not that eager to teach me, I can tell you.'

Erin sighed.

'Oh, Patrick! But I still don't see what you hoped to gain by running away.'

The boy moved restlessly. 'I thought I might find work somewhere to suit me. As I said, I've got to support the others if not you, Erin. It's my fault, after all, that we're in this position.'

'What do you mean?' Erin said sharply.

'What I say. It's my fault.' Patrick's face was dark, the misery and guilt written there all too clearly. 'I was supposed to be watching that night when the convicts came. If I'd done my job properly perhaps none of this would have happened.'

'But that's foolish, Patrick!' Erin began, but the boy interrupted her.

'No, Erin, it's the truth. I've had to live with it, every day, knowing that because of me Father is dead, you're married to a man you despise, and we're all living on his charity.'

'That's not true!' Erin protested. 'You mustn't feel that way, Patrick. I don't blame you, and

244

neither do Grianne or Brenna. So you must stop blaming yourself. As for Brett...' Her voice tailed away. How could she explain to him her change of heart? She could hardly explain it to herself. 'Patrick, when Brett comes home I'll tell him how you feel,' she promised. 'He may be able to suggest something. He has so many people working for him in so many different capacities I'm sure he's bound to have some ideas.'

'I don't want his help,' Patrick said stubbornly. But Erin touched his arm.

'Try him, Patrick. You may find he is not the ogre you think him,' she said gently.

But Patrick only shrugged. 'I'll think about it, Erin,' he said, and she knew that for the moment that was the most she could expect.

The days passed, the rains continued, and Erin's life fell into a routine. There was so much to do looking after William she had little time for brooding, either about Patrick or her own future with Brett. And as the river rose higher and higher, filled to overflowing with the endless torrent that streamed down from the leaden skies, Erin discovered to her amazement that Mia-Mia was regarded as a haven by those whose own homes were in danger of flooding. They began arriving at the door asking for shelter, and before she could turn around there were three families beside her own sharing the accommodation the 'big house' could provide.

'It happens every time the river bursts its banks,' Henry Stanton told her. 'They come and stay as long as they can, getting something for nothing.'

Although she had lived a long while on the river, Erin was amazed by their audacity. She would have died, she thought, before she would have imposed herself on Brett's hospitality this way, and privately she labelled them 'scroungers'. They ate Brett's food, they slept in Brett's beds, and all with an air of graceless resentment and a determination to squeeze the last ounce of charity from Mia-Mia. Worst of all, they patted and poked at William as if they owned him, trying to buy her favour by cooing over her baby.

'I'm certain they would be less ready to put on us so if Brett were here,' Erin decided. 'At least he would keep them in their place as I cannot.' But Brett was not here, and as mistress of Mia-Mia it fell to her to keep up the pretence of hospitality even though beneath her cool exterior she boiled with indignation.

One morning, when the river was so high it threatened to swamp the whole of the road, cutting Mia-Mia off from the rest of the world, Erin saw a horseman riding up the drive.

More refugees! she thought wearily, but as horse and rider came nearer she realized this was no farmer seeking shelter but an officer of the New South Wales Corps.

At once her heart began to beat a tattoo and her imagination worked overtime. A Corps officer could sometimes mean trouble or bad tidings – and to be riding this way in weather such as this must surely show his mission was of some importance.

By the time she reached the kitchen he was already inside, dripping rain onto the floor and gratefully drinking from a cup that Patrick, who happened to be there, had offered him. As Erin entered the room his eyes narrowed appreciatively, running swiftly over her body, now returned to its former trim shapeliness, her neck, white and smooth after the long winter, and the inviting curve of her breasts above her low-cut gown. Erin, however, scarcely noticed his attention.

'Why are you here?' she asked sharply.

The half-smile froze on his mouth, then, as the fear in her eyes conveyed her meaning, he relaxed once more.

'Oh, I'm just passing, Mrs Wilde, on my way upriver and I thought to avail myself for a brief time of your hospitality. 'Tis cold and wet riding today, but a junior officer such as myself has little choice but to do as his superiors command.'

Erin's breath came out on a sigh.

'I see. For a moment I was afraid you might be the bearer of bad news. With my husband away at sea it is all too easy to fear the worst.'

The officer put down his cup, rubbing some life into his wet, numbed hands.

'Strangely enough I *can* give you news of your husband,' he said with a smile. 'His ship is the *Amber Fawn*, is it not? I saw it anchoring this morning in Sydney as I left.'

'You mean he's home?' Erin's heart leaped wildly and her pulses began to race once more, but this time in anticipation and joy. If Brett was

247

in Sydney, then it would surely not be long before he came to Mia-Mia! Though, knowing him, he would want to deal with his cargo first, finding buyers for the larger items and booking the rest into the stockroom at the store. And if he delayed too long, the river road could well be underwater, keeping him away until the rains stopped.

'I'm glad I could bring you good tidings,' the officer said, smiling at his thoughts. The colour that had risen in her cheeks had made her more desirable than ever and the gleam in his eye gave clear notice he considered Brett Wilde a lucky man indeed. But his reaction went unnoticed by Erin; her excitement blinded her to it, just as it blinded her to the black look that settled on Patrick's features.

'Brett home!' she repeated softly, and it was only when the door slammed that she turned to see that Patrick had left the kitchen. For a second his reaction made a small dent in her happiness, but it passed almost as quickly as it had come. Given the opportunity, Patrick would learn to overcome his mistrust of Brett just as she had done. She was certain of it. And now the opportunity was almost with them...

In a happy daze she saw the young officer on his way and to her surprise she found not even the lazy, inquisitive refugees could annoy her so much today. She hardly noticed them as she set to work organizing the convict women to cook, clean and tidy the house, for she wanted everything to be perfect when Brett finally rode up the drive to Mia-Mia.

When lunch was served, Patrick did not put in an appearance, but she did not worry too much. She knew he hated sharing his meal with the uncouth scroungers as much as she did, and as she doled out bowlfuls of steaming soup which they accepted greedily and without a word of thanks, she had little time for worrying about him. But when they had all dispersed and there was still no sign of him poking his head around the door in search of his share she began to be anxious.

'Have you seen Patrick?' she asked Brenna, but her little sister shook her head.

'No. He went up to his room when the soldier came but I don't think he's there now.'

'I'll go and see,' Erin decided.

She hurried up the sweeping staircase and pushed open the door of the room Patrick had used since coming to Mia-Mia. It was very much a young man's room, littered with the little wood carvings Patrick made to occupy his time when the weather was too bad to go out of doors. But today the room was empty and Erin was about to close the door again when a sheet of white paper pushed under the edge of the dressing table mirror caught her eye.

A small stab of foreboding made her catch her breath and she crossed to the mirror, jerking out the paper. Then, as the words leaped out at her from the page her blood seemed to turn to ice.

'If Brett Wilde is coming home, I don't want to be here,' the boy had written. 'Don't come after me, Erin. When I come back it will be because I am able to take care of all of you as I should. Your loving brother, Patrick.'

CHAPTER SIXTEEN

The words blurred before Erin's eyes and she clutched at the edge of the dressing table for support.

'Oh Patrick, you fool!' she whispered thickly. 'What are you trying to prove?'

'What is it, Erin? What's the matter?'

Startled, Erin looked round to see Brenna standing behind her. She had not heard the child come in on slippered feet and now she stood watching Erin with an anxious frown puckering her forehead.

'It's Patrick,' Erin said sharply. 'He's run away again.'

'Oh no! No, I don't believe you!' Brenna cried.

'Well, it's true, whether you believe it or not!' Erin snapped, angry as she often was when too much responsibility settled onto her shoulders.

'But he promised if he went again he'd take me with him!' wailed Brenna. But Erin scarcely heard her. Her mind was too busy with wondering how far Patrick would have got by this time – and how she was going to tell Henry Stanton that he had gone. The overseer would be furious, she knew.

Without stopping to reply to her sister she hurried out of the room and down the stairs. It was still raining, not so hard now, but still a steady downpour, and it blew miserably into her face as she crossed the yard to the stables.

Inside the horses shifted, restless for lack of exercise, but Erin pushed aside their thrusting noses, searching anxiously to see which one was missing. Then she drew a tight breath. Her father's horse Bess was not here. No one but Patrick would take Bess. And on the great black mare he would have got a good start, rain or no rain.

'Who's there?' a voice called from the doorway and Erin recognized the gruff tones of Henry Stanton. What an ear the man had for anything even slightly out of place! The last time Erin had seen him he had been up at the pens on the high ground where the livestock had been shifted for the duration of the flood; now he must have been passing the stable on his way back to the house and heard her moving about inside.

'It's me,' she said, emerging from the dim stall. 'Patrick's gone again – and it looks as if he's riding Bess. We'll need really fast horses to catch up with him. If I take Starlight...'

'No!' Henry Stanton's tone was as gruff as ever and he stood blocking her path to Starlight's stall.

She gathered herself up.

'What do you mean, no?'

'I mean I can't allow you to go anywhere, Mrs Wilde. With the river as high as it is it's too dangerous for you.'

Erin stared, horrified. 'But what about Patrick?'

'The young fool will have to look after himself. I thought after last time he would have learned his lesson. I won't risk men and horses going after him again. And I can't allow you to go, either.'

Anxiety for Patrick and fury at being spoken to in this way combined to raise Erin's temper.

'You seem to forget I'm the mistress here!' she said sharply.

But still Henry Stanton's stocky build blocked her path.

'That's as may be. But I work for Mr Wilde and I'm acting on his instructions to make sure you're looked after in his absence. This time you'll just have to let your brother go. He'll be back again, as like as not, when hunger begins to pinch his belly.'

'Oh!' Erin could have wept with frustration and anxiety but she realized the futility of arguing with Henry Stanton. He was quite capable of preventing her single-handed from taking a horse from the stables and if he chose he could be as stubbornly impossible as Brett himself. And without a horse she had no chance of catching up with Patrick. All she could hope was that the road he chose was well above the swirling river torrents and that when he was hungry enough he would come home as Henry Stanton had said.

If only Brett were here – he would know what to do! she thought, but deep inside she was sickeningly sure of Brett's answer. Today at any rate, it would be the same as that of his overseer – if Patrick was foolhardy enough to choose such a day to run away, then he must take his chances and endure the discomfort he would meet along the way.

But it wasn't easy for her to accept that sort of philosophy. He was, after all, her young brother and she was used to being responsible for him.

'Come along, Mrs Wilde, I'll see you safely back inside the house,' the overseer said firmly, taking her arm, and wretchedly Erin realized she had little choice but to do as she was bidden.

But as evening fell, and the lowering skies outside necessitated the early lighting of the lamps, she felt sick and heavy with worry.

Where was Patrick now? Was he holed up somewhere, soaked to the skin, shivering and hungry? Or was he pressing on, trusting Bess to ignore the dangers that were intensified a hundred times with the darkness?

The chatter of their uninvited guests and the hilarity of their children bore in on her now until she wanted to scream, and when William began to cry earlier than usual to be fed she even felt out of patience with him for once. At last she sought sanctuary in the kitchen, glad that now there were extra mouths to feed the convict women who worked there resented her presence less. They had relaxed, in any case, since they had discovered she did not want to move in and change their ways of doing everything, and today the air of sympathy with which they treated her told Erin they had got wind of Patrick's fresh disappearance.

During the afternoon the rain had eased to a misty drizzle, but just before dinner was ready to be served Henry Stanton came in and told them with a black look that he and the other men were going to have to go downriver on an errand of mercy – yet another house had been swallowed up by the swelling river and the occupants had been forced to climb to the roof to escape being drowned.

At his words, Erin shivered violently. In all her years on the river she had never known things to reach this pass before, and a feeling of nightmarish inevitability was beginning to pervade all her senses. Suppose the rain continued for another week – what then? Not even Mia-Mia would be safe and certainly not Kinvarra. The thought of flood waters swirling through the little farmhouse she had loved so dearly was almost more than she could bear. It was the last desecration, somehow, of all her mother and father had done here, and as bad almost as having Patrick missing...

Patrick ... Kinvarra! The thoughts came together suddenly inside Erin's head. Perhaps Patrick had gone to Kinvarra! What he could hope to gain from it she did not know but it could be he would think of it as a haven for the time being at least if he was unwilling to be at Mia-Mia when Brett came home.

The idea comforted her a little. It was something to hold on to. If Patrick was at Kinvarra, at least he would be safe, dry and warm. And tomorrow, when it was light, she would persuade Henry Stanton to let her ride over and see.

Cheered somewhat, she finished her preparations for the evening meal and asked one of the women to call all the children in to eat. But when they came trooping through the door, ravenous as usual, she noticed her small sister was not with them.

'Where's Brenna?' she asked, but no one seemed to know, and Erin despatched Becky Mabberley, one of the older girls, to look for her while she served cold meat onto the dozen or so plates.

A few minutes later, as the hungry horde began to eat, Becky came back alone.

'I can't find her,' she announced cheerfully. 'She's nowhere in the house.'

'But she must be!' Erin protested.

'No, she ain't,' Becky reiterated. 'I've looked everywhere.'

'You can't possibly *know* everywhere,' Erin retorted, irritated. 'You've only been here a week or so.'

'Long enough,' came the reply. 'She ain't in the house, I tell you.'

Small prickles began to raise themselves on the back of Erin's neck. If Brenna was not in the house, where was she?

'She's gone out to look at the animals in their pens, like as not,' Emily Mabberley, Becky's mother, said in answer to her unspoken question.

'Go and look,' Erin commanded Becky and a couple of the boys, but the trembling did not leave her and she was not in the least surprised when they returned to say they could see no sign of Brenna outside either. Brenna wouldn't have gone to the temporary pens, Erin knew. She was not at all interested in cattle or sheep – they were no novelty to her – and she would not have gone to the stables, either. No, there was only one suspicion niggling at the back of Erin's mind and gaining strength with every passing moment, and that was too terrifying a one to acknowledge. Yet for all that she did not even want to think of it, Brenna's wail of anguish when she had learned that Patrick had gone away kept drumming in Erin's ears and again and again she seemed to hear her sister's words: 'But he promised he'd take me with him!'

Murmuring some excuse to the others, Erin ran up the stairs to Brenna's room. Even now she was hoping desperately she might find her little sister there, hiding because she was upset by Patrick's disappearance. But when she pushed open the door and saw it was deserted the most sickening sensation of history repeating itself washed over her and a gasp escaped her lips as she saw a sheet of paper pushed under the dressing table mirror in exactly the same way as Patrick's note had been. With nerveless fingers she picked it up, already knowing what it would say, and the childish capitals leaped up at her.

'GONE TO LOOK FOR PATRICK. DON'T
WORRY. LOVE, BRENNA'

Erin's hand went to her throat. So she had been right! Brenna had copied the brother she adored even to the detail of the note and she had gone to try and catch up with him to be taken along with him as he had promised her. But sweet Jesus, there was no chance she would find him – none!

And outside the night was wild and dangerous with the river that could sweep away horses and cattle swirling darkly almost at their very door.

The room seemed to sway around Erin as the horrifying pictures danced before her eyes. She had been worried about Patrick, yes, but he was on the way to being a grown man who had been raised on the river and knew its moods. But Brenna was just a little girl. And how long had she been missing? Frantically Erin thought back to the last time she had seen her, not long after her discovery that Patrick had gone. It had still been daylight then, now it was almost dark. And somewhere out there Brenna's nerve would be failing her and she would be stumbling about in terror, surrounded by rain and darkness and swirling floodwater!

Erin ran to the window, her eyes raking the wild night, but there was no sign of human life in the rain-wet foliage and all too clearly she could hear the roar of the river. Never before had she heard it this clearly, and her blood ran cold as she imagined it rushing angrily along, taking with it everything in its path. Would Brenna go too close to it? Would it have encroached upon the road by now? Might she lose her balance and fall within reach of its angry torrents?

The nightmarish horrors shocked Erin into action. Brenna must be found – and found before it was properly dark. Once the inky blackness of night fell upon the river she would be in mortal danger. But Henry Stanton and all the able-bodied men on Mia-Mia had ridden off to help stranded settlers and Patrick was gone too. There were only the women to help her find her little sister – and for the first time Erin was grateful they were here.

Pausing only to snatch a wrap from her wardrobe she ran downstairs and into the room where the refugees sat tucking into the meal she had provided for them. They looked up curiously at her hasty entrance, but continued to eat greedily.

'My sister's gone,' Erin said, fighting to keep her voice from rising hysterically. 'Could some of you come and help me look for her, please, before it gets too dark?'

Eight pairs of eyes regarded her narrowly but not one person moved from the table.

'Don't you understand what I'm saying?' Erin repeated shrilly. 'Brenna's somewhere out there! I've got to find her and I can't do it alone.'

'You'd best wait till the men gets back,' Lizzie Cruse, a dark-haired slattern, told her calmly, and Erin's rage exploded.

'If we wait it may be too late!' she stormed. 'Either you come and help me look, Lizzie Cruse, or you can take your children and your belongings and go back where you came from, flood or no flood. There'll be no more hospitality here for you, I promise.'

'I just don't see the sense of it,' Lizzie complained, moving reluctantly, but Erin was no longer listening. She set the light to three lanterns, passing one to Lizzie, one to Emily Mabberley, Becky's mother, and taking the third herself.

'We'll spread out,' she instructed. 'You two look along the road to Kinvarra. I'll go towards

258

Sydney. Take care. It may be flooded in places. But be warned. We're not giving up until we find her.'

The women were muttering together, but she ignored them.

'If by chance she should come back, keep her here,' she instructed those left as the possibility occurred to her.

'Suppose she doesn't want to be found?' Emily queried. 'She could be anywhere.'

'Now it's getting dark, she's probably sheltering somewhere, frightened half to death. It won't seem such a great adventure to her now. So call till you're hoarse, do you hear?'

As they went out into the stormy night Erin strained her ears hoping to hear the sounds that would herald the return of the men, but apart from the wind in the trees and the ominous roar of the river all was quiet. Swinging her lantern from side to side she hurried down the drive, not waiting for the others, and her voice, as she called Brenna's name, seemed to be swallowed up by the wild night. Branches lashed at her face and soon the other bobbing lanterns were left far behind; but, too afraid for Brenna to be frightened herself, she ran on.

As she neared the road the roar of the river grew even louder, so that it seemed to fill her head with its thundering voice. But it was misty here on the lower ground, a thick, swirling blanket that hid the river and most of the road from view.

Erin hesitated, biting anxiously at her lips. She had not expected river mist to add to her problems and though she hated looking at the swirling currents and the carcasses they bore along with them, at least that was preferable to only hearing – and smelling. She wrinkled her nose as the stench of rotting flotsam reached her, then once more she quickened her step, calling Brenna's name again and again.

There was no water on the road where it joined the drive to Mia-Mia, but Erin knew from driving along it on many occasions that it passed a high point just here. Further along, in the direction of Sydney, there was more than one dip, and there, if anywhere, the river would have encroached.

Pulling her wrap more closely around her she hurried on, still calling, though her voice seemed to be thrown back at her by the mist. All the while she looked this way and that, straining her eyes into the fog and trying not to think of what might have befallen Brenna. If she allowed herself to really visualize the dangers, she would scream and scream and never stop, Erin knew. So she stumbled on, automatically following the only path she knew. Once or twice she twisted her ankle in a pothole and almost fell but it was only when she approached what she knew to be the first real dip that she slowed down, going cautiously and calling at the top of her voice to make herself heard above the raging of the water.

Halfway down and she knew her worst fears had been realized – the road was under water. How deep it was she did not know, but as she felt it swirling about her ankles she wondered

260

just how long it would be before Mia-Mia was completely cut off. Not long, judging by the rate at which the river was rising. That meant the men may have difficulty in getting back. Worse, if she went further on foot she might not be able to get back herself, and with William left behind at Mia-Mia that was something she dared not risk. Yet she *must* go on – she *must* find Brenna! She would never forgive herself if she did not do everything within her power to find her little sister and bring her safely home.

The first helpless tears of indecision stung her eyes and angrily she brushed them away.

Just a little further, she thought. Keeping to the side of the track that was farthest from the river she edged through the water, shivering as her dress clung wetly to her legs, but inching on. Then suddenly she stopped, her heart seeming almost to stop beating.

There was something in the bushes on the lower side of the road – as the mist lifted momentarily she caught sight of it for a moment, though it was now almost obscured once more.

'Brenna!' she called frantically, but there was no reply above the roaring of the water. 'Brenna!'

The heart that had almost stopped beating was thudding a tattoo against her ribs now as if to protest at the shock it had been given, and Erin held her shawl tight around her heaving chest. There was something there – she was sure of it! Could it be that her little sister had climbed into the crook of a tree out of reach of the water and become marooned? Perhaps now she had fainted, or fallen asleep there from sheer exhaustion – Erin did not dare consider any other possibility.

Bracing herself, she took a step towards the centre of the road, then another and another. As she neared the lower side, the water was deeper and the currents seemed to drag at her, but fixing her eyes on the spot she had seen the object she struggled on. Once her foot struck a boulder and she almost fell, another step and a pothole threatened to throw her off balance. And it was so dark and misty! If she could have seen properly it would not have been so bad.

Almost sobbing with the effort she reached the far side of the road, reaching out with her hands to grasp an overhanging branch and desperately looking around her.

Now – had the currents taken her downstream from where she had seen the object? She was not sure, but she thought they must have done.

Struggling against the water and hanging onto the overhanging branches for support she pulled herself slowly back upstream. She had no breath left for calling now – she could only hope if Brenna was near she would call out herself.

Suddenly, as she struggled, the mist parted once more and she had another glimpse of what she had seen before, much closer now, and disappointment rose to choke her. It wasn't Brenna, or anything like her – it was just a piece of light-coloured cloth caught in the branches. And yet...

Supposing it was her cloak! Erin thought, unable somehow after her supreme effort to let the idea go. She took one more step, holding out her lantern with one hand and grabbing at the branches with the other. But at that moment a log, or some heavy object being carried along by the flood, struck her legs, and the swirling eddies took the uncertain ground from beneath her feet. Her cry was drowned in the rushing of the water; crazily she grabbed out with both hands at the branches to prevent herself from being swept away and the lantern smashed against a tree trunk and went out. For a moment it seemed the water would take her, then her outstretched hand encountered scratchy bark and, heedless of her torn skin, she held on for dear life, while small sobs of fear broke in her throat.

As the confusion gradually subsided a new sort of panic threatened Erin – a panic for her own safety. Until now she had thought of nothing but the danger to Brenna. Now she realized for the first time that she, too, could be drowned. The thought shocked her – never before had she come so close to realizing that death did not only happen to others. And she did not want to die! Why, she had hardly begun living! What would happen to William if she should not return? And Brett ... she would never have the chance of trying to make him love her...

With an effort, Erin pushed the panic to the back of her mind. She could not stay here, she knew. Already the water was deepening, for although the rain had eased there was still so much to come down from the mountains. But to get back to the safe side of the road she would have to let go of her branch and once more abandon herself to the swirling currents. And her strength was beginning to fail. Her legs were tired and numbed and she was beginning to feel giddy. She couldn't make it just yet, but neither could she wait.

Her head singing, she clung to the tree while the water rushed by around her. She must think! She must! But thinking did not seem to help, and now...

Her lip held tight between her teeth, Erin cocked her head to one side, listening. The noise of the river was different than before, splashing, thundering. What was it? For a moment or two her numbed brain could not seem to work it out, then, all at once, she knew. Someone was coming! Someone was riding a horse along the road through the floodwater! There was a chance for her even now, if only she could make them hear her!

'Help me!' Erin shouted, but her words seemed only to echo around her head in the swirling mist.

Suppose the rider did not hear her? Suppose he should pass so close and never know she was there! But she could not trust her legs to support her any longer. Gathering all her remaining strength she shouted again: 'Help me! Oh, please – help me!'

The splashing came closer and faster. The mist broke slightly and she saw the figure of horse and rider. For a second she thought she was hallucinating. It couldn't be ... surely...

'Help me!' she cried yet again.

Then, as the dark world swam around her,

strong arms caught at her, lifting her from the knee-deep water, and as she felt the saddle beneath her she fell, with a sob, against the hard shoulder of Brett Wilde.

CHAPTER SEVENTEEN

'Erin, in God's name...!'

Brett's voice was almost lost in the roar of the water and for a moment Erin let her head rest against his wet jacket, relief almost overwhelming her. Then she levered herself away again, her breath coming in harsh sobs.

'Brenna's out here somewhere! She's run away! Oh Brett, we must find her!'

'*What*?' Brett's fingers bit into her arm. 'What are you talking about?'

'Patrick's run away again and Brenna's gone after him. I found her missing at dinner. Henry Stanton and the men were all out on rescue work. I've been searching and searching, but it's no use. I can't find her. Oh, Brett, I'm so frightened...' The words came tumbling out between her chattering teeth.

Brett's arms tensed around her as he pulled on the reins and she felt his horse begin to move forward in a crablike motion as the currents swirled about his feet.

'Brett – where are we going?' she cried.

'I'm taking you home. We can hardly stay here, can we?' His voice sounded brusque.

She caught at his coat, her nails digging into the cloth.

'But Brenna's out here somewhere I tell you! We must find her!'

He did not answer, concentrating on steering his horse through the floodwater to the higher ground and she beat at him helplessly with her hands.

'We can't leave her here! She'll be drowned! Listen to me, Brett!'

'Be quiet!' he ordered her. 'There's nothing you can do.'

'But...'

'Ride quietly, I say, or you'll frighten the horse.'

The tears came, blurring her eyes and running in hot rivers down her cheeks. He was heartless! Heartless! How could he leave Brenna out here alone? She would never forgive him – never!

As they gained the higher ground Brett urged Jack to a gallop, and, numbed as she was, Erin was forced to cling on for dear life. The roar of the water receded a little and before she knew it they were in the drive to Mia-Mia. Here, above the river, there was no mist. The lights of the house shone out welcomingly into the dark night and on the veranda she saw two bright bobbing arcs she recognized as lanterns.

'The other women – perhaps they found her!' she gasped. But as they drew closer she saw the way the women shrank back awkwardly, and knew they had not.

'Oh, Brenna, my little love!' she whispered brokenly.

Outside the house Brett brought Jack to a halt and dismounted, lifting Erin down to stand

267

beside him.

'Are Henry and the others back?' he asked the women.

They shook their heads. 'No. And we couldn't get anywhere, Mrs Wilde. The road's flooded between here and Kinvarra. We couldn't get through.'

'I don't suppose you tried very hard!' Erin flared, but Brett silenced her.

'They're perhaps not so foolhardy as you, Madam. Would you have everyone at Mia-Mia drown themselves?'

'If it would find Brenna – yes!' Erin choked. 'She's just a baby! And if you were a man, Brett, you'd be out looking for her, not standing there lecturing me!'

Brett's jaw tightened.

'I'm going to look for her, Erin, as soon as I have a fresh horse – and when I've established where she might be. There's no sense in charging about aimlessly on a night like this. Have you any idea where she might have gone?'

'She said she was following Patrick, that's all.' Erin was shivering violently now, so much so it was difficult to form the words. 'That's all I know. Unless...'

'Unless what?' he pressed her.

'I did wonder if Patrick might have gone to Kinvarra. Perhaps Brenna might have done the same.'

Brett nodded sharply.

'It's a good, sound thought. If I can get through where those women could not I'll check the farm – and the road that leads to it. And now,

Erin, will you get into the house and change out of those wet clothes before you catch your death of cold. Go on, now. Do as I say.'

He caught at Jack's bridle, leading him in the direction of the stable and she stood watching him go, too tired to care that the refugee women had heard the exchange between them, but still too worried to do as she was bidden and go meekly into the house to change although she was chilled to the marrow.

What chance had he of finding Brenna? she wondered wearily, and the overwhelming desolation seemed to shout the answer back at her. No chance. Not even Brett could find the child on a dark, wild night such as this. No, not even if he took Henry Stanton and all the men on Mia-Mia with him...

'Mrs Wilde...' Lizzie Cruse was approaching her tentatively and the thought of having to converse with the stupid slattern who was no doubt lapping up every moment of her troubles moved Erin where Brett's command could not.

'Not now, Mrs Cruse,' she said shortly, turning away to hide the tears that were once more threatening, but before she had gone a step, Emily Mabberley's voice brought her up sharp.

'Mrs Wilde, look! Look – oh, praise be!'

At her shout Erin swung round, then her hands flew to her mouth, stifling a gasp. Coming across the yard were two figures – one, the tall, unmistakable figure of Brett, the other a slight form that did not even reach up to his chest, whose head hung miserably and whose shoulders were hunched in an attitude of self-protection.

'Brenna!' Erin cried. Picking up her dripping skirts she ran across the yard towards them. 'Brenna! Oh, thank God!'

She bent to catch her sister in her arms and hold her close. Then, puzzled, she drew back, looking at her.

'But you're not wet, Brenna! You're bone dry! Where have you been?'

Brenna's face was tearstained; now her mouth puckered once more and she turned her head away.

'She was in the stables,' Brett informed her. 'While you were scouring the countryside, risking your life looking for her, this little madam was hiding in the stables. I've just found her there now. If I hadn't stopped to change horses I could have been off on a wild goose chase too. Why didn't you search the place properly, Erin, before raising Cain this way?'

'I – I sent the children to look outside,' Erin stuttered, as surprised by his attack as by the reappearance of Brenna. 'And she said in her note she was going. Why did you do it, Brenna?' she questioned the little girl.

'He went without me.' Brenna rubbed a grimy hand across her tear-wet face. 'Patrick's gone off without me. I went to get a horse to follow him, but I couldn't get the saddle on. And I could hear the river and I was frightened...'

'Well, you'd better realize the trouble you've caused!' Brett told her angrily and his tone sent her into a fresh spasm of weeping.

'Oh, leave her be!' Erin cried, putting her arms

270

around the little girl's shaking shoulders. 'Can't you see, she's upset enough without you making it worse.'

'So she should be upset!' Brett said coldly. 'As for you, Madam, I told you to get indoors and out of those wet clothes before you catch your death of cold. Perhaps you don't care if you depart this world and leave your child motherless. But while he's young and helpless, *I* do care!'

Erin's eyes widened. She opened her mouth to reply but no words would come and she stood for a moment staring at him speechless. She should know by now there was only one thing on his mind – his son and heir. But it could still hurt her – oh, it could still hurt!

She tightened her grip on Brenna's shoulder, lifting her chin and averting her eyes from his gaze.

'Come, Brenna. I'll take you inside.'

His voice followed her.

'Then leave her to one of the women and get out of those wet things *at once*, Erin!' he commanded.

In the hallway she gave Brenna a push in the direction of the kitchen.

'Go along, do as Brett says,' she managed, but the words were choking her and though she held her head high as she climbed the stairs, turmoil was seething within her.

How dare he speak to her that way, especially in front of their visitors? How dare he order her about as if she were a servant – or a convict? But then, Brett cared for nothing and nobody. He

271

was quite insufferable. And it was her misfortune that she should not only be married to him, but that somewhere along the way she had also been careless enough to fall in love...

She stood in the centre of the bedroom, her fingers making tight knots of anger in the wet fabric of her dress. When she heard the door open she swung around, her eyes blazing fire.

'You're heartless, Brett!' she flung at him. 'When are you going to stop using us all?'

A muscle tightened in his cheek, but he closed the door before replying.

'I wasn't aware I was using you, Erin. I would rather have thought the boot was on the other foot. I have given a home to your brother and sister and so far they have caused me nothing but trouble. I returned to Sydney to find Grianne entertaining her circle of friends in my house; Patrick, it would seem, has caused havoc here by taking it into his head to run off yet again; and Brenna very nearly cost you your life. And you have the insolence to say *I* am using *you*!'

Erin had the grace to look a little shamefaced, but knowing Brett was right in this respect at least did nothing to alter her feelings.

'How could you speak to me so in front of those horrible women?' she cried.

Brett shrugged. 'In my own house I shall speak as I like. Besides, it's the only way to get through your thick head.'

'What do you mean – thick head?' she squealed indignantly.

He had left his wet coat downstairs; now she saw him unbutton the collar of his shirt, massaging at his neck as if it was stiff from riding in the wind and rain.

'Every time my back is turned, it seems, you do something foolish,' he said nonchalantly. 'You seem intent on killing yourself, Erin, my love.'

The sight of him standing there stirred something within her, but the sudden stab of longing only fuelled her anger and made her reckless.

'And that would never do, would it, so long as William is young enough to need me,' she said bitterly. 'After he's old enough to put out to a nurse, I dare say I can do as I please.'

Brett froze, his hand tightening on the neck of his shirt.

'What did you say?' he demanded.

She laughed, a small, choking sound that seemed to catch in her throat. 'Oh, it's all right, Brett, you don't have to pretend with me. I know very well why you married me. It must be a very great trial to you, having to put up with my foolishness and all for the sake of your son. But I dare say you'll find a way to rid yourself of me as soon as he no longer needs me.'

Brett took a step towards her, his hands shooting out to grip her arms. 'Have you taken leave of your senses? Why should I rid myself of you?'

'Because you hate me!' She knew she sounded half-hysterical but now the words were tumbling out so fast there was no way she could stop them. 'You take every possible opportunity to make a fool of me. And you don't want me as your wife the way a husband should. When you're at home you sleep in the room next door with never a thought to me! You find your pleasure elsewhere, I suppose.' She tossed her head back and in the candlelight her eyes gleamed like sapphires above her flushed cheeks.

Dear Lord, if only she knew the truth! Brett thought, and her beauty stirred all his senses. A moment ago he had been angry with her for risking her life; now looking at her small, up-turned face with the black hair hanging in damp, curling strands around it, he was consumed with desire.

'Erin ... you're wrong,' he murmured thickly. 'There is no one else. There never has been from the moment I set eyes on you.'

'You expect me to believe that?' she cried. 'Why, I even offered you to come into my bed and you refused!'

His lips curved slightly. 'You, Erin? When was that?'

'When William was born. You know very well when.'

His smile broadened. Her beauty and spirit were exhilarating him as they always did. Oh, he remembered that night as she said – remembered too how he had wanted her, yet knew that for her well-being he must not take her. But for the moment he did not want to tell her that. He liked to see her eyes flashing with anger – liked to see the toss of her head.

'Do I?' he teased.

She tried to shake herself free of his grip.

'You're playing with me. I hate you, Brett!'

She had said it before and hurt him. Now, for

the first time, he looked beyond her words.

He pulled her closer to him so that the small, upturned face was directly below his.

'Do you know you're beautiful when you're angry?'

Her mouth puckered and he ached to kiss it. Instead he slid his hands around to the fastening of her dress. At once she jerked away.

'What are you doing?' she demanded.

'I told you to get out of these wet things. If you won't do it yourself, I must do it for you.'

'No!'

He saw the fear come into her eyes, felt the tensing of every muscle in her body. She was still afraid, then. In spite of herself, in spite of the passion he believed to be there, as potent as her temper, the fear the convict had begun in her still remained. His stomach churned with love for her.

'It's all right, my sweet,' he said, speaking softly as if to a child. 'I won't hurt you, I promise. And if I'm worried about you, it's not on William's account, whatever I may say. My concern, I assure you, is purely selfish.'

She hesitated, her eyes wary, and he went on:

'I wish to keep you safe for myself, Erin.'

'But ... you don't want me,' she whispered.

His hands on her arms were firm now but gentle.

'Come to me, my love, and let me show you how I want you.'

Beneath the urging of his hands she took a step towards him, still searching his face for any hint that even now he was deceiving her, teasing her, setting her up that he might hurt her once more. Instead she saw only strength in the features she had grown to love, and a desire so potent it made an answering desire dart deep within her.

'Brett...' she whispered.

One hand released her arm, moving to rest on the nape of her neck beneath the wetly curling hair. The touch of his fingers sent small shivers down her spine and her legs seemed to turn to liquid beneath her. Gently he urged her closer still until her toe ran against his boot and she put a hand onto his broad chest to steady herself. How hard it felt beneath her fingers, the muscle unyielding as a rock! Breath seemed suspended within her, and when she felt the touch of his lips on her forehead a tremor ran through her. She tipped her head back and saw the angular lines of his nose and jaw in sharp relief. Oh, the planes and shadows the candlelight cast! Oh, the tricks it could play, making his skin translucent bronze and his eyes liquid silver...

A small gasp escaped her, making her lips tremble like corn before a breeze. His breath was a whisper upon her cheek, a whisper that formed into words:

'I love you, Erin. You must believe that.'

From somewhere deep within her, the tiny spark of light fanned to a glow, sending rivers of warmth through all her veins.

'I love you, Erin. Believe me.'

'I do,' she murmured. 'I do.'

How could she not believe, when he held her this way, and the glow seemed to spread so that it no longer surrounded only her body, but his too? How could she not believe when they hung, suspended together in time? It was as if she was awake, suddenly, as she had never been awake before, every nerve in her body sharp and singing, with their nerve-endings reaching out to extend her. Yet the world seemed to have shrunk to a ball just large enough to encircle the two of them.

His arms were about her, holding her close, and the muscles of his back were taut beneath her exploring fingers. She moved her head to nestle into the crook between his shoulder and chin, then lifted it again as she realized his lips were seeking hers. Slowly, like pins to a magnet, they drew together, and the quiver of expectancy seemed to draw her soul from her body. Then, as their mouths touched and fused, all the waiting, all the tender realization of love, all the longing, exploded into a blaze to light the sky.

Her eager lips parted beneath the pressure of his mouth; she tasted him sweet and heady as she had never tasted him before. His hands were in her hair; as they tugged at the wet tangles she might have cried out, but she only twisted closer, for even the pain was exquisite.

His lips left hers, moving down her throat and she arched her back, unwilling to give up any part of him. Slowly, sensuously, his hands encompassed her, one moving over the tight-drawn lines from her waist to shoulder blades, the other seeking the curves of her breast.

She moaned as the small thrills of fire followed where his fingers touched and this time as he fumbled with the fastening of her gown she made no protest. What was it but a piece of stupid wet cloth that came between them? She wanted to be free of it, to press her body close to his, to feel him against her skin. The fastenings came away in his hands and as he pulled the gown down over her shoulders she wriggled her body to make it fall more easily.

She heard him groan then, an animal sound that might, only hours ago, have frightened her. No longer. Now it only exhilarated her, making her feel powerful and strong as well as desirable.

His arm slid down her bare back, coming to rest beneath her buttocks, then, with one swift, sure movement, he swung her up, carrying her bodily across the room to the bed. He knelt beside her, covering her body with kisses from the soft curve of her breasts to the valley between her legs and back again. As his lips brought every inch of her to sharp, singing awareness, she moaned softly, catching at his head and pulling it down hard between her breasts. But it was not enough. Her thighs moved restlessly while an aching longing grew deep in the most secret parts of her.

'Oh Brett, come to me!' she whispered.

He needed no second bidding. He straightened up and she reached out for his hands, unwilling to give up the touch of him and ridiculously afraid that this heaven might yet be suddenly snatched from her. She heard him laugh, low in his throat, a mixture of exultation and desire, and in the candlelight saw him rid himself of shirt, boots and breeches. As his form loomed over her she opened her arms to him, and felt his

278

hard, lean body mould itself to hers. His hands went beneath her, lifting her hips, and she spread her knees to accommodate the weight of him. As he slid between her legs she thought she would scream with the desire that surged within her and as he thrust deep into her she gasped softly with relief. Then it seemed the need was more pressing than ever, sweeping her along like the flooding river, drowning all her senses but the one that made her move in unison with the rhythmic working of his body, and swirling her further and further into the whirlpool of passion until at last, when she felt she would die of escalating need, it exploded in a myriad of sparkling light.

When it was over she lay stunned and breathless, basking in the warmth that seeped in where before there had been molten desire, and feeling the tremors that still ran through her deepest parts. Brett, too, lay motionless for a moment, then he rolled sideways to ease the weight from her slender body and she lay her face against his chest, tasting the salt of his moist skin and rubbing her nose in the matt of thick hair.

Briefly, through the blissful haze, she felt a stab of disquiet as she remembered that Patrick was still missing. What sort of a sister was she to be so happy when he could be in danger? But almost as soon as it was born she thrust the thought away. Patrick was almost a grown man. The time had come for her to allow him to make his own decisions – and respect them, whether she agreed with them or not. And he was no fool. He had lived on the river long enough to know its dangers and anticipate them. No doubt he had taken himself to safety before the flood became too serious. No, the time had come to allow Patrick to live his own life. Her first duty now was to Brett, her husband, and their child.

His hands ran the length of her back, lingering on the narrow flare of her hips and caressing her long, slim thighs. She lay with a smile curving her mouth, enjoying every touch.

'You see now how it can be?' Brett asked softly, against her hair. 'I knew from the first time I saw you we could reach the heights together, you and I. But it was no easy task convincing you!'

She stretched a little, luxuriating in the way her damp skin clung to Brett's.

'I had my baptism in a hard school,' she murmured. 'Forgive me, Brett. And forgive me for being so pig-headed and foolish.'

'No, I am the one who needs forgiving. I don't always stop to consider how my words and actions affect others, I'm afraid.' His hand cupped her breast, squeezing gently at its rosy tip. 'I could promise you to try to change, but I doubt it would do the slightest good. Tomorrow, with the best will in the world, I shall no doubt be as rude and surly as ever.'

She snuggled against him.

'And I shan't mind one bit. After all, I must be able to recognize the Brett I have come to know and love, mustn't I?'

There was the smallest pause.

'Love?' he said roughly.

'Of course. I thought you knew.'

280

He laughed, a small, gruff sound of relief.

'Why should doubts be the prerogative of the female of the species? If you love me, you have sometimes had an odd way of showing it.'

It was her turn to laugh. Her face felt rosy, her lips full.

'And that, my love, is something I will likely be as powerless to change as you.'

'Then while we're here, in harmony for once, I dare say we'd better make the most of it.'

Brett pulled her towards him and laughingly she wriggled free.

'Brett – no – the people downstairs – what will they think if we don't soon go down?'

'Really, my dear, I haven't the least idea. Nor do I care one jot!' he replied.

And for once, as she gave herself up to his arms, she felt only glad of his ability to disregard the opinions of the outside world.

CHAPTER EIGHTEEN

When she awoke next morning Erin saw that the sky above the mimosa trees was pale, washed-out blue, and she knew that the rains were over and spring was well and truly on the way.

It seemed to her like an omen, as if the storms had passed at the same moment their love had begun, and with every passing day it blossomed just as the yellow bloom on the trees spread and grew beneath the ever-strengthening sun.

Winter was over now, the river had receded, leaving only rich mud flats to show where it had been, and the families who had boarded themselves at Mia-Mia went home to plant their fields and count their livestock.

Erin thought it was impossible to remember a time when she had been happier. Brett, after such a long absence, found plenty to do organizing the farm, laying plans and checking accounts with Henry Stanton, so that for most of the time he was never far away from her sight. William grew daily – and at Erin's request Lucy Slack, the convict woman who had been such an invaluable help in Sydney, was sent for to become his special nurse.

Only one thing marred her peace of mind – the continuing absence of Patrick. Though Brett rode out to look for him with the express purpose of satisfying her, and though they made inquiries far and wide, no one seemed to know of his whereabouts. He had not been to Kinvarra, that was plain. As soon as the floods receded enough Erin herself rode over with Brett to search the buildings, but they were damp and unoccupied and it was clear no one had used the farm for living purposes since the Kellys had moved out.

'He'll turn up one day,' Brett assured Erin. 'If anything terrible had befallen him we should have heard.'

Erin, however, in spite of her determination to allow him to live his own life, could not help worrying. 'I can't help being afraid he might have drowned,' she murmured anxiously.

But Brett shook his head. 'If he had been his body would have been found as soon as the water went down,' he told her, though he did not go on to detail the number of animal carcasses he had seen caught in the crooks of trees, nor to mention his own anxiety – that Patrick had gone into the wild, unexplored country that was well within reach of Mia-Mia, lost his bearings, and starved to death. 'He'll be coming home rich, I shouldn't wonder, after making his fortune at something or other.'

Erin nodded, trying to smile, but the anxiety still niggled at her. Why hadn't Patrick been in touch? Didn't he know how worried she would be? He was a dreamer, yes, but in his own way he was thoughtful.

Ridiculously, perhaps, she felt she had somehow failed him, and failed to keep her promise to her dead mother. Sometimes, while Brett slept beside her, she lay awake and wondered what she could have done to change things, but the darkness never gave her back an answer.

Patrick had not wanted her to marry Brett, but she had had no choice, and now nothing in the world could make her regret that.

She smiled softly in the darkness, curling her body around his long, muscular back and remembering how she had once hated him. How glad she was now that he had forced her into marriage! If he had not, she would now be struggling to raise William alone, and she would never have known the glory that could come from loving a man such as he.

Poor Patrick! she thought. Poor, stubborn Patrick who had never given himself the chance to get to know Brett. If he had, he would have discovered what she, Brenna and Grianne had discovered – that beneath the tough exterior was a man who was as remarkable for his compassion as for his strength, and who would drive himself ceaselessly in an effort to do his best for those he loved.

As for Grianne, Brett had arranged for one of the officer's wives to chaperone her so that she could remain in Sydney, and secretly Erin was glad. Of late she had found it all too easy to quarrel with her sister, something which grieved and upset her, and since the day when she had seen her trying to make up to Brett she felt the two of them were better under separate roofs.

It wasn't that she didn't trust Brett – she did.

He had sworn to her that there had been no one else in the long months they had not lived as man and wife, and she believed him. But she was embarrassed to think that Grianne could behave so – throwing herself at any man who could offer her the lift in society she was seeking.

'I wish she could find herself a husband and settle down,' Erin thought, but for some reason it seemed Grianne could settle herself with no one.

It wasn't for lack of admirers – indeed not! A girl as pretty as she was greatly in demand. But none of the men who tried to woo her seemed to come up to the standard she desired, and Erin suspected she compared them all unfavourably with Brett. Not that she could be blamed for that, thought his besotted wife. There couldn't be another man in the whole of Australia with his attributes, for though there may be some who were as good looking, they were usually the newest and most penniless officers of the New South Wales Corps, and though there were others with land, wealth and position, most of these were too old, or too ugly, to interest a young woman of Grianne's tender years.

However, while she was in Sydney, there was always the chance she would meet someone to take her fancy and then, thought Erin, the problem of her wilful ways would be the problem of her husband, whoever he may be.

At the end of an idyllic two weeks, Brett informed Erin he would have to go into Sydney to make sure of the smooth running of the store.

'Oh Brett, must you go?' she asked, unwilling

to see an end to these lovely, timeless days warmed by the freshness of their new love.

He brushed her hair aside from her face with a gentle movement, twisting one curl into a corkscrew around his finger.

'I must, love. You know that. I would take you with me, but I know you hate Sydney.'

'I don't mind where I am, Brett, so long as I'm with you,' she whispered.

He smiled, still delighted to hear her say so.

'Careful, Madam! Such protestations will go to my head!'

'Will they? I don't mind – as long as you promise never to leave me.'

She put her arms about his waist and for a moment he held her close while the tide of desire that was never far beneath the surface surged through him. Then, with a deliberate movement, he held her away.

'You and I both know that now you're here at Mia-Mia it's best you stay until William is older. At the moment it would mean moving him and Lucy as well as yourself and the upheaval would not be good for him.'

She nodded. She was no longer jealous of his concern for William. She knew now she had no cause to be.

'I don't intend to stay longer than I can help, in any case,' Brett continued. 'I don't care for being tied to any of my business enterprises. Mia-Mia I know I can safely leave in Henry Stanton's hands and I'm well satisfied with Captain Edwards' capabilities as master of the *Amber Fawn*. What I need now is someone to whom I can entrust the running of the store, leaving me free to oversee all sides of my business and come and go as I please.'

'You think you will find such a man?' she asked.

'Undoubtedly,' he assured her. 'Those who decide to make a new life here are for the most part ambitious and resourceful. If I can find one who has failed to prosper through no fault of his own, and is also honest, then I suggest I shall have my man.'

'I see,' she said, thinking that anyone given the opportunity of working for Brett would be a fool not to grasp his chance with both hands. Hard he might be, but he was also fair. And success seemed destined to follow his ventures.

When Brett had gone she could have wept with loneliness. Such a short time they had been truly together, yet now she felt as if her right arm had been cut off. But on the second day she was surprised to see a large wagon trundling up the drive, and even more astonished when she saw the men unloading the piano that had occupied pride of place in the house in Sydney.

'Lawks, Mum, I never thought the master would have that moved!' Lucy Slack cried when she saw it and Erin's heart melted with warmth for Brett.

She hadn't thought he would have it moved, either, especially after the fuss he had made when he found her playing it, and that he should have it sent here for her was an act of love that brought tears of happiness to her eyes.

'When can we begin our lessons again, Lucy?'

she asked, and Lucy, who had gained in self-importance with every day since she had come to Mia-Mia, beamed benevolently.

'Just as soon as young William is bathed and changed, I reckon, Mum!' she replied.

The days passed more quickly now, though at night Erin lay in the big bed aching for Brett's arms around her.

It was a week or so later and Erin was sitting at the window that overlooked the drive when she saw a horse and rider trot into view. She leaped to her feet, spilling needlepoint and silks in an untidy heap on the floor while her heart began to beat an excited tattoo. Brett! It was Brett! No one else that she knew sat a horse that way – no one rode with such easy control. But there was another horse trotting behind Jack on a leading rein – a black horse that from here looked for all the world like Bess.

Gathering up her skirts Erin ran down the stairs and out onto the veranda and as Brett came closer she could see the second horse was indeed her father's beloved Bess. At once her heart came into her mouth and a thousand thoughts began chasing through her head.

If Brett had found Bess, did it mean he had also found Patrick? And if so, where was he now?

Hardly daring to breathe she went to meet him. He slid out of the saddle, pulling her close into his arms and kissing her until her senses reeled. Then he held her away, looking at her, and hating herself for being able to think of something other than him, she indicated the horse.

'Brett – that's Bess! Where did you find her?' His face sobered.

'In Sydney, my sweet. I took Jack to be fitted with new shoes and saw Bess tied up behind the smithy. When I asked about her I was told a young man had left her there a few weeks since. He answered Patrick's description. But more than that I was unable to discover. The young man had sold Bess to the smith with no explanation as to where he was going or why he wanted to sell the horse.'

'I don't understand,' Erin breathed. 'But it must mean Patrick reached Sydney safely, mustn't it? He wasn't drowned or lost.'

'That's true,' Brett agreed. 'It is a good sign, though I fear we are no closer to finding Patrick. But knowing how much the horse meant to you I bought her from the smith and brought her back upriver where she belongs.'

'Thank you,' Erin whispered, tears sparkling in her eyes. 'It's true, she was my father's pride and joy, and I couldn't bear to think she might fall into the hands of someone who would ill treat her. And she's too old for the bustle of Sydney. Like me, she prefers the quiet life.'

'I hope that does not mean you consider yourself old, my sweet,' Brett teased. 'If so, 'twill not take me long to prove to you how wrong you are. Just let me stable these brutes and we'll go back to the house.'

'I'll come with you,' she suggested, unwilling to leave his side.

Holding onto his arm she went with him to the stable, standing by while he unsaddled Jack and

289

hung the bridles and reins of both horses on their pegs. As she watched she was deep in thought, but gradually the lithe rippling of his muscles beneath his shirt began to work its magic on her. Patrick and his fate slipped to the back of her mind, for while her stomach did these disturbing twists there was no room for thought, only for feeling.

As if sensing her gaze upon him Brett looked up and as their eyes met the magic sparked again. He stood motionless, his hand upon the bridle, and the tide of desire rose within him, warm and demanding. All the way home he had been longing to see her, this girl who had come into his life and taken it over, and he silently thanked all the saints in heaven for making Therese reject him. If she had not, he would never have spoken to Erin that night at Alice Simmons's rum parlour, never known her as anything but a fledgling whore. And if Therese was here now, he could not imagine he could possibly feel the happiness he felt with Erin. Therese would have wanted to remain in Sydney, that much was certain. Whatever he did for her, no doubt she would complain ceaselessly about the new country. For all that he had thought that he loved her, she had never occupied his whole heart and soul as Erin did. Why, when he was away from her, her soft Irish accent had echoed inside his head like a haunting melody, and the memory of her clear blue eyes had stirred him over and over again. As for her body, he wanted nothing but to feel it close to his, smelling the sweetly scented skin, feeling its white smoothness that yielded so readily to his touch.

'Erin, come here,' he said softly.

She took a half-step towards him, then stopped.

'Why?'

He laughed, deep in his throat.

'What do you mean, why? So I can kiss you, of course.'

'But supposing someone should come?'

'They won't. And if they should I shall tell them, if it's any of their business, that *I* am master here and if I wish to kiss my wife in my own stable, I shall do it! Now, are you coming here, or have I to fetch you?'

It was Erin's turn to laugh.

'Fetch me.'

'All right. But don't say you haven't been warned.' He reached out, slipping a strong but lazy hand around her neck beneath her hair and pulling her towards him.

'Brett!' she protested, but she had no choice but to do as he bid her. He relaxed his hold on the bridle, taking her chin between his hands and holding her face steady beneath his.

'A good wife does as she is told,' he teased.

Her lips pursed a little; he could see the light of mischief shining in her eyes.

'Do you mean I am not a good wife?'

Her nearness had set his body throbbing with desire; her softness and warmth made the blood pound in his veins while the scent of her hair in his nostrils made his senses reel.

'I'm not sure that I can remember. Remind

291

me,' he murmured.

Beneath his lips hers were soft as ripe fruit and her body crushed against his, moulding and pressing as if nothing mattered but that they should fit close together. His hands slid from her neck to her waist, tracing the line of her shoulders and spanning the rib cage that felt so fragile that it seemed he could crush it between his hands like a walnut, then on down to the soft flare of her hips, sliding to the curve where her buttocks became the uppermost part of her thigh, and tucking her close against him so that the desire to possess her became unbearable.

With a swift, determined movement that left nothing of the decision to her, he lifted her in his arms, side-stepping the shifting horses and carrying her to the farthest corner of the stable. Then gently he laid her down in the soft, scratchy straw, bunching her skirts about her and kneeling astride her.

For just a second, as he looked down into her face, he thought he saw her flinch and he had no way of knowing how ghosts from the past were rising to haunt her then. He spread her legs and lowered himself onto her, taking the weight by placing his hands on either side of her head.

'No arguments, now,' he murmured. 'No one will come, love.'

He felt the tension stretch at all her muscles for a moment longer, then suddenly, with a cry, she wound her arms around his neck, pulling him hard down onto her. His mouth covered hers again as his manhood drove deep into her and love and passion overwhelmed him. He moved within her and felt her answering movement, angry, desperate, and hungry for he knew not what. Together they moved towards a climax that seemed to rend the sky with its intensity and, as the fire exploded within his own body, he heard her echoing sob, and then and only then he found himself wondering about the emotion that had driven her.

'Is the hay too rough for you?' he murmured, rolling onto his back and taking her with him so that she lay above him.

She did not answer, but to his surprise he felt something wet fall upon his face and putting up his hand he found it was a tear.

'Erin, what is it?' he asked, concerned suddenly.

For a moment she could not answer. He heard the words choke within her throat.

'Erin!' he lifted her so she was cradled in his arms, holding her close and looking down into her puckered face. 'Erin, what's wrong? Tell me!'

She swallowed hard. 'Don't take any notice of me,' she stuttered. 'I'm being foolish, I know. But I never thought I would be taken in a stable again.'

'What...?' He broke off, cursing himself as he realized her meaning. 'Oh, Erin, my dear love, I never thought! Oh, sweet, I'm sorry...'

She shook her head and to his surprise her mouth curved into the beginnings of a smile.

'Don't be sorry, Brett. It wasn't like the last time, I promise you. It was quite different. And this is the time I shall remember.'

'Oh Erin!' The love rose in him again, shot through with tenderness and a desire to protect her and see that nothing ever hurt her again. 'My sweet love, don't be afraid. You're my wife now.'

'I know,' she murmured. 'But if it had not been for that other time, I might not be.'

And as they both acknowledged the truth of happiness grown out of fear and terror, and a new life built from the ruins of the old, past, present and future seemed to merge into one within the circle of their arms.

A few days later Erin was nursing William at the window that overlooked the rear yard when she saw Brett round the corner of the house in the company of another man. For some reason something about the set of his shoulders made the skin prickle on the back of her neck and she clasped William tightly to her, peering down at the pair of them.

Who was the man – and why was he having this effect on her? From his clothes he gave the appearance of a fairly well-to-do traveller, and yet ... and yet there was something about him that was disturbingly familiar.

As she looked, Brett motioned towards the house. The man turned round and as she caught sight of his face, Erin froze, a startled cry dying on her lips, her hands tensing around William's firm, round frame.

Holy Mary, surely she must be mistaken! The face was clean shaven after all, where before it had been bearded. And those clothes were as different from a convict's rags as was possible. But the eyes – those wicked, narrowed eyes – they looked for all the world like the eyes of the convict who had raped her!

Trembling from head to foot Erin backed away from the window. It couldn't be! Oh, surely, it couldn't be! He would have put as many miles as possible between himself and the scene of his crimes – if he had not been recaptured.

But certainly he had not been among those recaptured convicts she had seen in chains behind the soldiers' horses the day they had passed by Alice Simmons's rum parlour. And if he wanted to return to the rich land he had known as an assigned labourer, perhaps he had been confident that no one would recognize his changed appearance.

'No one but me,' thought Erin.

For his face had been burned into her memory with a brand of fire. She would never forget it. How could she?

She stood for a moment biting at her lips until the blood ran. What should she do? Go down and challenge him? But if the stranger and the convict *were* one and the same, and Brett attempted to apprehend him, heaven alone knew what would come of it. The convict who had taken her had killed before. She had no doubt but that he would kill again – and Brett might not be prepared for him.

And what if she was wrong – and the man was as he appeared, an innocent traveller? Brett would think she had taken leave of her senses!

Yet if she was *not* wrong, the man could not be

allowed to walk away! If he was who she thought he was it was her duty to hand him over to the military so that they could hang him as they had hanged his filthy friends, and ensured he never raped or terrorized or murdered again.

Willing her legs to move steadily she crossed to the cradle and put William down. Then, gripping on tightly to her self-control, she made herself walk down the stairs. Everything within her was shrinking away from meeting the man, but somehow she went on.

Through the door and onto the veranda she went, then stopped, her fingers gripping at the wooden surround. For there was no sign of the man now. Brett was alone in the yard, adjusting the girths of his horse. He looked up at Erin's approach, but the sun was in his eyes and he did not notice her white, drained face.

'I'm just going to ride over to Kinvarra,' he told her matter-of-factly. 'Stanton and I want to decide what's to be done with the land.'

Erin looked around her, her eyes bright specks of fear.

'Where is he?' she asked sharply.

'Henry? Already at Kinvarra,' Brett replied, puzzled.

'No, not Henry. The man who was here.'

'Oh, you mean Morgan Jagger. He was just passing through on his way to Sydney.'

'Morgan Jagger,' Erin repeated in a trembling voice. 'Is that his name?'

Brett's eyes narrowed a little and he looked at her questioningly.

'That's right. Why?'

'Because ... oh, I know it sounds silly, Brett, but I thought I'd seen him before.' She followed the statement with a little laugh, but it hardly hid the tension in her voice.

Brett shook his head. 'I should think it's unlikely you have seen him, Erin. He's only just arrived here from England, and he came to look me up.'

It was Erin's turn to look surprised.

'Why should he do that?'

'Because he knew me back in the old country. When I was a boy I spent some time on the road with my mother's troupe of players, and we stayed a week or more in the village where he lived.'

'I see.' Erin's heart was still thumping. 'And you remembered him, after all this time?'

Brett smiled. 'I must be honest. I would never have recognized him if he had not made himself known to me. But I suppose that's not surprising. To me, he would have been just another boy in another village, while I to him – well, I suppose I was something a little out of the ordinary compared with most of his friends. However, be that as it may, when he arrived here and began looking for work he heard my name mentioned and decided to look me up.'

'Thinking you would give him a job, I suppose,' Erin said.

Brett shrugged. 'Maybe. But I don't see him in the mould of a farmer. I told him I thought he would be better off in Sydney.'

Erin breathed a sigh of relief.

'I'm glad, Brett,' she said softly. 'He frightened me.'

'Frightened you?' he queried. 'Why?'

She hesitated. Should she tell him of the panic she had felt when she had thought she recognized the man as her attacker? No. It sounded too foolish. If he was fresh out of England, and known to Brett into the bargain, it was clear she had been wrong. Now there was no point in raking up the past. She did not want Brett to think she was obsessed by what had happened to her. And neither did she want to talk – or even think – about it.

'Oh, I don't know,' she said with forced lightness. 'I told you – I was being silly, Brett.'

He looked at her for a long moment, then swung himself up into the saddle and leaned over to kiss her lightly on the forehead.

'I must go now then, love, if I'm not to keep Henry waiting, and wasting his precious time. I'll be back by dusk.'

She nodded, forcing a smile to her lips. But as he rode away, her legs were still trembling a little from the shock of seeing the man.

'Forget him!' she told herself firmly. 'He damaged your life enough without letting him haunt you for ever more.'

Then, with a determined toss of her head, she turned and went back into the house.

CHAPTER NINETEEN

For all her good intentions, and although she did not mention the strange Morgan Jagger to Brett again, he continued to haunt Erin's thoughts.

As often as she told herself she must have been mistaken – the smartly dressed settler could not possibly be one and the same as the convict who had raped her – the doubts continued, and when Brett returned to Sydney to attend to the business of the store again she found herself waking at night from nightmares where she saw the man riding up the drive to the house.

Sometimes he was bearded, sometimes clean-shaven; sometimes he wore the rags of a convict, sometimes the frilled shirt and breeches of a well-to-do settler, but always his eyes burned with the terrible lust she remembered so well, and always she knew him for the danger that he was. Yet in her dream she could never run away or call for help, for when she tried her legs and her throat were paralysed with fear. And she knew that when he reached her, the man would show her no mercy ... none at all...

'I declare I'm going crazy!' Erin told her reflection in the mirror one morning after a disturbed night had left her pale, heavy-eyed and still weary. 'Why should I begin worrying about the convict again now, just when I'm so happy? He's either hundreds of miles away, living in luxury, or else his neck has been stretched like the others who took part in that break-out. And the man who came here is just who Brett said he was – Morgan Jagger, fresh out from England, with not a stain on his character, poor man.'

But still she was not easy in her mind. It was one thing to force logical, sensible thoughts to the surface. The others still lurked beneath, making her restless and anxious, and disturbing her sleep.

One afternoon, while she was checking the household linen that was stored in a cupboard at the head of the stairs, Brenna came running up in a high state of excitement.

'Erin – it's Grianne! Grianne's here!'

'Here?' Erin echoed, then, dropping all the linen, she ran after the little girl down the stairs. Difficult Grianne might sometimes be, she was still her sister and it was a long while since she had seen her.

'Where is she?' she cried, hurrying through the house.

'I'm here!'

Erin spun round to see Grianne coming through the doorway, her dark beauty enhanced by a brand new riding habit of sapphire blue – and the glow that the ride had brought to her cheeks.

'Oh, Grianne, what a lovely surprise!' she began, then broke off with a gasp. For standing in the doorway behind Grianne was a figure who seemed to have stepped right out of her nightmares!

'What are you doing here?' she tried to say, but no words came, and as she stood, her lips working foolishly, Grianne caught at the man's arm, pulling him into the room beside her.

'Erin, I don't believe you've met Morgan Jagger,' she murmured. 'He's an old friend of Brett's, and when he learned I wanted to ride out here to collect some of my things he kindly offered to escort me.'

Her heart beating a tattoo, Erin looked from her sister to the man beside her, then she almost gasped aloud. For the smile had died on his face and as their eyes met the recognition flared and panic rose to choke Erin. Holy Mother, she had been right when she had suspected Morgan Jagger was in reality the convict who had raped her! Though before she had tried to tell herself it was imagination only, now she knew it was not. For he had confirmed it himself by recognizing her – and by showing that he had recognized her.

Waves of horror engulfed her so that for a moment the room and everything in it seemed a long way off. Her throat felt constricted, as if a scream was trapped there, yet sheer, blind panic prevented it from escaping.

He must not know she knew who he was! she thought wildly. If he did realize the recognition had been mutual, heaven alone knew to what lengths he would go to preserve his new identity and his fresh start in life. He had killed before – he would kill again without a second thought, and there was no one here to protect them. Brett was in Sydney, and Henry Stanton was at

Kinvarra with a workforce of men, and would be staying overnight at least.

With a supreme effort of will she extended her hand towards him.

'Thank you for escorting my sister, Mr Jagger. It was kind.'

His lip curled and as he took the hand she offered she noticed that his right arm was twisted as if the muscle had been injured at some time and no longer worked as it should.

I did that! she realized in horror, and as clearly as if it were being played out even now before her eyes she saw herself fumbling in the hay for her father's gun, finding it and firing at the figure in the doorway of the barn.

'Thank you kindly, Mrs Wilde.' His voice was as she remembered it – not even the effort of making it refined could hide the soft, snarling menace in its tones – and she shivered violently. But Grianne seemed oblivious of the menace that underlay his smooth exterior. Even as Erin gazed through horror-struck eyes she saw her sister's hand tighten on the thick, linen-covered arm, and heard her soft, flirting laugh.

'I'm sure in the future you'll be seeing a good deal more of Mr Jagger,' she said triumphantly.

Erin dragged her eyes away from the man and back to her sister's smiling face.

'What do you mean?' she asked, fighting to keep her voice level. But it was the man who answered her.

'Brett has offered me a job,' he said, his guarded eyes scrutinizing her narrowly. 'I am to manage his store in Sydney.'

'You?' Erin breathed.

He smiled, looking more like a dangerous animal than ever.

'Yes. I knew Brett in the old country when we were boys. 'Twas a lucky chance for me to find him here.'

Erin held her trembling lip taut between her teeth. A lucky chance indeed! This man had deliberately sought Brett out, she was sure, to trade on his old acquaintance and worm his way into a position in his empire. Why, what was to say he even knew Brett? His recent arrival in Australia was a complete fabrication; perhaps the previous meeting was invented, too, to fit in with what he knew of Brett's past. Brett had not remembered him, after all. He had admitted to her it was Jagger who had made himself known to him, and there must have been many such casual acquaintances for a boy who travelled as he had done with a troupe of players.

'I am sure that Brett blesses his good fortune as much as you do!' Grianne put in. Her hand was still on Jagger's arm and she was smiling up at him in the teasing way that somehow managed also to convey her admiration. Erin felt her stomach turn.

To see her sister flirting with this man, while the memory of what he had done to her still burned raw within her, was almost more than she could bear. Of course, Grianne knew nothing of the truth about him. To her he was exactly what he said he was a gentleman fresh out of England, and a good-looking one to boot! Not only that, with Brett's seal of approval, Grianne

303

would see him as someone likely to rise to a position of importance in the ever-growing Wilde empire – and that made him worthy of her attentions.

'I must warn her!' Erin thought desperately. But for the moment, for the sake of the safety of both of them, she must somehow stomach his presence and pretend that she had not recognized him as her attacker.

'What was it you came home for?' she asked Grianne.

'Oh, some of my summer bits and bobs,' Grianne replied airily, but a slight bloom rose in her cheeks and her eyes avoided her sister's. Erin's heart sank a little. She knew Grianne's way well enough to see straight through that ploy. No doubt her sister had used going home for her 'summer bits and bobs' as an excuse to get Morgan Jagger to herself. If she was already trying those tricks, there was no time to be lost. She must be warned – and warned right away.

'You're staying the night, of course,' Erin said, determined to get some time alone with Grianne, and the other girl acquiesced readily enough.

'Yes, of course – if Morgan can spare the time, that is,' she murmured coyly.

He nodded, unable to conceal the look of sly triumph, and bile rose in Erin's throat.

How clever he must think himself, to have wormed his way back into a society that he had such a short time ago plundered and ravaged! Oh, if she had a gun handy now she would shoot him through his black heart and finish what she had begun that night! But she had no gun. She had only her own wits to see her through this unexpected and unwelcome development.

She excused herself to go to the kitchen and arrange for two extra dinners to be prepared, but the sick trembling still shook her, and she was only surprised the convict women did not seem to notice. Then came the ordeal of putting William to bed as usual while that evil man sat downstairs, and then, even worse, the nightmare of sitting through dinner, trying to force the food down her protesting throat while he sat opposite her, grinning, pleased with himself, and Grianne hung onto every word he spoke.

'Why can't she see through him?' Erin wondered. 'Is she so blinded by his good looks and the manner he has put on with his new clothes that she cannot see the evil that lies beneath?'

But then, how could she blame Grianne if Brett had also been deceived?

At last the meal was over and Erin knew her best chance of a talk with Grianne was approaching. Making some excuse about supervising the clearing-away, she dragged a reluctant Grianne to the kitchen with her, leaving the vile Morgan Jagger to smoke a cigar in the comfort of the dining room. As soon as the two girls were alone she caught urgently at her sister's arm.

'Grianne – I must talk to you.'

Grianne's face puckered bad-temperedly and she glanced back towards the dining room, obviously anxious to return.

'What about? You're not going to start on about Brett again, are you?'

'It's nothing to do with Brett.' Erin's eyes too

flicked to the dining room door. It was firmly closed, she'd seen to that, but she didn't want to risk Jagger overhearing any of what she had to say to Grianne – and there was always the danger that he might become bored with his own company and come looking for them.

'Can't we go outside for a few minutes?' she suggested. 'It's a clear evening.'

Before Grianne could refuse she opened the door, leading onto the veranda and down the steps. It was dusk already, and all the outbuildings looked dark and solid against the murky sky. Grianne shivered a little.

'What is this, Erin? Have you taken leave of your senses?'

Erin stopped, pulling on her sister's arm to bring her around face to face and her fingers gripped so tightly that Grianne winced.

'For the Lord's sake, Erin...'

'Listen, Grianne, and listen carefully. What I have to say to you now is very important.' Erin swallowed at the painful lump in her throat, then continued: 'Do you remember the night Father was killed?'

Grianne's lips tightened a shade.

'I wasn't at home. I was at the Percys'. Do we have to go over this?'

'Grianne, listen please!' Erin urged her. 'It's difficult enough without you making it worse.'

'Why?' Grianne muttered. 'Hurry and get it over with, whatever it is, if you must. I want to go back inside with Morgan.'

'That's just it, Grianne – you can't! You mustn't have anything more to do with that

306

man!' Erin whispered urgently. 'He's not who he says he is – and he certainly hasn't just arrived in Australia. He's been here a year at least, and he didn't come as a free settler – he came as a convict.'

For a second there was silence, then Grianne threw her head back and laughed.

'Oh, Erin, what nonsense! Whatever gave you that idea?'

'It's no laughing matter!' Erin flared. 'I know he's a convict because he was one of those who overran Kinvarra the night Father was killed. Some were caught, but he couldn't have been. And now he's given himself a new identity and tried to wriggle his way in with Brett.'

'You're crazy!' Grianne returned, her voice still amused. 'Anyone can see he doesn't look in the least like a convict.'

'Not now, perhaps,' Erin agreed. 'He's shaved off his beard and got himself some decent clothes. But it's him, right enough. I'd know him anywhere. And he recognized me, too. I saw it in his eyes.'

Grianne's lips tightened and her gaze became shrewd.

'You're really serious, aren't you, Erin? You really believe what you're saying.'

'Of course I do!' Erin cried. 'And if you'd been here that night you'd remember him too. Why, I saw his face quite clearly – in the full lamplight in the kitchen when he ripped Mama's locket from my neck, and then...' Her voice tailed off into a sob. 'Well, thank God you weren't there, anyway, Grianne. Thank God you weren't.'

Grianne took a step closer to Erin, peering narrowly into her face.

'What do you mean?'

Erin shook her head.

'No, Grianne, don't ask me, please.'

It was Grianne's turn to grip her sister's arm.

'But I am asking you. You can't make accusations like this against someone and then only tell half a tale. What happened that night? And what has it to do with Morgan?'

Erin swallowed hard, fighting an inner battle with herself. She hadn't wanted ever to have to reveal to her sisters or brother the brutal truth of what had happened to her in the barn that terrible night. She had wanted to put it out of her mind forever. But now, if it would make Grianne see the hateful Morgan Jagger in his true light, then she would have to face it all once again.

'I hoped I'd never have to tell you this, Grianne,' she said wretchedly. 'But perhaps if I do you'll know why I could never forget that convict as long as I live – why I'd know him anywhere. When the convicts left the house I ran to the barn where I knew Father was lying injured. But I was too late. Father was dead. Then I heard someone making off with the horses – Father's horse, Bess, and Starlight. It was him – Jagger. I tried to stop him – I even managed to shoot him in the arm. Have you noticed there's something wrong with it? But that just seemed to madden him. He attacked me in the barn. He ... he raped me, Grianne. He was like a brutal animal. And that's why you can't go back in there alone with him – why you must be on your guard. And why we must be careful not to let him know that we know who he is. If he realized he was in danger of being turned in, our lives wouldn't be worth a candle to a man like that.'

For a moment Grianne stood motionless and in the quiet of the evening even the sounds of the river seemed to be stilled. Erin's heart lifted with hope. If she had convinced Grianne then at least she would have an ally – at least she would not have to fight this battle alone.

'You do see now, Grianne, don't you?' she whispered urgently.

Grianne's head came up with a jerk and to her horror Erin saw that her eyes were blazing blue fire.

'Sweet Jesu, you *are* crazy, Erin!' she cried harshly. 'I knew you'd go to any lengths you could to spoil things for me. You always have. But I never thought even you would stoop to this!'

Erin stared, horrified, and Grianne ranted on.

'I suppose you're jealous to think I'm on the point of making a good catch for myself. You can't accept I'm old enough now to make my own decisions instead of having you make them for me. Well, this time you've overstepped yourself. I won't let you poison my mind against Morgan, and you might as well accept it.'

'But Grianne...' Erin raised horror-stricken eyes to her sister's face and as she did so she caught sight of a small, glowing light in the darkness on the veranda. Holy Mother, was it him? Had he come out looking for Grianne –

and if so, how much of their conversation had he overheard?

'Grianne, please!' Erin whispered urgently, but the younger girl did not answer. Shaking herself free she marched furiously back towards the house and Erin, afraid that Jagger might indeed be lurking on the veranda, dared not run after her to pursue the matter.

What now? she wondered wildly. It had never occurred to her for a moment that Grianne would not only doubt her word but openly refute it. And now she was at a loss what to do to save her sister from the clutches of this evil man.

'Why bother to save her?' a wicked little voice whispered inside her. 'If she can dismiss you as a vicious and spiteful liar, then why not leave her to discover the truth the hard way?'

But even as this small devil prodded at her, her mind was returning as it did so often to the promise she had made to her dying mother.

If Mama was here now, she would do everything in her power to make Grianne see the error of her ways. No matter how Grianne abused her, it would make no difference because she would still want only the best for her. But Mama was not here. And she had entrusted the younger ones to Erin's care.

'Promise me, Erin, promise...'

'I promise, Mama...'

Never had the echoing words seemed more apt than they did now!

In the dark yard Erin stood with her hands pressed to her mouth while her mind churned desperately. Why, oh why, had the evil man returned? And why did he manage to be so plausible? To have taken in Grianne, who clearly wanted to be taken in, was one thing. But he had also misled Brett to such an extent that he had offered him the responsible job of store manager.

No, there was nothing for it. If she was to prevent him from worming his way into their lives she must find some way of proving that he was the man she knew him to be – a cheat, a murderer and a rapist. But how? Perhaps Brett would dismiss her story as Grianne had done. Perhaps he would think her head had been turned by her experience and she had to have a scapegoat for the awful things that had happened to her before she could put them behind her for ever.

What she needed was some concrete evidence that Jagger was not who he said he was. If she had that they would have to listen to her. Without it – why, she was even beginning to wonder herself if she was going mad!

She glanced towards the house. The door had closed after Grianne and there was no sign of either her or Jagger. Perhaps, thought Erin, this was her best chance. If she went to the stables where Jagger had left his horse she might find something in his saddlepack to incriminate him. It seemed a vain hope. If he had indeed taken a new identity he would surely have gone to great lengths to make sure every trace of his old life was left behind him. But it was just possible he had saved some keepsake or memento. Sometimes the tougher the man the more sentimental a streak that lurked at his core.

Making up her mind, she crossed quickly to the stables. The door had been closed for the night, but with shaking hands she unlatched it and went inside.

The horses shifted at her entrance, thrusting curious noses over their stalls to nuzzle her, but she went on to the end where Jagger's horse was tethered. Above him, on a peg, hung the saddle and the saddlepack. Carefully, Erin thrust him aside, pulling an empty box into position to enable her to reach the saddlepack. Then, hardly daring to breathe, she inched her fingers inside.

Though she knew that Jagger was evil and her reason for ransacking his belongings was the best one in the world, she could not help but feel guilty as she probed through his personal belongings. Determinedly she pushed the feeling aside, concentrating on trying to recognize what object, if any, could give her the tie-in to the past for which she was searching. But all his things were new – too new – though she supposed if challenged he would simply say he had acquired them since coming to Australia.

It was hopeless, she thought bitterly, hopeless. She had been expecting far too much if she thought she might find something to incriminate the man. One last time she thrust her hand into the saddlepack, probing the corners, and suddenly her fingers encountered something small and hard. Scarcely daring to breathe, she extracted it. As she opened her hand and the lantern light illuminated the object that lay glinting in her palm, a small gasp escaped her lips.

She had prayed for proof – and now she had it – her mother's locket torn from her neck on the night of the attack! Brett would have to believe her now – and Grianne too!

She stood for a moment looking down at the locket. Why Jagger should have kept it she did not know – perhaps as a gift for someone, perhaps simply because he had been afraid to dispose of it. Whichever, it was as if her mother was helping her, she thought.

A sound in the yard outside startled her, and she stiffened, eyes widening in alarm. She thrust the locket deep into the pocket of her gown, then stretched up to replace the saddlepack exactly as it had been. It wouldn't do for Jagger to suspect she had been prying. But her shaking hands could no longer hold the pack steady. To her dismay it slipped from her grasp, falling to the floor and spilling the contents beneath the hooves of Jagger's horse.

Swiftly she climbed down from the box, scrabbling to collect his scattered possessions. But as she did so the shifting of the horses nearest the stable door attracted her attention. Heart hammering, she spun round on her haunches.

A dark shadow was moving up the aisle beside the stalls and as she recognized its bulk fear rose within her in a cloud so thick and black she thought it would overwhelm her.

Sweet heaven it was him! And here she was, alone, defenceless, and surrounded by his possessions!

CHAPTER TWENTY

As Jagger approached her, Erin crouched motionless like a mouse who sees the hawk circling above.

She knew that if she tried to scream no sound would come, and even if it did there was no one to hear her. And there was no escape for her, either. The bulk of the man blocked the narrow aisle between the stalls and the stable wall and it would be useless to try to slip past.

'Well, well, Mrs Wilde!' His voice was the same evil snarl she remembered so well, all pretence at refinement forgotten. 'And just what do you think you are doing?'

She swallowed at the lump of fear that seemed to be choking her.

'I thought I heard intruders. I came to see...'

Jagger brought his fist down hard onto the wooden surround of the stall so that the horse within whinnied and shied away.

'Liar!' he spat. 'You're prying, aren't you? Prying into things you'd have done best to forget.'

'No...' she protested weakly.

'Yes!' He towered above her, his face ugly with hate. 'You want to spoil everything for me, don't you, Mrs Wilde? Or can I call you Erin, since we're on such intimate terms?'

Erin gasped. So he knew she had recognized him and he was taunting her with it. Further pretence was useless now. Her mind flew back to that other time when he had towered above her in the barn and her flesh quailed. But every instinct within her cried out against letting him see she was afraid. A bully such as he would revel in her fear, and enjoy every moment of grinding her underfoot. Well, she would not give him that pleasure whatever happened.

'You scum!' she grated recklessly. 'If you think you can deceive Brett for long, you're much mistaken!'

Jagger laughed unpleasantly. 'Oh, and what's to stop me?'

'Brett's not the fool you think him,' Erin asserted. 'And besides, *I* know the truth...' She broke off, her hand flying to her mouth as she realized the folly of her brave words.

'That's so, my dear Erin.' Jagger shifted himself and the menace was obvious in every controlled movement of his frame. 'A pity, in truth, for it means I shall have to dispose of you.'

Erin's throat closed with fear, but somehow she fought it down.

'You won't get away with it. How could you?'

He laughed again.

'Easily. I know a hundred ways to make sudden death look like an accident.'

Her skin crawled at the cool reason in his tone. 'You wouldn't...'

'Oh yes. A pity, when you are so lovely – but then, Grianne is lovely too. I'm sure I can console myself with her.'

At his words, sudden anger flared alongside her fear. How dare he! How *dare* he! On the wall behind her hung a riding stick. She knew it was there, though in her previous panic she had not contemplated using it. Now, with one swift movement she levered herself up, grabbing the stick and striking Jagger full in the face before he was even aware what she was about.

She heard his cry of pain, saw him stagger backwards, and desperately tried to slip past him. But he was too quick for her. His hand slid out to grasp her arm, the fingers biting painfully into her soft flesh.

'Bitch!' he snarled. 'Hell-cat! You'll pay for that, I promise you!'

With a sharp jerk he pulled her towards him, holding her for a moment so close that she felt his breath on her face. It was not the fetid breath of a convict now, but it still turned her stomach, reminding her as it did of that other time, and the horror of how he had used her. Something warm and sticky dripped onto her chin and she realized it was his blood, running from the gash her riding stick had opened along his cheek.

Desperately she tried to strike out again, but he held her pinioned with ease, and as she kicked at him her soft slippers made no impression on his hard, muscled calves. Then, with an oath, he began to drag her along the aisle beside the stalls, his eyes darting like a smake's in the lamplight.

One of the stalls was empty; he kicked it open roughly and threw her inside. A mound of straw in the corner broke her fall, but her head cracked back against the wooden partition, half-stunning her. Then the stall rocked as he threw himself down on his knees beside her and instantly, terrifyingly, she was fully conscious once more.

Holy Mother, it couldn't be! This fearful replay of her worst nightmare couldn't be happening!

'No!' she gasped as his hands caught at the neck of her gown, ripping it as he had ripped it once before. 'No, you pig, leave me!'

But he only laughed, the same evil laugh she remembered so clearly.

'You've spirit! I like spirit! Your sister falls like a ripe plum, but you ... I shall be sorry to have to kill you!'

'No – no!' she screamed, almost incoherent now, and her cries seemed to unsettle the horses. They stamped in their stalls and whinnied. But Jagger seemed unaware of them. His lust had blinded him to everything but the lovely girl who lay half-naked in the straw, clawing and fighting with every ounce of her strength. He would have to kill her, of course. Since she knew who he was and could put a rope about his neck, there was no other way. But first, he intended to enjoy her as he had enjoyed her before – and as he had enjoyed no other since her...

With one ham-like hand he held her back in the straw, with the other he ripped the remnants of her dress from her flailing body. Then, with a groan, he threw himself down onto her. But at that very moment a sound from behind made him start. He raised his head and Erin drew in air

317

in a shuddering gasp. Then, as she saw a shadow fall across the lamplight, hope burst in her. With renewed energy she struck out again at the face that was now half-turned away from her, arching her back and thrusting wildly, and to her astonishment the crushing weight lifted from her body, twisting away.

'You bastard!'

The voice was Brett's.

Jagger, still scrambling to his feet, twisted round and Brett's fist connected with his jaw so sharply that he was almost lifted from his feet by the impact. Erin screamed and turned aside as he hit the back of the stall and collapsed full length into the straw beside her. Then her scream became a sob of horror as he dragged aside his coat and with a swift movement pulled out a gun.

'Brett – look out!' she cried as the gun pointed wickedly at him. But Brett ignored the warning, coming towards Jagger with the slow, determined gait of a tiger about to pounce.

'Oh no!' she screamed, covering her face with her hands, and in so doing she never saw Jagger swing around as a change of plan occurred to him.

The first she knew was the sharp jab of a ring of steel in the soft flesh of her neck, just below her ear, and the upward jerk of her chin as thick fingers fastened around her throat. Her cry of fear came out on a strangled sob as Jagger roughly forced her to her feet.

'Any closer and she's a goner!' he snarled, and the menace in his tone told Brett it was no idle threat. He stopped in his tracks, fists balled at his sides, eyes narrowed as he took in the situation.

'Harm her and you'll suffer!' he warned.

'Hah!' Jagger spat viciously. 'You'll do as I say, Wilde.'

With a quick, panther-like move he shifted the gun to the right of Erin's jaw, at the same time doubling his left forearm across her throat to hold her in front of him. 'Now, saddle my horse for me, damn you, and be quick about it.'

For a moment Brett stood motionless and he jerked his head impatiently.

'Come on, now, hurry up and do as I say and let me get away from this bedevilled place. Or as God is my judge I'll kill the witch!'

Brett swore softly, though Erin was too bemused by terror to know what it was he said. Her head was tilted backwards by the pressure of the hard forearm and as if through a distorted mirror she saw Brett go past them to the end of the stable where Jagger's horse was tied up. She heard the creak of the saddle leathers and the shifting of the horse's hooves on the hard-baked floor, then, above the ringing in her ears, Brett's voice:

'Here you are then, Jagger, he's ready for you.'

Jagger laughed unpleasantly.

'Oh no! D'you take me for a fool, Wilde? No, I am not ready to do the exchange here. Let it be outside, my friend. Bring my horse out now, and no tricks. My gun is cocked, do not forget, and pointed at the most vulnerable spots on your wife's fair throat.'

He backed into the stall, dragging Erin with him. As his arm tightened round her throat, she

319

sobbed in fear and pain, her eyes following the sound of the horse's hooves as Brett passed by down the aisle. Then Jagger pushed her forward roughly so that she gagged, and the cold steel muzzle of the gun bit painfully into her neck.

The terror was intense in her now, sharper and clearer. 'He can't let us live,' Erin thought wildly. 'He'll kill us anyway once his getaway route is clear – he'll have to. For he must know Brett would track him down wherever he flees...'

The stable door swung open; she saw the patch of star-studded sky as Brett led the horse out. Then she felt the cold rush of air on her bosom and remembered with a shock that she was half-naked.

'Here you are, Jagger!' Brett yelled. The former convict pushed her forward across the stable yard until she was so close that the pungent smell of the horse was in her nostrils and the glow of his body warmed her face. Then with a violent thrust he sent her spinning, at the same time turning his pistol on Brett. She heard its sharp retort as the muddy yard rushed up to meet her and she turned her head in time to see Brett sway, grabbing at his shoulder with the blood already running out between his fingers.

Erin's scream of horror was echoed by another. Unnoticed by any of them, Grianne had come out onto the veranda and now she stood watching with her hands pressed to her mouth.

Although Brett reeled backwards as the shot tore into his flesh, Jagger knew at once that in his haste he had fired high. Brett was not dead and the pistol was now useless. With an oath he hurled it away, turning his horse swiftly on its rein and leaping to its back. But as his weight hit the saddle the horse screamed and reared violently. Unknown to him, when he had saddled the horse Brett had cleverly slipped a sharp spur beneath the saddle. Now, taken utterly by surprise, with one foot only in the stirrups, Jagger had no chance of retaining his seat. For a long moment he seemed to hang suspended against the laws of gravity; then with a crash he fell heavily and the horse plunged forward across the yard.

As soon as he hit the ground he rolled over, catlike, but Brett was too quick for him. Before he could defend himself, Brett was upon him, seemingly oblivious to the wound in his shoulder, dragging him to his feet and driving a solid punch into his face. Jagger staggered backwards beneath the power of the blow and Brett followed, but this time Jagger was ready for him. His flying fists smashed into Brett's face and the two men locked together, punching and gouging, while their blood mingled and ran down in the dusty yard.

Erin, who had somehow managed to scramble to her feet, shrank back under the veranda, clasping her torn gown around her and sobbing with fear as the two men battled first on one side, then the other. In the half-light it was almost impossible to make out what was happening but the thuds and cries made her blood run cold.

The fight had taken them back by the outbuildings when Erin saw Jagger grab something that had been lying back against the wall, and a scream rose in her throat as she realized what it was – a pitchfork one of the farmworkers had used to clear out the stables and left lying outside.

Shouting in triumph the former convict lunged at Brett with the vicious weapon. Quick as lightning Brett side-stepped, but he knew he could not long escape the jabbing prongs, and he backed away towards the stable. At least within its confines Jagger would be able to wield the fork less freely.

For just a second Jagger held back in the doorway, suspecting a trap, and the delay was enough for Brett. With a swift sideways movement he reached for one of the saddles that hung on the wall and threw it with all his might at Jagger. The heavy leather caught the man full in the face and, arms flailing wildly, he staggered back. His boots slipped in the mud created by an overturned bucket of water and he went down heavily, his head cracking back against the wall.

Without pausing for thought Brett was upon him once more, knocking the pitchfork from his numbed hand and raining blows upon him. Helpless now, Jagger was unable to retaliate or even defend himself. His head jerked from side to side on his rubbery neck, while groans and whimpers escaped his bloodied lips. But still Brett drove blow after blow into his face and body, fighting like a madman and extracting his revenge on the creature who had threatened his wife.

Erin, watching, turned as cold now with fear

for her attacker as she had been a moment ago for Brett.

'Stop – stop – you'll kill him!' she cried.

But Brett ignored her. All his energy, all his efforts, were concentrated on making a bloody pulp of Jagger's face.

'Brett – please!' Gathering her skirts, Erin ran across the yard towards them and in response to her screams Grianne came too. 'Brett, don't! He's not worth it!'

Desperately she grabbed at his one arm and Grianne the other. At first Brett brushed them aside like flies, but they caught at him again. 'Brett, don't ... don't kill him! Hand him over to the authorities. They'll deal with him!'

Abruptly Brett straightened and Erin could hardly believe he had given up the fight so easily. Then he reached out for the pitchfork that lay on the ground beside them, placing it at Morgan's throat.

'You're right. The Corps will hang him. Why should I have his blood on my hands?'

His tone was so cold Erin shivered.

'Brett – are you all right?' she whispered.

For answer, Brett merely jerked his head towards the house. 'Find some rope so we can tie this bastard up,' he grated. 'For tonight we'll lock him in one of the convict's huts, but though they're strong enough to contain six such as he I won't take the chance of him escaping.'

The man on the floor groaned and Erin felt a stab of something almost like pity. The military would hang him without a doubt. It was no more than he deserved, but for all that the certainty of his fate sickened her.

Hardening her heart she went into the house for the rope and Grianne followed her.

'Oh, Erin – I'd no idea – none!' the younger girl wept. 'When you told me, I thought it was just sour grapes. Oh, I'm so sorry...'

'Never mind that now,' Erin said shortly. 'Let's get him into the safety of a shed so Brett can rest. His shoulder needs tending.'

'I'll help,' Grianne offered, and marvelling at her changed attitude Erin left her to look out clean linen and set water to boil while she took the rope to Brett.

He looked a little unsteady now, she thought, and the light of the moon that had risen showed his face to be milky-pale. She watched anxiously as he trussed Jagger, noticing how he gritted his teeth against the pain as he secured the knots, and followed nervously when he manhandled the former convict at pitchfork point to the strongest of the huts. But it was only when the door had been locked and bolted that she saw him sway, resting for a moment against the wall.

'Lean on me, Brett,' she whispered urgently. 'I must get you back to the house.'

With an effort he lifted the corners of his mouth into the ghost of his usual smile.

'That sounds, my love, like an offer I would be a fool to refuse.'

She put her slender arm about his waist and felt her knees buckle beneath the pressure of his weight on her shoulder. But somehow she supported him, uncaring that his blood soaked her dress, up the veranda steps.

Grianne was hovering in the kitchen. She was close to tears but Erin had no time to spare for her now. She eased Brett down into a chair, motioning Grianne to bring the candelabra closer so that she could examine Brett's shoulder better, and gasped with horror when she saw the hole that the bullet had torn in the flesh.

How had Brett managed to stave off Jagger's attack when he was so badly injured? she marvelled. And how fortunate it was that the former convict had missed his aim and fired high! For he had been shooting to kill, she was sure.

But now the ball was embedded in Brett's shoulder and it was plain from the sweat beads rolling down his face that it was causing him great agony.

'The shot must be removed, Brett,' Erin told him anxiously. 'But there's no doctor within miles and Henry Stanton is over at Kinvarra.'

Brett's grey eyes, clouded with pain, met hers.

'Then you must remove it, Erin.'

'Me – but I couldn't!' she whispered, horrified.

Brett's lips curved slightly. 'My love, I believe you could do anything if you put your mind to it. And Grianne will help you. With two such pretty nurses...' He broke off, gritting his teeth as a wave of pain washed over him and Erin almost sobbed with distress. 'Just give me a drink,' he grated out as the spasm subsided.

Erin splashed rum generously into a glass and held it to his lips. As he drank her mind worked furiously. Brett was right, as always. The shot must be removed. But could she do it, with only Grianne's doubtful help? Why, if Brett was to move as she probed...

She shuddered, and as if reading her thoughts he drained his glass and set it down.

'I'll remain still for you, don't worry. It won't be easy, but preferable I dare say to spending the night in agony.'

She nodded. For him she must try to do it – no, not *try*, she must succeed. She motioned to Grianne to bring the things she had laid out ready and with her sewing scissors she began to snip away Brett's shirt from around the wound. It was a painful business; in places the fabric was firmly stuck by congealed blood. Erin held her lip tight between her teeth to aid her concentration – and to keep from crying out as he winced beneath the ministrations of her fingers. But at last his shoulder was laid bare. Gently she cleaned the wound, then with the scissors she began to probe for the bullet.

Several times, as he groaned deep in his throat, or drew a sharp, shuddering breath, she drew back, afraid of hurting him more. But he roughly urged her to return to her task and, steeling herself, she did so. Grianne, she noticed, though she held him steady, gently but firmly, had her head turned away, and Erin wished she could afford the same luxury. But somehow she worked on, probing more deeply and trying to ignore the sweat that poured down his face and neck as he held himself taut against the pain.

At last her scissors encountered the ball and gripped it firmly. Then, terrified she might lose it again, she inched it out of the gaping hole. Grianne was ready with a pad to staunch the rush of blood that followed and Erin stood looking down at the bullet as if she had never seen one before. Then she set scissors and bullet down on the table with a clatter.

'Now you must rest,' she told him, relief of tension making her voice tremble. 'Grianne and I will help you up to bed.'

'Not tonight, my love.' Already Brett's glazed eyes were clearing and he looked more like his old self.

'But, Brett,' she protested. 'You're hurt!'

He laughed shortly.

'I'll be all right. But I don't trust our friend Jagger one inch. The convict huts may be as safe as we can make them; I still prefer to take no chances. Bring me a pistol now and help me move my chair closer to the window. Then you, at least, can retire for some rest.'

'I certainly shan't go to bed without you!' Erin said heatedly. 'If you insist on staying here then I shall remain with you.'

He caught at her hand with his good arm, pulling her close to his chair and leaning his head against her breast.

'And much good may it do you! Though if it were not for this shoulder you'd get little sleep wherever we chose to spend the night.'

A small, choking sound reminded them of Grianne's presence and Erin, cheeks flaming, prised herself from Brett's embrace.

'You go to bed, Grianne,' she advised. 'There's no need for the two of us to remain here.'

'No, I can see that,' Grianne muttered, then suddenly turned and ran to her sister, catching at her hands.

'I'm so sorry, Erin,' she sobbed. 'I feel this is all my fault! I know I've been nothing but a worry to you, but things will be different from now on, I promise.'

'Oh, Grianne, don't upset yourself now,' Erin murmured gently, embracing her sister. 'Everything will sort itself out, you'll see.'

When the younger girl had gone she turned to Brett, sinking onto the floor at his feet and leaning against his legs with her arms resting in his lap.

'Poor Grianne,' she whispered, but Brett only shrugged.

'Perhaps the shock of discovering the true nature of the man she was about to give herself to will bring her to her senses,' he said coolly.

'But you were taken in by him too,' Erin protested mildly.

'For a while only. I had already set in motion the procedure for checking his credentials before giving him employment on the strength of his word alone,' Brett said, his fingers playing in her dark curls.

'But he said you were making him store manager!' Erin told him. 'They both seemed to be under that impression.'

'Wishful thinking only,' Brett reiterated. 'If fact my inquiries have revealed that his past is dubious indeed. That was one of the reasons I rode home tonight – I did not care to have the two of you left in the company of a man such as he, and when I learned Grianne had left for Mia-Mia and taken him with her I followed at once.

And thank merciful heaven that I did! God alone knows what would have happened to you if I had not arrived when I did.'

Erin held her breath. He did not know then that Jagger was the same convict who had raped her before. His brutal assault on the man had been motivated by what he had believed he was *about* to do. Well, she would not enlighten him now. If she did, like as not he would go storming out to the huts, weak as he was, and throttle the evil Jagger with his bare hands.

'You said one of the reasons,' she murmured, trying to turn his attention to safer subjects. 'What is the other?'

His fingers slid along her jaw, turning her to look at him.

'What would you say if I told you I have news of Patrick?' he asked, smiling as her face lit up in pleasure and disbelief. 'Only today I have discovered that he had gone to sea, as a cabin boy on a merchant trader. By chance I talked to the man who signed him on.'

'Patrick – at sea?' she marvelled.

He nodded.

'Yes. I was surprised, too, at first, but the more I think about it the more sense it makes to me. Since he hates the land so, might it not follow he would have an affinity with the sea? And those starry nights on the deep might suit a dreamer such as he.'

'I suppose so,' Erin murmured. 'But what of the future?'

'I have a ship now,' Brett reminded her. 'If Patrick has found his sea legs he could be of

329

great use to me on the *Amber Fawn*. I could do with someone from the family – someone I can trust.'

Erin, relief and happiness making her mischievous, smiled.

'And what makes you think you can trust my family, Brett?' she teased.

He pulled her around so that she was kneeling between his long, hard thighs.

'Why, because they have such a redoubtable sister!' he smiled.

She sighed with contentment, leaning closer to twine her arms around his waist and press herself against his body, and Brett's hands moved to loosen her torn gown once more.

'If he had touched you I would have killed him,' he murmured, his voice low with passion as he cupped her breasts in his hands.

Erin shivered slightly but she said nothing. She simply pressed his hands tighter around her breasts until the tips stood taut against his palms and her heart seemed to be beating in his hand. These were the only fingers that would touch her now. His was the only body that would know her.

'Forget him, Brett,' she whispered.

And as she reached up to kiss him she knew that from this moment on the past, for her, would be securely locked away where it belonged.

Nothing mattered now but the future.

It was a week later and Erin and Brett were riding together to Kinvarra. To all intents and purposes Erin was with him for the exercise only, but in reality there was a dual purpose behind her suggestion to accompany him – firstly because although his shoulder was now healing fast she still did not like the idea of him riding alone in case he should get a sudden bout of pain, and secondly because she wanted the opportunity of making a certain suggestion about the future of her old home.

Since she had come back to Mia-Mia, Grianne had begun seeing David Percy again, much to Erin's relief. It seemed that at last her sister had realized her folly in chasing wealth and position and come to realize that all that glitters is not gold. But Erin knew that if she and David were to make a match of it times would be hard for them, for David would be too proud by far to accept any kind of settlement or dowry from his brother-in-law.

But there was still Kinvarra. It was, after all, Grianne's birthright, and since the family no longer lived in it, Erin could see no objection to Grianne and David making their home there.

'Besides, it needs to be lived in,' Erin thought, lovingly remembering the house her father had built for them all to begin their new lives in Australia. 'It needs to be restored to what it was before Father's drinking brought ruin to us all.'

But how to raise the subject with Brett? Though there were no barriers between them now, Kinvarra was still a thorny question. The house was in a state of disrepair, of course, but since it had fallen into his hands Brett had utilized the land to stop it from returning once more to wild forest and scrub, and knowing how possessive Brett could be over what was rightly his, Erin was afraid he might be unwilling to lose what he might now look on as part of his estate.

As the horses reached the entrance to the drive Erin swallowed at the sudden lump that rose in her throat at the view that greeted them. She had thought of the house often, but she had forgotten how beautiful were the trees that guarded it. Now, in spring, they were at their best, the eucalypts stretching tall arms to the blue sky, the yellow blooms of the mimosa seeming to catch the sunshine and bring it down to earth.

Tears sprang to her eyes as she thought of those she loved who would never see the blossom again, and suddenly through the blur she saw Brett rein in Jack and turn to face her.

'Erin, I'm glad you came today. There's something I want to talk to you about. David Percy had intimated to me that he and Grianne might be going to make a match of it and if they do I would like to suggest that they make their home here at Kinvarra. But it's your home, not mine, and I wouldn't put forward such an idea without your consent. Why...' He broke off suddenly as he noticed the tears rolling down her face. 'What's wrong, my sweet? Why are you crying?'

'For happiness, Brett,' she whispered.

'Then you don't mind Grianne and David having Kinvarra? You don't mind that it will not be William's?'

'Oh, Brett,' she murmured, 'William has enough. And if there's one thing I never could abide it's a spoiled child.'

He smiled, reaching for Starlight's bridle and pulling him close to Jack.

'There's little danger of that, my love,' he said softly. 'For I plan to give him plenty of brothers and sisters to share his good fortune.'

'Do you indeed?' she teased.

Ignoring the pain from his damaged shoulder, he leaned over, reaching for her, and she leaned to meet him. Briefly their lips met and love and desire sparked within her. Would it always be like this, she wondered, this magic fusion of hearts and bodies? And how could she ever have wanted it any other way?

'I'm so glad now that I'm your wife, Brett,' she whispered. 'Promise me you'll never let me go.'

He smiled at her, a smile that had no need for words, and the sun, slanting through the mimosa, bathed them in golden light.

It seemed like an omen for all the years to come.